JOSEPH COULSON

Of SONG and WATER

A NOVEL

archipelago books

Archipelago Books
232 Third Street, #A111
Brooklyn, NY 11215
www.archipelagobooks.org

Coulson, Joseph.
Of Song and Water : a Novel / Joseph Coulson. – 1st ed.
p. cm.
ISBN: 978-0-9819873-8-5
1. Fathers and sons – Fiction. 2. Great Lakes (North America) – Fiction.
3. Middle West – Fiction. 4. Jazz – Fiction. I. Of Song and Water.
PS3553.O827O36 2007
813'.54–dc22

Distributed by Consortium Book Sales and Distribution
www.cbsd.com

Material from Tudor, Steven *Haul-Out: New and Selected Poems*, pp. 5, 18, 26, 27, 30, 32,
43, 44, 49, 50, 106, 111, 137, with the permission of Wayne State University Press.
Material from *The Aeneid* by Virgil, translated by Robert Fitzgerald, copyright © 1980,
1982, 1983 by Robert Fitzgerald. Used by permission of Random House, Inc.
Material from "Orpheus Alone," *The Continuous Life* by Mark Strand © 1990 by Mark Strand.
Used by permission of Alfred A. Knopf, a division of Random House, Inc.
"The Sidney Greenstreet Blues," *The Pill Versus the Springhill Mine Disaster*, Richard Brautigan.
Copyright © 1968 by Richard Brautigan. Reprinted by permission of
Houghton Mifflin Company. All rights reserved.
Lines from "September Song" (Anderson/Weill), "Stardust" (Carmichael/Parish), and
"I've Been Loving You Too Long (To Stop Now)" (Redding/Butler) appear in italics.
All possible care has been taken to secure permission for copyrighted material.

Cover art: Edward Hopper, *Rooms by the Sea* (1951), Yale University Art Gallery,
Bequest of Stephen Carlton Clark, B.A. 1903.

This publication was made possible with the support of Lannan Foundation
and the New York State Council on the Arts, a state agency.

NYSCA

Manufactured at Thomson-Shore, Inc. in Dexter, Michigan
Visit Thomson-Shore on the web at www.thomsonshore.com

for Stephen Tudor, 1933–1994,

lost on Lake Huron

Acknowledgments

In writing this book, I am indebted to the poems of Stephen Tudor, my teacher, mentor, and friend. As a tribute to Steve, lines and phrases from *Haul-Out: New and Selected Poems* appear occasionally throughout the story. My thanks to Ellie Tudor and Wayne State University Press for permission to use words from "Haul-Out," "A History of St. Ignace," "Depth Sounder," "Overnight Solo, Lake St. Clair," "Sailing Vision," "The Gott Locks Through," "Falling Overboard for You," "De Tour Reef Light," "Boatspeed," "Blue Water Bridge," and "North of the Blue Water Bridge."

Other indispensable resources were *Richardson's Chartbook and Cruising Guide for Lake Huron* and also *Lake Erie, The Practical Mariner's Book of Knowledge* by John Vigor, *The Sailor's Illustrated Dictionary* by Thompson Lenfestey with Captain Thompson Lenfestey, Jr., and *Images of America: Detroit, 1930– 1969* by David Lee Poremba.

I owe thanks to the first readers of this book, especially Jill Schoolman, Jim Baldwin, Charlene Coulson, Mike Levine, Seoni Llanes, Alison Park, Lynn Pierce, and Greg Smith. Finally, I am indebted to my brother, Phil Coulson, for his comprehensive knowledge of twentieth-century music, jazz guitars, and all things nautical.

And there he tried three times
To throw his arms around his father's neck.
Three times the shade untouched slipped through his hands,
Weightless as wind and fugitive as dream.

Virgil, The Aeneid, Book VI

And, then, pulling out all the stops, describing her eyes,
Her forehead where the golden light of evening spread,
The curve of her neck, the slope of her shoulders, everything
Down to her thighs and calves, letting the words come,
As if lifted from sleep, to drift upstream,
Against the water's will . . .

Mark Strand, "Orpheus Alone"

Coming up under the bridge into
you, Huron, at Sarnia, the first
time was the same as entering an
ocean. But that's not true now. I
cannot love the finite with that

infinite love I'd saved for the
ideal. I know you too well.

Stephen Tudor, "North of the Blue Water Bridge"

Of Song and Water

chapter one

HE CLIMBS without faith, the ladder unsteady, the wooden rungs brittle, each step filling the air with the sound of old bones. Don't look down, he thinks, watching the slow drift of his shadow, seeing its darkness on the long white surface of the hull.

He stops, checks his grip, and struggles to turn his head, the cramp in his neck burning. He strains again, harder this time, until something moves – a snap – at the base of his skull. The stiffness gives way. Clusters of stars whirl, trail off, and vanish.

He reaches the top and steadies himself before loosening the cover. Two days ago, he found the boom tent dusted with snow. Tonight, it's dark and dry. He waits for the smell, the heavy scent that begins with canvas, a strange mingling of wood smoke and old skin, but it doesn't come. Too cold, he thinks. He clambers onto the deck and crouches on one knee, listening to the stillness.

From his perch, he looks toward the channel. Everything visible is white, silver, or gray. Untouched snow covers the buildings and docks; it clings to the empty cradles and the towering hoist. Snow reflects the light from a few tired lamps, imbuing the dark with a spectral glow. Swirls of low-lying fog, impossible in such cold, rise up around rusty trailers and fuel tanks, moving through the marina like men in long coats. The shifting outlines make him uneasy. The ghosts of sailors, he thinks. They're here to pass judgment. Call him an imposter. Tell him to give it up.

He's in Michigan, downriver from Detroit. It's the beginning of the twenty-first century.

Though it can't be seen, he knows that HUMBUG MARINA, in letters large enough for a roadside billboard, hovers above him. He marvels at the correctness of the name.

HUMBUG: the word under which he labors; the word that in winter seems inescapable; the word that in his coming and going is always the first and the last.

His grandfather used to say that a great name guarantees success. "It shouldn't be a placeholder," he insisted, "or a catchall for loose ends. It shouldn't be given lightly, whether to a boy, a boat, or a business, not when dreams, even fate, hang in the balance."

He rubs the top of his right hand behind the knuckles. On some days the pain is general, difficult to pinpoint or describe. On other days it grows like a rolling fire, waves of misery that pressure and pills cannot relieve. He finds it intolerable when both hands go off at once, because then the most familiar routines – shaving, taking a shower, putting on shoes – deplete what little he has in terms of humility and patience. When the pain is constant, he sweats to make deliveries, the hours dragging, and by the time he punches out and gets to Humbug, having stopped at Blue Moon for a bottle, his fingers are cramped and rigid, too clumsy for the simplest chores.

The only safe haven is Humbug, he thinks, especially for a guy with bum hands. It's a refuge of faded glory, an anchorage filled with practical buildings and unfashionable clientele, a business that takes pride in being cheaper than the Ford Yacht Club. He mentions the savings whenever he calls Maureen to ask her for more time.

Alone in the cold, kneeling on the white deck, he hears her voice. "You can't do this anymore," she says. "You're late six months out of twelve. What am I supposed to use at the grocery store? My good looks?"

"You could," he says, almost smiling. He still thinks of her as beautiful.

"That boat," says Maureen, "is more important than your daughter."

"Not true," he says.

"But it makes no sense. For God's sake, Jason, you don't even like sailing."

"You'll get the money," he says. "Nothing comes between you and your money."

"Humbug," says Maureen.

He regards it as mean-spirited, her refusal, after marriage, divorce, and child support, to call him by his adopted name – his stage name. From the beginning, she took sides with his mother, insisting that he be Jason, over-ruling the friends and strangers who braved late hours and bad weather just to hear him play. To those people he was Coleman Moore.

He is Coleman Moore.

HE REMEMBERS his first lesson – though no one would've called it that when it happened – having seen the guitar with its black body and ebony neck resting in a silver stand and then picking it up without thinking and trusting the weight of it in his hands and knowing, as if by communion, that it was already under his skin, that he felt more like himself just holding it, though his fingers were at a loss for what to do.

He sat on a stool, the guitar cradled in his lap, and looked up at Mr. Young, a man with dark eyes, coffee-colored skin, and yellow teeth. He heard Mr. Young's voice, raspy but melodic. "That'd be Lucille's sister. She's been here since before you were born."

He nodded, feeling grateful, realizing in a flash that seeing the guitar and touching it were matters of pure chance. He'd started to walk off, taking his pay for cutting the grass, when Mr. Young said, "You got a minute? I could use some help in back."

So he followed Mr. Young down the hall and through the kitchen and out the back door to the small shanty that sat in the corner of the yard.

After moving two or three boxes, he saw that the shanty was some sort of studio stuffed with sound equipment, microphones, and tapes. A few records were framed and hanging on the walls. Then he walked over to the guitar and picked it up, forgetting to ask permission.

"I'll teach you," said Mr. Young. "You need a guitar?"

"Yes."

"All right. We'll use that one until you find your own."

"I don't know, Mr. Young. Getting my own may be a long shot."

"You can drop the Mr. Young routine. Call me Otis."

He remembers the way Otis made him feel at home and the first notes on Lucille's sister and the lessons, week after week – once his father agreed and talked to Otis about what instrument to buy – and then the hours of practice between the lessons, losing himself in the scales, the grips, and the patterns. He believed that learning music would make him a better person – that it would change him in some essential way so that he could move beyond his neighborhood, beyond the wishes of his mother and father, beyond the lives of the people he knew.

After each session, he'd ask Otis one question after another, careful to call him Otis rather than Mr. Young, wanting to know more about the black-and-white photos that cluttered the studio, about the old days, the gigs with Duke

Ellington or Dizzy Gillespie, about working as a sideman with John Coltrane – names that had little or no meaning to an uninitiated boy. More often than not, the stories ended abruptly, usually in midsentence. "What are you waitin' for?" Otis said then, his voice like sandpaper. "That's all there is to it. Don't count on a second ending."

HE FEELS his legs aching. He drops into the cockpit and sits on the starboard seat, unzips his coat pocket, and pulls out a flashlight. He sets it down, the beam pointing toward the stern. He reaches into his other pocket and carefully unloads a pint of vodka and rests it on his thigh. He tries to open it but the fingers of his left hand seize up. He clamps his teeth on the cap and turns the bottle.

Maureen is constant, he thinks. She takes for granted the solidity of things. He sees her now much as he did before, a woman of disciplined habits living without indecision or clutter. She appears to be the same person in the morning and in the afternoon, at work or at home, at the post office and at the grocery store. He judges this to be a monumental, if unnatural, achievement. The self he sometimes knows as Coleman seems to waver, to change pitch, to move faster or slower depending on the conversation, the weather, or the room.

Maureen calls him unstable. "I've spent my entire life in Gibraltar," she says, "but you didn't stay long enough to be a husband or a father. I'm telling you, a lack of routine makes a person thin and indefinite."

When he did materialize, she took it as a blow to her system. "You don't understand," she said. "Each time you step through that door, you're a man I can't quite recognize." She attributed the changes to his itinerant profession, to the convenient and well-heeled women, to the harsh lights.

He listened to her judgments but didn't believe that his poorly defined self had anything to do with music or the ways of a musician. It went back almost to the beginning. He was a joker in math, a vandal in chemistry, and a dreamer in English. He could be any combination of these traits even then. The years had only added to the list. He didn't cultivate these qualities as some sort of perverse game. This was simply the way he was. The way he is.

ONCE, after he'd cried all the way home, unable to pull himself together, he got obsessed with the idea that his cheek would never stop burning, so he opened the faucet and ran water into the flower bed until the rich, black soil turned to mud. Then, sinking to his knees, he plunged his hands into the wet darkness and smeared his face with it, the earthy smell filling his nostrils. With his chin dripping, he ran into the house, rushing past the washed-out faces of his mother and father, and locked himself in the bathroom, staring into the mirror like an actor worried about his makeup, wetting his fingers and trying to cover the blank spots, but all of it looking worse for the effort as the mud dried and became brittle.

He remembers how his cheek kept stinging and his heart continued pounding and his breathing wouldn't slow down, having been caught off guard after Levina, a girl he barely knew and would never see again, had invited him in, and her mom had poured two glasses of milk and arranged fresh cookies on a plate. Levina had said, "This is Jason. He lives close to the water and has two sailboats, and he says that someday I might be able to go out on the big one with him and his grandfather."

"Are you sure?" said Levina's mom. "Why would anyone need two boats?"

"One belongs to my dad," he said. "The other one – the big one – belongs to my grandfather. He keeps it here but lives in Saginaw."

"Oh, I see," said Levina's mom. "But my baby girl can't swim."

He gulped his milk and put down the glass. "I'll swim for both of us," he said.

They finished their cookies and Levina walked him to the front door. In the hall were photographs filled with black faces, most with dark hair and others with white.

"See ya," he said.

"When?" said Levina. "When school starts, you won't come around."

"Why wouldn't I?" he said.

He was already on the front walk, having heard the door close behind him, when Levina's big brother, a muscular boy with a midnight face, decided to block the way.

"You're Jason Moore," said Levina's brother. "What are you doing here? You slumming?" He narrowed his eyes. "My sister ain't for sale."

He didn't like the smell of the older boy's breath. He didn't know what to do or say, so he stepped back and began to smile. That's when the boy slapped him, the open hand landing with enough force to turn the head of a statue.

THE VODKA warms the back of his throat. He considers the chores that need doing, but now, after the exertion of climbing aboard, he's lost his ambition.

He sits here two or three evenings a week, smelling the canvas and drinking vodka. He looks forward to it. He likes the boat resting in its cradle, no pitching or rolling. No immediate demands. With tanks cleared, engine drained, and compartments left open to the air, it's a good place to think, to hunker down. He likes being hard to find.

He comes to the marina straight from work in an effort to avoid the kids who collect signatures or sell magazine subscriptions, to escape the bow-tied Christians who, for the redemption of his soul, say that they'll provide a personal introduction to Jesus. There'd been no talk of solicitors, religious or otherwise, when he submitted his application for the house – a two-bedroom ranch with an attached garage – and the landlord, a woman anxious to reveal her spiritual fervor, had kept her ecstasy under wraps, kept things low-key until she had a signed lease and the first month's rent.

He'd lived in the house for forty days when, as a concerned proprietor, she made her first unannounced visit. She wore a white tank top over a deep, coconut-oil tan. The slope of her breasts led to a book, a Bible, which she squeezed with both arms like a child. She created a place for the Bible on the kitchen table after brushing bread crumbs and granules of salt onto the floor.

Later, when she came by again, her tan darker and her hair shorter than before, she remarked that the Bible hadn't been moved. She put a sticker on the wall above the phone. "This is my number," she said. "For emergencies."

On her third visit, she wore tight shorts and a thin T-shirt and asked him if he'd accepted Jesus as his personal savior.

Now he tries to avoid her by leaving the house in darkness and going to the boat as often as obligations and weather allow. On some nights, he conjures up the scent she left behind and the moist warmth of her breathing, but in Humbug's yard, surrounded by snow, he drops the fantasy and sails high and dry. He keeps an almost perfect solitude.

HEATHER'S the only one who visits him here, and he suspects, though she'd hardly admit it, that duty is a large part of her devotion. What choice does she have? "You're my dad," she's fond of saying, "for better or worse."

He feels too often that she's trying to save him, if not from loneliness then from the bald realization that he's a middle-aged failure. Exactly when she became so wise and sophisticated is impossible to say.

His daughter, already seventeen, drives her own car and waits tables at the Lighthouse Diner, a young woman so blessed with her mom's best features that it makes him wonder what part he played in bringing her into the world. Her figure is Maureen's – only more so. She has her mother's red hair, her freckles, and her green eyes. Their smiles are the same too, but lately Maureen obscures this detail with a fixed expression, an artful mix of disappointment and disgust. Naturally, she reserves this face mostly for him – for terse meetings in coffee shops where they talk about parenting or money and where she stubbornly calls him Jason, as if Coleman had never been.

Heather, on the other hand, smiles easily. She's in the habit of stopping by on weekends. When she doesn't catch him at home, she drives over to Humbug and usually finds him on the boat.

He wants her to turn up now, despite it being the middle of the week, a school night, but he knows the notion would go against her better judgment. He moves his foot and knocks over a plastic bottle; it rolls across the floor of the cockpit. It's the one Heather brought up here on Saturday, he thinks.

She held out the bottle as soon as she came aboard. "Want some? It's spring water from a faraway mountain."

"Too pure for me," he said.

He led her down into the cabin and they sat across from each other at the teak table, an electric heater keeping out the frost and damp. She spoke in a low, soothing voice, as if she were visiting a sick friend in the hospital. She touched the top of his hand and the swollen joints of his fingers. The warmth of her skin astonished him. She went on about her plans for college and made a passing reference to her new boyfriend. The part of him that felt fatherly pushed for taking a little interest in the guy, but the larger part, the not-so-fatherly side, argued for writing the kid off. As always, he skirted the issue, choosing to avoid questions that showed him up as defensive or absurdly jealous.

Heather reached into her bag. "I bought you a present," she said, pulling out a CD. "I know you don't listen to music anymore, but I heard this and thought of you."

Maybe a year ago, when they were looking at his old LPs, he'd made the mistake of telling her that he'd stopped listening to music. Since then she'd bought him a dozen or so albums, an attempt, no doubt, to stave off his precipitous decline.

"And the next time we're at the house," she said, "would you play me a song? Something ancient and slow."

"It's hard to do," he said, rubbing the heel of his left hand.

"You're lying," she said.

"Maybe. I haven't changed the strings in a while."

"You told me old strings are bad for a guitar."

"That's right."

"And rough on the ears, too."

"I guess no one listens better than you."

She smiled. "That's what you always say."

Too much talk about music, he thought. He longed to give her some useful advice, a few words she could save for later. "As for college," he said, "you'll figure out the right move. Don't worry about me or your mother. Take yourself as far from here as you want – as far as you can. Don't look back."

"Not so fast," says the sandpaper voice. "There's more to it than speed. When I say attack, it isn't about fighting. It's about feeling."

He plays the phrase again, slower this time, alert only to the sensation of strings beneath his fingers. For a moment, the sound flows from him like water. When he starts pushing the tempo, Otis shakes his head.

"You're like those boys in the Big Apple," says Otis. "In a hurry. You think you got somewhere to go."

He wonders how Otis could live in a place like New York and then give it up and settle here. Why would you do that? he thinks. If I ever get to a city, I'll stay there. There's no place to play in a little town.

After collecting his sheet music and closing his guitar case, he points to a picture on the wall. "Is that New York?"

Otis rubs the gray stubble on his face, his hand a little unsteady. "That's Grand Circus Park," he says. "Detroit."

"Why don't you live there?"

"I would – I was born just a few blocks away. But I left when I was your age, and when I finally went back, it was gone."

He looks at Otis looking at the picture.

"You have to find a safe haven," says Otis. "If you can't find a real place, then you have to make one, up here." He taps his temple with a long finger.

"See you next week, Mr. Young – I mean – " The screen door of the studio slams. "I appreciate your time."

On this day, like all the others, he stops and glances back to see Otis standing at the door in his crisp white shirt and black pants. The silence is awkward. He wants to fill up the space, say something to ease the tension, but always in that moment the old man turns and disappears.

LATER, three of his classmates surround him in the school lavatory.

"We saw you," says one of the boys. The others look on with suspicion.

"So what?"

"You're supposed to be cuttin' grass."

"So what?"

"Cuttin' his grass is bad enough. Now you're goin' inside."

He dries his hands and steps toward the door but can't get by the others, big boys with strong Midwestern shoulders.

"Are you that nigger's nigger?" says the tall one.

The boys laugh.

"What do you do in there?"

"Nothing."

"Does he take you out to his little shack?"

"No."

Putting his head down, he tries to squeeze between two of the boys, but sharp fingers dig into his arms.

"For Christ's sake, Jason, we know you're lying. I suppose when you're out there on the edge of town you think we can't see you. But we can. We've all seen you, even when you said you weren't going." The boy pretends to be thinking hard. "I know, maybe you can clear up a little rumor we've heard. Is that man your real daddy?"

The lavatory rings with laughter.

"No."

"You can't deny everything," says the first boy who spoke. "How do you expect to stay in our good graces if you don't tell us the truth?"

He struggles against their grip. "He's a teacher," he says, staring at the floor, one arm pinned to his side, the other twisted and cramped. "He's teaching me to play guitar."

"That coon's a picker?"

He nods slowly.

"Well. All right then. The man's an entertainer. You should've said so in the first place."

"I'm taking lessons." He looks at the faces of the three boys. "But only until I can afford someone better."

The fingers let go. The boys nod approval.

Two of them disappear into stalls and urinate while the third waits. The boys flush, zip, and check themselves in the mirror; then the one waiting opens the door and the three leave together.

HE BRINGS the vodka to his lips. No wind tonight but something in the air sounds like a muffled voice. Heather won't be here anytime soon. He thinks of her now, sleeping in her mother's house, dreaming the dreams of the young.

He remembers his first leave-taking, turning away from his father, driving to the East Coast in a rusty Dodge and looking for a place off campus.

He arrives late for orientation and sits beside a woman wearing a white jacket. "I'm Jennifer," she says. Her long straight hair is black, swept to one side, and secured with a silver clip.

They meet for coffee and later she listens to him play. After a while, she offers a corner room, a single bed that's been pushed against the wall and covered with thick pillows.

He sleeps with her and cooks oatmeal in the morning, smells the sweetness of her body in his own clothes, and they stay in the tiny room for days at a stretch, especially in winter, lighting candles while the snow swirls and drifts in the street below.

The rhythm of her body, her movement, stirs in him new sounds and he composes with perfect ease, ignoring the changing light, making melodies that tumble and turn like clear water.

She comes through the door with a bag of groceries, unpacks the fruit and vegetables, and puts a small bottle of vodka on the table. He pours a shot into a short glass, feels the bite on his tongue.

There's no memory as sharp as this, he thinks. She will not go away, even in the face of inexplicable years.

His frigid legs rest heavy on the fiberglass seat. The chill seeping into every inch of the boat and into his bones is familiar. He lifts one foot and then the other to keep his blood moving and pictures again how their love affair begins in winter and ends in winter, the cold streaming in under the door.

She walks with him to the station, hands in her pockets, shoulders hunched in the blowing snow. He carries his guitar and a tattered suitcase. She's silent until they reach the bus.

"Can't you postpone it?" she says. "Why should I spend the day apologizing for you? C'mon, Cole, I want you to be there with me."

"I have to go," he says.

"If they're serious, they'll wait. It's a tryout, not a job."

"If I don't show up for the audition, they'll use somebody else."

"But you'll miss – "

"Miss what? A lousy band?"

"Miss me."

"Have fun at the wedding," he says. "Tell your sister I'm sorry."

Departures and arrivals echo through the station.

"I work here," she says. "It isn't so easy to leave."

"I'm not asking you to quit," he says. "It wouldn't make sense anyway. This whole thing's a long shot."

"I know that," she says.

Jen stands in front of the door, shivering in her thin jacket. She doesn't say anything about the nausea or the test.

A blast of wind pushes him against the bus. "It's time," he says.

"Are you going?"

He's struck dumb by her stubbornness. He kisses her on the mouth and then steps onto the bus. She begins to follow him, moving like a sleepwalker, but he turns and the shock of his turning startles her. She backs away from the door and another passenger rushes aboard.

The boat beneath him seems to lurch. Still no sound except for a vague whisper. "It's bitter cold," he says out loud. His words trail off and disappear. He slips the bottle of vodka into his pocket. "It's bitter cold," he says again.

The flashlight flickers, begins to fade. He picks it up and bangs it on his leg. It goes out. He unscrews it a little, setting off slow waves of pain in his fingers. He tightens it up and pushes the switch back and forth. "Jesus," he says.

A faint glow creeps in where the boom tent is open. All the rest is darkness. In the absence of light, the canvas above him appears to recede; it becomes for him an immense black ceiling, a night sky without stars. He searches for a point of reference, peering at the empty heavens, unable to comprehend the meaning of his position. Something like this has happened before. He feels the familiar strain on his neck, knows that in looking up he will see nothing but a blank slate. A touch of vertigo washes over him then, spins him slowly at first. He's aware of the deck rolling beneath his feet, the fixed objects of his world sliding away, and a weight on his body, not so much gravity now as water, as if he were drowning, caught in the vortices of a sinking ship.

HE SEES himself as a boy, as Jason, kneeling on the starboard seat of his father's sloop, a stiff wind out of the northwest making him shiver.

His father says, "Prepare to come about – use the winch handle."

He tries but turns it the wrong way. He knows where the edge of the lake should be, but he can't distinguish between sky and water. There's only one light in the distance.

"Jason," says his father, "I don't want you going below. Your grandfather's not there."

The galley's dark. The mark to be fetched is Port Austin Reef. The boat leans and picks up speed.

He realizes that if not for his grandfather, he would still be in bed – no order to tumble out, no reason to set sail in the middle of the night. He feels anxious and out of sorts and hears his dad saying for the second time, "Your grandfather has no face."

He looks up. No moon. Not a single star. Barely visible is a low ceiling of gray clouds. The sky shudders from one horizon to the other. No face, he thinks. Heaven has no face and my grandfather has no face. Dad says it's so.

The eyes in the photograph, fixed on something outside the frame, are discerning and troubled. He likes the mustache and believes that in the future he'll grow his own. Someone printed H.M. in the corner of the picture. Handkerchiefs and cuff links bear the same letters. So do the trophies in the glass case. On the trophy for the singlehander's race is HAVELOCK MOORE. It's a strong sound. He says to almost everyone he meets, "Havelock Moore is my grandfather's name. My dad calls him H.M." He suspects that H.M. is the only man his father fears.

"There'll be no going below," his father says again. "I need you to give a hand."

He wants to get out of the wind, but with the weatherboards in place and the hood closed and latched, he's stuck. He accepts the fact that Havelock's not in the cabin. Havelock's not in his berth – the old man's sleeping somewhere else.

Over the wind, he hears his father say, "If you found H.M. on the street, you wouldn't know it was him."

He tries to understand, but the words create a white space in his mind. The whiteness scares him. Needing to fill it, he recalls the old photograph – first the initials, then the face, and finally the eyes, black pools touched by a spark of light.

"No stars tonight," he says, looking up.

"Just as well," says his father.

The face in the picture is full of deep sadness. How can it be that Havelock Moore has no face?

"It's gone," says his father.

"Why do you say that?"

"Because it is."

I'm sailing in a plastic tub, he thinks. It's smaller than my grandfather's ketch. He remembers going in headfirst when the big boat rose and fell. He'd like to do it all over again – prove to everyone, once and for all, that he's no longer a boy.

He sees himself on the ketch and his grandfather's face unworried.

"This is an old man's ship," says Havelock. "It isn't for racing. She's made of wood and she's proud. Fiberglass is cheap. You can't call it a boat when it's built of such stuff." He scratches his nose and smiles. "Your dad's sloop is a white whale. I'd call it a plastic tub."

Havelock looms overhead, trying to explain the vagaries of wind. "You must keep your canvas on the verge of luffing," he says. "It's easy to pull in a sail too far by mistake. If you do, the boat'll stall."

They watch the forward edge of the jib.

"A Moore never sinks," says Havelock.

He smiles at the old man and nods.

Havelock says, "Be proud of your name. A good name guarantees success. Jason was a great hero. He sailed the world looking for the Golden Fleece." The jib begins to ripple. In the next instant, Havelock makes the correction. "Mind the telltales, too."

He follows his grandfather's order and worries that his eyes aren't big enough. He can watch only one part at a time. He has to know about wind and where he's going. And somewhere there's a Golden Fleece. He wonders what it is and whether or not he should be looking for it. On the ketch there's too much to do, too much to think about.

On land, his grandfather doesn't do everything at once. He sits at the kitchen table and sorts the mail into three piles: letters, bills, and solicitations. If it's personal, he holds it in his hand for a while, examines the return address and the stamp. Finally, he opens it with his pocketknife, careful not to damage the envelope. On the water, though, his actions overlap. He trims and steers and checks his bearing all in the same breath.

Conditions on the lake change quickly. There's no rocking in a steady wind. But in calm, the swells come up and the ketch rolls and the sails flap and jerk. He stumbles and grabs a lifeline.

"Enough noise," says Havelock. "Lower the sails and let go the anchor."

He knows he's too small to help. He's been out many times, but the sun still hurts his eyes. It's hot on the water with no wind, he thinks. He enjoys the ketch rising and falling, the deck slanting like a floor in a fun house. He wants to jump when the deck lifts him up to see how high he can spring. On his shoulder, he feels his grandfather's hand. He turns and finds suddenly that there's nothing either behind him or below.

He soars spread-eagled through the air and then plummets, all the heat and glare collapsing into cold and dark. He doesn't thrash or kick. He falls through water, the lake filling him until he is deaf, until he is mute, and then his body stops, suspended between two worlds. Though it's impossible to explain later, something here takes hold of him, buoying him up, so that slowly at first, through no effort of his own, he starts to climb. An ache for breath, for speech, swells in his throat. He begins to think. He breaks the surface, arms and legs moving, and sees his grandfather's face.

"Sink or swim is the only way," says Havelock. "You can scuttle the boat, but a Moore never sinks."

I'M ON a white whale, he thinks. One hour out and searching for deep water. Havelock's not in the cabin. Havelock's not in his berth. He sees his father looking up, navigating without stars. The wind drives the sloop on a broad reach.

"There's no turning back," says his father. "It won't keep. He'd want it this way."

After the reef, the bottom yawns. The water is deep and goes deeper still. He wonders what depth his father is hoping for. He dreams bright gardens of fish and then a circle of sailboats – red, yellow, and blue – floating on the air. He listens to the hull slicing the lake, to the steady sigh. My grandfather had a face, he thinks. He journeyed upriver, through the narrows, to sail on an inland sea. Huron was the lake he loved.

The boat turns into the wind. It stalls and they douse the sails.

Now the hood slides back and the weatherboards come out. He follows his father down into the cabin. In the berth is a long canvas bag lashed with line and weighted with heavy stones. They haul it up the companionway. They let it rest in the cockpit, catching their breath. Facing each other, they lift it over the starboard winch and balance it on the gunwale. The boat rocks like a cradle. He knows why he is here. He puts one knee on the starboard seat. His father holds the bag with both hands. "I'm sorry," he says. "You were disheartened on this boat. It should've been the ketch that carried you." And then his father lets go and the bag rolls over into darkness.

HUMBUG feels colder than before. Snowflakes shimmer in the gap of pale light. He shudders. He senses a subtle shift, a change. The refuge he seeks is not to be found. Perhaps he's come here too late on too many nights. Perhaps he's used it up, overstayed his welcome. Somehow, he's ill at ease. The marina's empty, he knows. No cars in the parking lot when he arrived. Not a soul stopping by to check on covers or equipment.

A thud rises from below. It's like a log striking the hull. Sailors are superstitious, he thinks, but I'm not a sailor. He waits. He hears himself breathing and feels the bottle of vodka resting on his hip. A wind starts in from the channel. Maybe that was it – a current of air nudging the boat. Now sheet metal and cinder block drone.

Nearby, three or four boats stand against winter with their masts and rigging in place, and in the wind they make a strange music, shafts and crosstrees keening, stays and shrouds whining, the slapping of loose lines. To the trained ear, these are the sounds of danger, of foreboding, of foul or heavy weather. And these are the very sounds that his father managed to ignore.

Those that sailed with the great Dorian Moore said he could read the sky better than any man. He could taste rain long before it fell. So he defied instinct and experience, made himself deaf to the alarm, when he slipped out at dusk under a press of sail, the storm gathering in the west.

A vessel isn't built to be empty. It's appalling to see it, to bear down on a grounded boat and find everything in place but its captain. It was stranded like a beached whale. He couldn't sail it back with his father adrift – with his father inconceivably lost. It was too soon. Too sudden. A less ghostly disaster would've been easier. Why not a wreck in the cove at Great Duck Island? Why not a rudder torn away on Hangdog Reef? But a reef, he realized, might've been worse. His father had been very clear about the challenge and temptation of reefs. With a reef dead ahead, a sailor might gamble. He might trust the water to reveal its mystery, risking the hazard of green shapes, gray knees of granite, driven toward lust, greed, avarice, envy, though there's never much warning.

He hears the noise again, a thud from below, a fist hitting a wall or a door closing. He should leave. He wants to sleep, to dream. It's bitter cold, he thinks, and I am sick at heart. Maureen won't find him here. Heather knows where he is, but she sleeps the sleep of the young. He hears the sound of wood groaning, as if the boat were settling for the first time in its cradle. The wind is up. He's had too much to drink. Going down the ladder will be difficult. He slides forward and lifts himself off the starboard seat. Another thud. The cabin calls to him. A black cave.

On the water, he's the embarrassing son of Dorian Moore. He's no better on land. He remembers walking with his father in a city park, where a man in a priest's collar stood preaching beneath a tree. "Lord, create in us changed lives," said the man, "even as we drink deep, and thirst, and drink again – whatever the cost."

He watched his father listening to the prayer.

He saw his father's confidence, the purposeful stride, the steady gaze, and the hands, waterworn but strong, scored by taut lines and the constant hauling.

"The boy's hands," Otis had said, "are made for a fingerboard and strings."

His father worried out loud. "Whatever skill or talent you're given," he said, "use it for its own sake. Don't cheapen it. Don't use it to go somewhere or get things."

He stares into the dark cabin. He can't see his hands. He rubs them together. Chewed up and worthless, he thinks.

He works his way to the opening in the canvas. He crouches on the deck and peers at the windswept yard. A footfall thumps in his ear. Someone is on the companionway.

He turns. He sees his father climbing up from below.

He shuts his eyes and tries to clear his head. When he looks again, his father is still there, water dripping from his face.

He gasps. He puts out his hand but fears losing his balance, tumbling backward and down the ladder to be found beneath the keel in a broken heap. He believes that he's gone too far, spent too many nights sitting on the starboard seat drinking vodka. What will Heather do when she catches her foot on a frozen lump? Or will he shatter, scattering across the ground like the pieces of a tedious puzzle? What can he do but choose? The only way is to choose – take sides with truth or memory, sanity or madness, the real or the imagined.

He opens and closes his hand. He wants to lean toward the companionway and touch the shadow that's standing there. But then, in the next moment, it fades. There's nothing now but black, gray, and silver. He listens. Not a breath of wind. Even the shrouds are silent.

chapter two

IN DETROIT is a large subterranean nightclub, difficult to locate and forever untouched by the neighborhood's decay, where the waiters, bartenders, musicians, and patrons live their lives in black and white. Men and women dressed in bright colors walk through the door and then slip into comfortable duotones. The room admits fedoras and berets, zoot suits and bell-bottoms, pocket watches and piercings. The terraced floor descends gently to a stage; the bar, handsome and well-stocked, dominates the rear; and the tables, arranged in perfect rows, offer white linens and soft silver lamps.

Waiting on stage, brilliant in a wash of light, is an archtop guitar. Always a classic instrument from the 1930s or '40s, usually a Gibson, maybe an L5 electric or a Super 400, it stands as an open invitation.

Those who finally take the stage do it as a kind of ceremony, a rite of passage, having earned admission to the club. All the old masters sooner or later turn up. This is where they perform, now when the world has spun away and become something strange and inhospitable.

Coleman knows all this and often spends time at the bar. He watches the people come and go speaking of Tony Mottola or Barney Kessel, of Art Ryerson or Charlie Christian. He gazes at the L5 bathed in light and imagines what it would feel like in his hands, resting against his body.

He likes to think of his father in this place. He buys him a drink. In the smoky haze, they talk about what matters. Sitting at a table on solid ground, he explains, in terms his father appreciates, the anatomy of a fine instrument, how each part has a purpose and a very particular name. He points to a legendary guitar, describes its quirks, tells how it speaks or shouts for the person who plays it. He says what he believes, that a great guitar will challenge the limits of what's possible.

After a while, he tries a different tack. "I've seen you at haul-out," he says, "with the boat in its slings. You stood there fretting about the gel coat and the frayed lines. You said, 'It's my life, this beat-up plastic heap.'"

His father stirs his drink. "I wanted more children," he says.

Something in the room tilts.

He sees his father's sadness and wonders how their conversation arrived here. "Why?"

"I always wanted a brother or a sister. I wanted you to have that. It wasn't easy being H.M.'s only child."

"So what happened?"

His father shrugs. "After you came, your mother lost interest."

"That's hard to take."

"Why? It had nothing to do with you."

"If you say so."

"I would've traded my boat for a brother," says his father.

"Is that the truth?" He raises his vodka and drinks. "Why didn't H.M. and Grandma have more kids?"

"She wasn't able."

"That must've stuck in H.M.'s craw."

"Maybe," says his father. "But he never said a thing about it. At least not to me."

"H.M. taught you to sail. He made you a singlehander."

"That's right."

"That's something that most people can't do."

"It isn't so much."

"You're being modest."

"And what about you?"

"Only classical players go solo."

"I didn't mean that," says his father. "I meant – " He lowers his voice. "Was there anything you learned from me?"

His father shifts in his chair. Most of the nearby tables are empty. The lights come up for a moment and then the Black & White Club goes dark.

He puts down his glass. It's Saturday. The faucet lies in pieces on the kitchen counter.

As it turns out, the new washers are the wrong size, and this gives him a reason for another vodka and tonic, his second of the afternoon. He isn't going to the boat. What happened there the last time makes him stay away. If the snow keeps up, he'll have to shovel the driveway. He wants it clear in case Heather comes by.

In the garage, he keeps pickle jars filled with screws, nuts, and washers. To find exactly what he needs is purely a matter of chance. He dumps the washers on the workbench and spots a couple that might fit.

He walks through the living room on his way back to the kitchen and sees his black guitar case leaning against the wall. It looks like a small sarcophagus. A curious echo of what his father said runs through his brain. He goes over it, rehearsing it like a difficult lyric. "It's only my life," he hears himself whisper.

"This thin, hollow-body guitar, banged up and scratched. There's a head and neck, too. Even a bridge." That's it, he thinks. I should've mentioned the bridge. So much of what we loved was the same. It would've been easy to explain had I found the right word.

He rarely meets anyone new at the Black & White Club. No one ever buys him a cocktail. On a slow night, he thought he heard a woman who was three sheets to the wind ask him why he was there. "Waiting for Bogart," he heard himself say. "Really," she said, "I had no idea." He likes to use this line whenever he can.

He admits now that wherever he is, regardless of the hour or the company, he finds himself waiting for Jennifer. Or is it Brian he's waiting for? The possibility that either will appear or wish to do an encore in his life strikes him as pretty far-fetched.

It's because of Jen that he actually knows a few things about living. "What stays with us for the long haul?" she says. "Not books. Not photographs. Not even music. It has to be something bigger – an early thaw, maybe, or a lightning storm." He pictures her in summer with the sky growing dark and the smell of damp earth floating in the air. She sits at a window and listens for the first drops. And when the trees rustle and the rain begins, she rests her cheek on the sill and observes, in a sudden illumination from childhood, that nothing important has changed.

I spent a lot more time with Maureen, he thinks, but somehow no essentials remain. He can only dig up bits of practical advice, common wisdom about cleaning the house or raising a child. But Jennifer persists, her scent, her way of seeing the world.

She asks him to stand in an open field at dusk and watch for the rising moon, but the vast, featureless sky makes him dizzy. She calls to him.

He turns but loses sight of her in the turning. She can't be far, he thinks. I can hear her breathing. I can feel her heart moving under mine. He wants her to stay with him, the generosity of her smile, the way she lifts her arms to gather her dark hair and pin it. And her words, so many still in his head, but always the last words she spoke when he walked out of the orchard in October, the ripe apples waiting to be picked.

He'd looked for anything that would cause her pain, because to his young mind needing her was a kind of weakness, an admission that he was no good on his own. He told her that none of it mattered, that he didn't know when he'd return, that getting away from where he found himself was what drove him, kept him from drowning in his father's life. "Come back or not," she said. "You won't find me." He hesitated, feeling himself torn in two for the second time, not realizing that all this was familiar and final. She held him then, giving him the words that never leave. "It happened too fast," she said, brushing her cheek. "For a while, everything was whole."

His mind begins turning. He drifts to Chicago and the last years with Jen, the two of them just out of college and glad to be in the Midwest once again.

He likes Chicago for the musicians and the clubs; Jen's returned to salvage what family she can. She wants to settle down in the city, away from her parents, both of them tired and bitter, but close to her sister and a few old friends.

They take an apartment in Wrigleyville. He eventually gets bookings in some of the better rooms around town. She teaches high school part-time.

Jen seems forever young. Her face is round with brown eyes and a Roman nose. Her olive skin is smooth. Her black hair falls long and straight over her shoulders and breasts. She wears tight jeans and sleeveless shirts. The whole of her body achieves a perfect rhythm when she walks. Jen is always this woman.

On most nights, she comes to hear him play and brings to bear a remarkable concentration, concerning herself not only with the guitar but with the other instruments as well, drawn to the shifting qualities of tone and phrasing. She'll go anywhere, the hotel lounges, the seedy, out-of-the-way places, but the Green Mill soon becomes her favorite. She likes being on a first-name basis with the people there. She enjoys the no-nonsense authority of the bouncers and waitresses. She respects the audience for jazz: small, eccentric, and reliable.

They meet Brian James at the Green Mill, and Jen invites him to the apartment after the show, after listening to a perfect balance between guitar and bass, a sublime counterpoint rising from the stage that she recognizes as chemistry, as some sort of communion.

BRIAN sits at the kitchen table drinking bourbon neat. "Here's to you, Cole."

"And to you," he says, returning the favor, his vodka like polished ice. "And for Jen, too."

He suddenly feels at home, nearly satisfied and calm, taking in Brian's dark skin, the deep resonance of his voice, the rhythm of words, of laughter, and the careful raising and lowering of drinks. At the Green Mill, they fluently went back and forth, trading licks and choruses, speaking for each other in a new language. Now, in the kitchen, he feels the same way, confident that if he started a thought, Brian would finish it.

Brian admires the pictures taped to the fridge, the cupboards, and the walls. Most are black-and-white: street scenes, old women, CTA stations, vintage guitars.

"Jen's the photographer." He pours more vodka for himself.

"I need a new camera," says Jen.

Brian leans over and takes a close look at a street lamp glazed with ice. "Not bad," he says. "How long you been here?"

"Just over a year," she says. "I can hardly believe it."

"I heard something about Boston," says Brian. "Where's the accent?"

"We met in Boston," she says. "Boston College. I'm from here and Cole's from Michigan. He grew up mostly in the thumb and then downriver Detroit."

"Thumb . . . ?"

Jen shows Brian the back of her hand, four fingers together and the thumb out. "You know," she says, "this is Michigan." She points to her thumb. "Cole raised some hell around here."

Brian looks over her shoulder. "That lake," he says. "Is that in Michigan?"

"That's Lake Erie," she says.

Brian wraps his long fingers around his drink. "I stay out of the water," he says. "I keep it out of my booze, too. And who's the big man in the picture?"

"Cole's father," says Jen. "Dorian. Dorian Moore."

"All right, Cole, I gotta know. Was it him that gave you your name?"

"Why do you ask?"

"Well, I knew some guys on the South Side named Coleman, but I haven't met any from the thumb."

"My parents named me Jason," he says. "I'm the one who picked up Coleman."

Brian sips his drink and waits.

"It was a club owner in Detroit. My first decent gig – right after high school – an upscale room with good acoustics. Anyway, he thought Jason Moore was a little flat. He thought we'd attract a better crowd if I had an interesting name."

"Once in a while I get the same shit," says Brian. "I'm a man with two first names. Seems to confuse people."

"I like it," says Jen.

"I plan to keep it," says Brian.

Jen cuts her bourbon with water and ice. "I'm hungry," she says. "I wish we had some food in the house."

"We could go somewhere," says Brian. "I know a good after-hours place. Sometimes they pull a trio together. I've been hoping to play with a trio."

He clinks Brian's glass. "Me, too."

Jen looks at both men staring at their drinks. "So find a drummer," she says. "Then you'll have a trio."

HE THINKS of the early days when they went out searching for gigs and Brian's string bass seemed larger than life – a mirrorlike finish, sloping shoulders, and a deep, unequivocal voice. Brian made graceful and surprising moves, walking, running, and flying on the fingerboard, playing fragments of melodies and sudden chords, the music moving through him as if the bass and his body were fused.

He remembers too the first year working with Brian, living without sleep, picking up local gigs and then going on the road, doing the rust belt tour – Cleveland, Buffalo, and Detroit. In the end, they both returned to the Green Mill, to Jennifer.

He understands now, though he'd prefer not to, that wherever he went, through good clubs and bad, he traveled with a burgeoning self-doubt, a feeling that any value or substance he had, any claim to authenticity, came from playing jazz with a black man. In the back of his mind, he wondered if he was really an imposter, a fraud – a white man posing with a jazz guitar.

Every so often this feeling rose in him and made him act in ways that were awkward and self-conscious – like the year he drank only what Brian was drinking and wore the same color clothes, imitating Brian's style, though not so much in music as in the way Brian walked or the way he cocked his head.

In those days, he imagined the possibility of dyeing his skin, an elaborate scheme that led to a new father, black women, and circuitous conversations with Charlie Parker. He invented a black town where he walked all night without worry and practiced his black voice, his black expressions, and paraded in front of voluptuous women, each of them magical and dark, who returned his gaze and measured him with their eyes and smiled and clapped their hands. After such long and drawn-out dreams, he felt like a man in a haunted house, like a pale fool who thinks it's a fine idea to open the basement door, his arms and legs trembling, his thoughts teeming with excitement and shame, possibility and fear. Almost always he welcomed the shaking and the fact of being overwrought, because only in those moments did he see his position and begin to understand that the people and places he desired came from a bottomless need, a yearning to be someone other – someone that didn't look, act, or feel like himself. He decided then that his only hope was a fresh start, a life without boundaries, the capacity to show the world a face not his own – a face not inscribed by history.

He thought at some point he'd confess all this to Brian, but he never discussed it with anyone, not even Jen.

ON HIS hands and knees, squinting at the yellow linoleum floor, he looks for the washer that slipped out of his fingers. He finds it just under the stove, uses a screwdriver to pull it out. With it comes a coil of greasy dust. He wishes it hadn't happened. It was fine not knowing about the crud under there. Now he has to think about it. Consider whether or not it's worth it to move the stove and scrape the stuff up. He figures ants will want their share sooner or later. Years of buildup – like the bottom of a boat that needs a stiff brush.

He holds the washer between his thumb and index finger. When a faucet leaks, he says to himself, a tenant usually calls the landlord. But I'm in no mood for a catechism.

Oddly enough, the landlord's last visit did involve maintenance. She'd made up her mind that the living-room curtains needed cleaning. When she came to collect them, she spotted his guitar case – the black sarcophagus – leaning against the wall.

"The talk," she said, "is that you're a musician."

"Who's talking?" he said.

"Some friends of mine. They say you used to play all over Detroit and elsewhere."

"Do you believe everything you hear?"

"Why would they make up something like that?"

"I don't know."

"They also said you were tall, dark, and handsome."

"I was young then." He liked the way her short hair revealed her face and shoulders.

"You're not so old," she said.

"I'm turning gray."

"Salt and pepper looks good," she said. "Besides, you're the only man I know who doesn't have a gut hanging over his belt."

"Thanks."

"Where do you play now?"

"I don't."

"It's God's gift," she said. "Don't be ungrateful."

He watched her hips as she walked across the room. "Can I help you with the drapes?"

She shook her head. She took down both panels and slipped them into a shopping bag. "Don't abandon your gift," she said, standing at the front door. "And until these are clean, don't go running through the living room naked."

The screen door slammed. She walked to the curb and squeezed her hand into the pocket of her tight jeans and then turned to display the perfect silhouette of her breasts. She opened the door of her station wagon, slid into the driver's seat, and started the engine, her rosary dangling like an air freshener from the rearview mirror.

He gets the washers and the hot-and-cold lever in place. It occurs to him that his hands feel fine, that he managed the job without stiffness or pain. He runs the water as a test. The steady leak seems to be fixed, but a slow drip remains. The heavy drops hit the stainless-steel sink with a decided thump. He knows he'll be able to hear it in the bedroom. He'll have to keep the door closed. He moves the spout over the drain. It isn't so loud that way.

It's always the trivial noises that bother him, a telephone ringing or a dog barking, someone talking or coughing during a beat of silence in a song. He grimaces at the pop of a bad cord or the humming and buzzing of amplifiers.

Setting up before a gig, he'd often tell Brian, sometimes more than once, to reverse the polarity on his amp.

"I will," said Brian, "but it won't help."

"Where's it coming from?"

"Who knows?" said Brian.

"I'm telling you, I can't start until we fix it."

"Ignore it," said Brian. "Pretend it's not there."

"I can't," he said. "It's not possible."

WHEN Tom Traynor came in on drums, he invented the group's name, the CBT Trio – an acronym that put Coleman and Brian first.

"We ignore whatever's new," said Brian, answering a question on a local radio show, trying to explain the trio's style. "We simplify. We break the music down and discover how the songs were built. Even the arrangements are lean."

They made no apology for what some people called the "elegiac mood" of CBT's repertoire. They didn't have to. It was the trio's interpretations of the great ballads that audiences recognized with energetic applause: "Misty," "In the Still of the Night," "Someone to Watch Over Me," "Cry Me a River," "I Get Along Without You Very Well," "Come Rain or Come Shine."

Coleman showed a gift for melody, stating the theme but then leaving it, traveling sad and complex distances until he reached an isolated world, a strange land where virtuosity mattered more than being part of any group or scene. At that point, having used up most of what he knew, he'd return in unexpected ways, playing familiar strains that seemed part of some deep and reawakened memory. Brian laid down the bottom with a steady poise, but when he took the lead, busting out with his smile and his exuberant assurance, the music changed direction, moving into a realm that felt like church, as if a divine revelation were close at hand. He was also, along with Tom, an arbiter of dynamics, building the moment to a crescendo or reducing it to near silence. Tom kept all this together, marking time, using the brushes like a magician, reigning in the guitar or bass when he thought either had gone too far.

A well-known critic described the trio as "elegant and spontaneous – an island of spare beauty."

After a while, the boys became regulars in two or three of the better rooms in Chicago. They did a few tours in the Midwest, enough to pick up a following. They started to write, slipping some of their own compositions into the middle of established sets.

There's proof, he thinks. In the closet are four reel-to-reel tapes and a box of black-and-white photos. Jen got a lot of CBT on film. Out of the corner of his eye he senses her movements, her curiosity, as she looked for a fresh angle or an expression she hadn't seen before.

He shuffles through the pictures. He appears to be a happy man. Don't get sentimental, he thinks. Nostalgia is a fool's game. Even so, the contentment on his face is undeniable. It's a fair record – Jen gets the credit for that – but a large part of the story can't be seen. The images, he realizes now, capture no background, no context, none of his attitudes, beliefs, or betrayals – none of the forces that carried him headlong toward damage.

It begins in Chicago. The CBT Trio opens for three nights at the Mill. Meredith Moore is in from Detroit to hear her son play.

She sweeps into the apartment with an aristocratic bearing that isn't the least bit pretentious. Tall and stylish, a thin woman with long auburn hair, she puts down her bag and takes in the entire place, especially the dust and disorder. "Your father wanted to be here," she says. "But he's up on Lake Huron again – another extended trip."

"You mean cruise," he says, kissing her on the cheek.

"Do I? When I say cruise I think of ocean liners and distant lands. Not a dinghy in the middle of Lake Huron."

"A thirty-six-foot sailboat is hardly a dinghy," he says.

"Let's not argue," she says.

He hangs her coat on a peg near the door.

Jen smiles and steps in Meredith's direction, but she snags her foot on the edge of the rug and stumbles. Meredith catches her. Without being the least bit flustered, she says, "I'd love to, my dear, but my dance card is full."

"I greet all my guests this way," says Jen, laughing and trying to regain her composure. Meredith's strong, she thinks. It must come in handy on the boat. She says, "Are you meeting up with the cruise later?"

"Heavens no," says Meredith. "I can barely dip my toe in a pond, and I've never been on a boat."

"I had no idea," says Jen. She looks embarrassed and confused.

"Mom doesn't sail," he says. "She's afraid of the water."

"You're unkind to say it."

"But it's true," he says.

"It isn't so much fear," she says, "as wisdom."

Jen wonders why a man like Dorian Moore would choose a woman who cringes at the sight of water. Of course, she should've realized before this – and after several visits to Detroit – that Meredith never goes out, whether for a day or an evening sail. She'll make an excuse, report a sudden headache or discover a forgotten but long-standing appointment. It's all an extravagant game. Dorian, naturally, is too tight-lipped to say anything about it. But Cole could've let her in on the joke. The knot in Jen's stomach starts to loosen. She says, "Would you like a drink?"

"I've had more than I need," says Meredith. "Where's the concert tonight? What time does it start?"

"It isn't a concert," he says. "We're doing three sets at the Green Mill. We'll probably start around nine."

"Fine. Where can I take you to dinner?"

"I don't eat dinner," he says.

"That's absurd," she says.

"I don't eat before a show."

"So when do you eat – 2:00 A.M.?"

"More or less."

"You'll wind up with ulcers," she says.

"We can grab a salad before the show," says Jen.

"Absolutely not," says Meredith. "If Jason's crazy enough to eat in the middle of the night, then I can be just as crazy."

"Mom, how many times – ?"

"I know. Coleman. Coleman. Coleman. What do you expect? I called you Jason for almost twenty years. Now, if you'll kindly point me to the guest room, I have some freshening up to do."

Carrying her bag, she glides down the hall and disappears.

"She's hydrophobic?" says Jen in a loud whisper. "You never mentioned it."

"It didn't seem important."

"Not important – in your family I'd say it's very important. For Christ's sake, Cole, that's like forgetting to tell me you play the guitar."

"Not exactly."

"Did your father know? I mean, did he know before they got married?"

"I suppose so."

"And he still married her?"

"She swept him off his feet. It's that Swedish thing. He probably thought he was marrying Ingrid Bergman."

"Even so. He spends so much time on the lakes. It must be difficult."

"Maybe he likes it that way."

"Maybe she's a sexual athlete," says Jen.

He shakes his head. "I can't think about that," he says.

HE ANTICIPATES a long night at the Mill, but the sets run smoothly from one song to the next, the music flowing like water, and it seems they've just begun when Brian announces the last number, a request from Meredith, "Moonlight in Vermont."

Tom and Brian fall back, leaving plenty of space, and so he takes the opening, finding new turns and dark corners in the song and creating a world all his own. He plays a cascade of diminished runs that electrifies the air. It sparks a small flame of tenderness and fills the room with audible light.

When the music stops, he glances at his mother and notices that something in her face has changed. Rather than the usual distance and pride, he sees sadness, even helplessness, but when he looks again the vulnerability is gone. Her eyes still sparkle, he thinks. She still commands attention.

Afterward, Brian and Tom politely explain that they've made other plans for dinner. Jen suggests an Italian restaurant on Halstead.

"It must be interesting," says his mother, "to live so close to a baseball park."

"We have friends," says Jen, "who can watch games from their rooftops."

"Do they sell tickets?"

"Some people do," says Jen. "But it's considered bad form."

"There are many kinds of bad form," says his mother, "but that, I think, is not one of them."

"If we had a driveway or a front lawn," he says, "we could charge people for parking."

The waitress brings three glasses of red wine and a basket of bread.

His mother raises her glass. "Here's to the success of CBT," she says.

He dribbles wine on his white shirt.

His mother dips her napkin in a glass of water. "You need to deal with that right now," she says, "or it'll never come out." She dabs the stain.

Pretty soon most of the shirt is wet and clinging to his chest.

"I have an audition," he says. "The Robert Shore Quintet is looking for a new man on guitar."

Jen's face fills with exasperation.

"That's wonderful," says his mother. "And is Robert Shore somebody I should know about?"

"He's in the big leagues. Tours the country playing major rooms."

"Chicago's certainly filled with musicians."

"Shore's based in Philly. That's where I have to go for the audition."

"CBT is doing so well," says Jen. "Why now?"

"Because that's what boys do," says his mother. "At least the boys in the Moore family. They're never satisfied with their station in life. You should've known Jas – I'm sorry – Coleman's grandfather. The man was pure ambition."

"It's a long shot," he says. "I probably won't get the gig anyway."

"Have you told Brian?" says Jen.

"Not yet."

"I don't get it," says Jen. "You won't be out front if you go with Shore."

"It's the experience," he says. "I'll be in the same circuit with guys like Joe Pass and Kenny Burrell. I'll get more notice."

The waitress sets three steaming plates on the table. Jen picks up her knife and fork and starts cutting her sausage. "When are you leaving?" she says.

"Don't worry about it," he says. "Like I said, it's a long shot."

In a different summer, on a day thick with humidity, Otis in a crisp white shirt and black pants opened the door and peered through the screen. "You been lost?" he said.

"I'm sorry, Mr. Young."

"For what?"

"For not showing up."

"It's no skin off my back. And the name is Otis. Or maybe you forgot that, too."

"I'm sorry," he said.

Otis crossed his arms. "You done?"

"I wanted to give you this." He unrolled a magazine. "There's a story in here about Coltrane and they mention you."

Otis opened the door. He looked at the cover. "Thanks," he said. "Maybe you should come in?"

He stayed put. "And I wanted to tell you – " He cleared his throat, an attempt to hold down his feelings. "We're moving away."

"Who is?"

"I am," he said. "And my family."

"What about the store?"

"My father closed it. The one in Saginaw, too."

Otis tucked the magazine under his arm. "You always said he never liked it much. I guess you were right."

"I was right about that," he said.

"You still practicing?"

"All the time."

Otis smiled. "Too bad you don't keep in touch. I'd like to hear how it goes."

"I'll let you know," he said.

Otis chuckled. "I guess I'll read about it when you crack the big time."

"Maybe."

A tired expression filled Otis's face. "Don't be a fool, now. Don't count on it. It's – "

"I know," he said. "It's a long shot."

"Yes it is," said Otis.

He wanted to hug the old man. "When I get back here, I'll stop by."

They shook hands.

"You do that," said Otis, "by all means."

Before he'd gone far, he stopped and thought about turning around, but this time he was afraid. He waited for the creak of the screen door, heard it close, and then kept walking.

WITH the afternoon light almost gone, he begins shoveling fresh powder and watches for Heather's headlights through the flurry. When he was a boy, he hated this chore; the sound of metal on concrete bothered his ears. These days he finds it enjoyable, almost peaceful, making a clean edge where the driveway ends.

He looks up and down the street. Of the houses he can see, most remain dark. His neighbors are either out for the day or waiting for the snow to stop before they shovel. Two or three inches so far, he thinks, and no sign of it letting up. His fingers are cold. When he played for a living, he wore gloves to protect his hands. Now he never wears them. Working on the boat or Maureen's house, summer and winter the same, his hands go bare against fiberglass, wood, mortar, and dirt. Heather scolds him about it sometimes. "You have to save your hands," she says. "Why save what's ruined?" he fires back.

He bumps the mailbox and snow falls between his sock and the top of his boot. He tries to brush it away, but before long he feels an icy wetness against his skin.

"My feet are freezing," he says.

"You got the wrong shoes," says Brian. "You can't be wearing wingtips in this shit."

"I know. Wet socks depress me," he says.

"Tell me, Cole, is the set list all you wanted to talk about? Because if it is, I'm not sure why we had to do it out here on this fine Chicago street."

He tells Brian that he couldn't say anything with Tom sitting there, too – that what he needs at the moment is fresh air and daylight. "It's only an audition," he says. "I'll be back before I miss anything important."

"But what if you get it?"

"No point in thinking about that. It's a long shot."

"But you've thought about it, haven't you? They could give you the green light. There's a chance. And I'm sure you've considered that and dreamt up another whole life for yourself."

"It could help both of us."

"That's shit and you know it. Shore isn't looking for a bass player. And that isn't the point. We've got something here. We've got a sound and people who come to hear us play. And this is a good town for music. And nobody's telling us what we have to do or when we have to do it. But you're willing to piss on that." Brian kicks the snow. "Like they say at the Mill, CBT stands for 'Chicago's Best.' Only you don't buy it."

"It's just a shot. I need to find out what it's like."

"I understand that. I do. But you could've let me in on it before you made your plans, before you dragged me out here in the snow and started complaining about your lousy socks."

"I'm sorry. Is that what you want?"

"No. I want you to go. Have a great audition. I hope you get the gig. It'll be great for both of us." Brian stops at the door. "Get the right shoes," he says. "It snows in Philly, too."

JEN's waiting in the kitchen when he gets home. She puts two bowls of vegetable soup on the table and throws the ladle in the sink. He fills a glass with ice, pulls out the vodka, and pours himself a double.

"So you told him," she says.

He sips his drink and nods.

"Is he happy for you?"

"As a matter of fact, yes. He said it'll be great for both of us."

"What else did he say?"

"He told me to get the right shoes."

"You mean he told you where to get off. Was he angry, hurt?"

"I'm not sure."

"Well, you can be sure about me – I'm angry."

He stirs his soup.

"It isn't what you want that bothers me," she says. "It's just that your timing is bad."

"Tom says I have a great sense of time."

She sweeps her hair to one side and secures it with a silver clip. "You're impatient."

"You've mentioned that before."

"You go too fast. You want everything right now."

"So what's the alternative? I suppose you'd like me at home doing the laundry or watching TV?"

"That's a ridiculous thing to say. The alternative is to find time for me, for your friends. Everything you do has an edge to it. Where's the joy?"

"It's hard for me to let things slide."

"That's because you're out to prove something."

"Can we eat?" he says. "The soup is getting cold."

"It's all about him," says Jen.

"Leave my father out of it."

"Why? You say you failed him. So until you decide otherwise, it'll always be about him."

"I'd like to change the subject," he says.

"All right," she says. "Let's talk about your mother instead."

"Fine."

"Too bad you couldn't take her to the airport. We had quite a chat."

"What about?"

"I'm not sure how to describe it. Social climbing, I guess."

"Her family's from Bloomfield Hills. It was a step down marrying my father."

"It wasn't that," says Jen. "She thinks when two people are in love, when they're committed to each other's dreams and doing good work, other people are drawn to them. She said it's dangerous to attract admirers with happiness and talent, especially when you're inexperienced. She said it's easy to get used."

He puts down his spoon. "I've never heard her say anything like that."

"Well, that's pretty much what she said – right before she got out of the car."

He pours more vodka.

"You're going to miss my sister's wedding."

"Your sister won't miss me."

"Probably not," says Jen.

ALREADY he sees a thin layer of snow where he just shoveled. He likes the look of it, inviting in a stark sort of way. When Heather comes, she'll have a good place to park. There's less visibility, he thinks, now that the wind's kicked up. He turns his back to the gust and tries to rub some warmth into his hands.

Through the blowing snow, he makes out a shape that seems to be a station wagon. I've paid the rent, he thinks, walking to the foot of the driveway, carrying his shovel like a weapon. I won't let her pull in – no time now for a visit. But as the car approaches, he realizes that he has it all wrong. It's a foreign job, elongated but sleek, and at the wheel is a gloved and bearded man, rather than his born-again landlord. The car glides by as if it were floating on the snow.

He hears a sound in the distance, maybe a chain saw or a snowblower – a nasal whine like a voice through a bullhorn, like a woman announcing the imminent departure of a bus.

The station overflows with people. His ragged suitcase sits on the wet pavement, but he won't put down his guitar. "You need to get a winter coat," he says. "Your lips are turning blue." Jen huddles against him.

"When will you be home?"

"Early next week," he says. "Tell your sister congratulations. When I get back, we'll go to the Green Mill for a drink."

She shivers but is otherwise still. She seems frozen to his body. He kisses her.

"It's time," he says. The wind pushes him onto the bus. He gives his ticket to the driver and then turns to see Jen, pale and stiff, disappearing into the crowd.

It's been a long afternoon, he thinks. He opens the garage, stamps his feet, and leans the shovel against the wall. He trips on a paint can and stumbles, catching his arm on the truck's side-view mirror. His workbench, tools, and accumulated boxes allow less and less room to maneuver. Parking the pickup in front of the house would be an easy solution, but he doesn't like the idea of turning his garage into an attic. He struggles to unlace his boots. He has the first one off when Heather pulls into the driveway. He hobbles out to greet her. She tells him to go inside. "You can't come out here in one boot," she says.

Heather follows him into the house brushing off snow and untying her scarf, and her red hair catching the hallway light makes the dullness of the afternoon and the tedium of the leaking faucet suddenly disappear.

He pours milk in a saucepan and sets it on a low flame. "No marshmallows for me," says Heather. He spoons chocolate powder into large mugs and puts blue paper napkins on the counter. "Hungry?" he says.

"Not really." She checks the photographs taped to the freezer door. "Look at you," she says, "with that long hair. And Brian James. Now *he* was a handsome man."

He keeps an eye on the milk. "Thanks a lot," he says.

She moves in closer. "Was this up the last time I was here? Jennifer took this, didn't she? You've been cleaning out your closet again." Heather tips her head and frowns. "You know, you can take down these old pictures of me whenever you want. Maybe you could replace 'em with my senior portrait."

He chuckles. "How'd it turn out?"

She picks up the napkins and walks over to the kitchen table. "Oh, the pictures aren't in yet. I'm not sure when they'll be ready."

He hands her a steaming mug. They sit across from each other stirring the hot chocolate.

"Has that new boyfriend of yours booked you for the prom?"

"No, he hasn't. And what's the deal? You never ask about boys."

"I know. I've decided to change my ways."

"Has Mom been talking to you?"

"Not about this. I just thought that if it's important to you, maybe I should know about it."

"Okay," says Heather. "So how's your love life these days?"

"That hurts," he says.

She puts on a serious expression. "C'mon, Dad. If it's important to you, I should probably know about it."

"You think you're pretty damn clever, don't you?"

"You can't blame me for inheriting your brains."

"First sarcasm and now flattery."

"I watch and learn," she says.

"What would you like to talk about?"

"I don't know." She looks out the window. "Why don't you tell me something I don't know anything about. A snowy day is good for that."

"Like what?"

"Like one of your stories about H.M." Her eyes wander back to the freezer door. "Of course, you've never said much about Jennifer."

"Havelock Moore was a pirate. I've told you that story."

"Well, Jennifer then. The only thing I know about her is that Mom says you should've married her."

"Your mother said that?"

"More than once."

He wants to ask if Maureen said it with bitterness or sympathy. But he knows better than to ask Heather for that kind of judgment. "How about Brian James?" he says. "You seem pretty interested in him."

"You bet," she says. "Let's move to the living room."

He settles on the couch and Heather flops down next to him. He balances the mug of hot chocolate on his leg and takes a moment to collect his thoughts. Then he begins the story of Crystal James, a blues singer, a churchgoer, and Brian's mother.

"Everybody who heard her sing and who knew her last name thought she was the sister of Etta James," he says. "'Crystal can make a hard man cry,' they said. 'If you listen too long, she'll break your heart and leave you with the pieces.'"

"That sounds like a song," says Heather.

"It is."

She smiles. She reaches over and presses his right hand between her two smaller hands.

He continues: "Crystal got married young. Her husband, a drummer, managed their band and booked gigs all over Chicago. Then Brian was born. He listened to his mother in church. He said she praised God and railed against sin. But the preacher didn't like it that two members of his congregation were 'prostituting their God-given talent.' So the preacher started talking to Crystal. He wanted to make himself the band's new manager – that's what Brian always said."

He sips his hot chocolate. "I could tell you a different story."

"No. This one's fine," says Heather.

"It isn't really about Brian. You sure?"

"Yeah."

"All right," he says, not entirely convinced. "Crystal went on singing and trying to explain things to the preacher. She sang until a new baby began to show, until the crowded clubs and the late hours made her sick. She ran a high fever and went to a doctor too late. When the fever spiked, she lost the child. The preacher said afterward that her loss was a punishment for wasting her God-given talent – 'for singing sinful songs in houses of sin!'"

"How old is Brian?" says Heather.

"Close to my age," he says. "If he isn't fifty already, he will be soon enough."

He watches Heather's face as she rubs the bones and joints of his hand. He hates that his fingers are crooked, almost swollen.

"After the miscarriage," he says, "she figured the Lord was speaking to her through the preacher, ordering her to sing only in church. When she told her husband, he picked up a lamp and threw it across the room."

He stops but Heather nods, urging him to finish. He says, "The band went for a while without a singer, but they eventually split up, and Brian's father drifted away, taking his drums and the family car. Crystal James sang only in church after that. By the time I met Brian, she no longer sang at all."

"Is that true?" says Heather.

"There it is – always the same question. Don't you believe my stories? Do you think I make them up?"

She giggles. "What about the Black & White Club?"

"What do you mean? What happens there is true." He smiles. "Well, maybe not all of it."

"Why are your stories always so sad?"

"Sad stories are easy to remember," he says.

"My life isn't like that," says Heather.

"That's a good thing. Do you want more hot chocolate?"

"No thanks. I want you to play a song."

He looks at the black case in the corner of the room. "Not today," he says. "The strings need changing."

"That's a crummy excuse. Next you'll say you don't know where you put the amplifier."

"I know where it is. But it hasn't been fired up in a long time."

"Well, let's find out if it still works."

Heather hurries across the room. She sees a thick layer of dust on the case. She grabs it and swings it around, steps between the couch and the chair, pushes a stack of magazines on the floor, and lays it on the coffee table. She opens the case.

She recognizes the guitar: the pear-shaped body with f-holes and a venetian cutaway at the top, the sunburst finish, a dark edge that bleeds to red and then yellow, and the gold-plated pickups. "It's beautiful," she says. "Even more than I remember."

He disappears down the hall and returns with a small amplifier. He slips off the cover and plugs in the power line. He pulls the guitar out of its case and rests it on his leg. "Open that compartment," he says, "and grab me a cord." He checks the action. The strings feel all right. He rearranges the extra pillows on his end of the couch, positions the amp and the coffee table so that the space feels uncluttered, and then flips the power switch and gives the tubes a minute to warm up.

He turns up the volume and starts tuning, making faces when the strings won't cooperate. Having come this far, he feels exhausted. The guitar sits heavy on his thigh and the neck is cold.

"How are your fingers?" says Heather.

"Okay," he says, wishing for a moment that she didn't know the truth. He shakes out his left hand like a wet rag. "What should I play?"

"An old song," she says. "Something you and Brian used to do."

He lets out a deep breath. He starts with three notes that to Heather sound almost uncertain, though afterward she'll think of them as leaves falling. Then he plays the first chords, a sound so rich that later when she learns the title, "September Song," she'll say that somehow she could picture the colors of autumn – bright reds and yellows, the warmth of gold becoming brown. But for now, she listens, hearing him sing a few words under his breath, watching his face for any sign of pain.

The song keeps him from thinking. *Oh, it's a long, long while from May to December.* He moves by instinct, hearing what his fingers produce in the second before he plays it. The only time is the beat, the temporal quality of the measure that he now seems to shorten or lengthen, phrasing and rephrasing the melody as the mood demands. *Oh, the days dwindle down to a precious few . . .*

As the final notes fade, he glances at Heather. He sees her curled up on the other end of the couch, her eyes closed.

The amplifier pops when he shuts it off.

"Don't stop," she says. "I'm not sleeping."

He rubs his left hand. "Did I pass the audition?"

Heather opens her eyes. "You always pass the audition," she says.

"Jesus – "

"What's wrong?" she says.

"That's what Brian said. More than once."

"Isn't it good to pass an audition?"

"Not always," he says.

"Why not?" says Heather.

"Forget it." He unplugs the guitar and puts the cord away. He wipes the neck and the fingerboard with a soft cloth. He lays the guitar in the case, flips the top down, and snaps the latches closed.

chapter three

HAVELOCK MOORE, drawn irresistibly to the radio, turns up the volume. He recognizes the tune, "Stardust," and finds himself speaking the words under his breath. *The melody . . . haunts my reverie, and I am once again with you . . .*

The music buoys him up. It carries him forward and back. He floats in time, returning to the river, the silver Detroit River, a luminous streak that inspires him, even at this juncture, to dream.

He stares at the gold dial.

He tries to stop thinking. He concentrates, hoping for a steady calm, but the borders in his mind give way. Now, no matter the effort, none of it can be forgotten, not the Great War or the wars that followed, not the crossings or the tricks of navigation, and certainly not the lies, expedient though they were, or the grim betrayals, the costs, the necessities of doing business.

Be smart, he thinks, hold fast to a line – but the song and the river run . . .

He takes up the planks and lowers the first case into the bilge.

The air is thick with humidity. A cold sweat streams down his face. He wears leather gloves and lifts one case at a time. He feels grateful for the weather: clouds, no wind, and a deep, impenetrable darkness.

It is 1932. He's made the crossing without trouble. Stepping off the boat, he turns and looks at Detroit.

He does most of his work after midnight. He starts from the Detroit shore and travels less than a mile without running lights to the Windsor shore, where he moors at an unlit pier and loads the waiting cargo. He moves with rehearsed precision and keeps noise to an absolute minimum.

When the work requires silence, he thinks of his mother mending a tear in his shirt or trousers and wanting him to stay with her in the hush of their apartment, only the two of them, his father dead before the War. He sees with the clarity of a picture the peeling brown door, its dead bolt thrown, the gap between the door and the threshold stuffed with a thin rug to keep out the winter draft. Then he sees his mother's long hair swept to one side, and her thick hands pushing and pulling a needle through coarse fabric, drawing and cinching the thread, the hypnotic rhythm of a woman stitching sails. And again, like a recurring dream, her breathing, the silence spun by her steady hands, and the longed-for peace of the living room vanish with the creaking of wooden steps, with footfalls that approach and finally stop at the peeling door. His mother looks up.

He starts the boat and shoves off. The water stretches in every direction like a black sky. He aims for his favorite light, a street lamp that stands taller and burns brighter than the rest.

When necessary, he tells people that he operates a shipping business and hauls merchandise for J.L. Hudson. He never considers himself a rumrunner, a name he finds distasteful. Instead, he calls himself a ferryman, an old boatman, exploiting the unruly freedom of the Detroit River, defying Prohibition with a pirate's guile.

In daylight, he appreciates the river as a guiding force, an instrument of fate, oddly attractive with its factories, sewage, and scows. But in darkness, without comfort of moon or familiar stars, the finite certainties of time and distance fall away, a condition made worse by his state of mind, by weather or fatigue.

His last crossing felt clumsy, as if he'd taken on too much. He kept hearing faint, inexplicable sounds. He wanted to push the throttle, skim across the water like a flat stone, but he held his course and struggled against the current. I may go under, he thought, believing then that the shoreline had somehow disappeared.

In his spare time, planning to outwit or outmaneuver any opposition, he explores the river from north to south, a thirty-two-mile stretch that rushes from Windmill Point to Lake Erie, an open border between Canada and the United States – a boon to free commerce, or so he likes to say.

He cuts the motor and drifts in deep channels to mark the shifting current. He sees slag heaps, stone fields, and rough-hewn wire that make a strange, but unmistakable, symmetry. A pile driver hisses and pounds. He floats past the sluiceway of a steel plant, the river roiling and steaming and turning bright red. He starts the engine.

When he reaches clean water, he reduces speed and floats slowly into the shallows. After a while, passing gingerly over rocks and debris, he finds what he always needs, a wharf where creosote and pigweed thrive, a deserted place where the launch can be moored and kept secret.

He wants the river for himself, a private resource, but there's no way to hinder or shut out the competition. When layoffs come or factories close down, rumrunners rise up like seaweed. They find cover in the coves and inlets, most of them outfitting old boats – schemes of dark paint, insulation, and bogus tanks.

Crossing to Canada, they fill the tanks with whiskey or gin. Sometimes they wrap special cargo with heavy line and lash it beneath their hulls. When a crackdown begins, they use submerged cables and metal drums, dragging the booze from Peche Island to the foot of Alter Road. Finally, in winter, with the river locked up, frozen by a subzero blow, they resort to carts and sleds, risking dim tunnels or the shifting ice.

He was cocky and green when he took his first job on the waterfront – learning the ins and outs, trying to steer clear of losers and thugs. By the next season, with a launch of his own, he began making runs as a freelancer, a supplier, servicing some of the blind pigs in Rivertown.

These days his setup is clean and predictable: Hiram Walker provides the whiskey and the Purple Gang launders the cash. When things get messy, he improvises. More often than not, he receives orders and collects his take from nameless go-betweens. He likes being one man removed.

A PEELING brown door, its dead bolt thrown, stands in his mind. It offers no safety or consolation. It fails to keep out the rising thump, the echo of someone entering the building and climbing the steps.

Footfalls stop on the landing. His mother looks up.

He imagines leather boots, the snow and slush melting, puddles forming on the doormat. No knock for now, but he believes he can hear a man breathing in the same way that he heard men breathe in the trenches, a shallow and cautious sound.

When did this begin? Was it after I shipped out? Why does he collect in person? He wants to ask his mother these questions, but since he's been home they talk less and less.

His mother stares at the door and holds her breath. Her silence is a strange comfort.

AFTER HE docks, secures the boat, and feels the safety of solid ground, he walks to the corner of Orleans and Franklin and stops at the Jackpot, an establishment that caters to raconteurs, cardsharps, and con men of all persuasions.

He recognizes the bartender who greets him with a booming voice and a handshake. He stands at the bar and the man next to him, a gambler in a silk shirt, takes a sudden interest in his name.

The gambler's never heard anything so high sounding and strange. He repeats the name to everyone within earshot. "Did your mama and daddy dislike you?" he says, laughing so much that he spills his beer.

He buys the gambler a whiskey and tells the bartender to leave the bottle.

"Don't mind if I do," says the gambler. "I'll drink to your highfalutin name. I've never once met a man named Havelock." He raises his voice. "If anyone here's ever heard the name HAV-E-LOCK, his drink's on me."

He turns and smiles at the gambler. Then he grabs the whiskey bottle by the neck, swings it in a perfect arc, and shatters the man's jaw.

Everyone in the Jackpot freezes.

He puts on his hat and straightens his coat before dragging the gambler across the floor and sitting him in a chair. "You can call me H.M.," he says.

He steps out of the Jackpot, the first leaves falling, and checks to see if he's being followed. It's the same here as on the river, he thinks. The odds are no different, especially when the wind picks up and the boat feels sluggish. He's been chased five times this season and turned away from landfall more than once.

Despite the risk, he never tires of the Detroit skyline: the Penobscot Building, the Union Trust, and the Barlum Tower. He considers it a privilege to see it so often from the Windsor side and from the boat.

For a long time, whether in daylight or after dark, he'd kept a close eye on the construction of the Ambassador Bridge. At the opening in '29, they called it the greatest suspension bridge in the world, one hundred feet longer than the one in Philadelphia. After that, they dug a wide tunnel so that trucks and automobiles could travel in both directions beneath the river.

Not even the crash – not even laborers drowning or being buried alive – could stop the march forward, he thinks. Not even ice storms or the water's will.

He remembers listening for a low and cautious breathing, waiting with his mother in absolute silence. Then a fist pounds on the door. His mother shakes her head, implores him to be still with a raised hand.

He freezes, tightening the muscles of his body as he once did, lying face-down in an open field with the sound of enemy boots close by. The knocking begins again, harder this time, more insistent.

Calling to collect at this hour is unusual. The city is bitter cold and the streets are empty. The knocking stops and starts.

He can hear the man breathing. He's heard it before. It's the sound a man makes when he's desperate for something – food or cash – when secrecy and stealth are no longer his concern.

The radio plays old songs, whets desire, drips sound like sweet liqueur – then the music fades and a voice floating on the air speaks of love and fresh-cut flowers.

He remembers how quickly it all happened, his first glimpse of Faya on a Monday and then meeting her father by the end of that week, how Faya had adored him and how her father had written him off as a man of insufficient means. The embarrassment pained him, of course, but it also spurred him to save money and stow it where it couldn't be found.

He'd made his first attempt at betrothal on a cloudless day after cutting his hair and buying a new suit, but Faya's widowed and pigheaded father dismissed the idea.

"You're a boy with an uncertain future," he said. "She will wait for a shop-keeper, for someone of real substance." He mopped his brow with a hankie. "But do come again if circumstances provide."

After that, Faya's father dispensed with formalities and complained about his feet. "No circulation," he said. "The tip of my little toe is black."

When Faya realized that her suitor had gone, she wept and threatened to run away.

Her father changed the lock on her bedroom door and kept the only key.

On the same day, he ordered new shoes, his third pair, from the finest boot maker in England. These, like the previous pairs, were too tight, stopping enough blood at his ankles to leave him standing on senseless feet. Having spent so much money on the shoes, he wore them everywhere, to work and to church, for a stroll near the river, even to the Jackpot, where the shiny leather commanded more respect than any man deserves.

A year or so later, Faya sent a letter, this one more urgent than the others. "My Dearest Havelock," it said, "I've now refused a well-to-do butcher and a middle-aged banker. If you don't come soon, I fear I'll be carried off."

Charged by the letter, he once again donned his suit and called on Faya's father.

He stood on the welcome mat and knocked.

After a long interval, Faya's father, red-faced and grimacing, opened the door. Shifting his weight from one foot to the other, he leaned and swayed, his swollen feet crammed into the shoes. He winced when he took a step. He hated to admit it, but several of his toes had turned black. "The leather needs more stretching," he groused. "How difficult can cowhide be?" He said he appreciated the visit but wouldn't discuss an engagement. "These feet are causing me too much trouble. Give it a month or two," he said, "and we'll see where things stand."

"Father can't hold out forever," said Faya. "Do what he asks."

"All right," he said, "I will. But it's all for you, not him."

In pursuing Faya, he'd been obliged to suffer a fool, a snob plagued by ill-fitting shoes, and so he felt nothing but satisfaction when he showed up for the third time, hat still in hand, and discovered that the old man could no longer answer the door. The gangrenous foot was gone, lopped off by a doctor who, according to Faya, dumped the shoes at the curb and burned them, expressing with some gusto his contempt for human vanity.

The patient suitor spoke his piece, refusing to sit, unruffled in his shirt and tie, while Faya's father reclined in a leather chair, his bandaged leg resting on a stool.

"Only one?" said the man without a foot. "What kind of shipping business uses one boat?"

"Someday I'll have a second. Maybe a third."

"Faya is my only child. Why should I give her up for 'someday'?"

"I've made a considerable sum. More than you hoped for."

Faya's father scratched his leg near the edge of the bandage. "And you can prove this?" he said.

"If I must."

"You realize, of course, that I can't go with you to the bank."

"It's not in a bank."

"Are you a fool? I should have for a son-in-law a man who stuffs money in a mattress?"

"That's not where I keep it," he said. "I don't keep it in the house."

"And where you keep it is safe?"

"Safer than a bank." He stepped closer to Faya's father and saw the old man, his red face twitching, shrink in his chair. "I plan to take her," he said. "She's packing her bag as we speak. So you can give us your consent, and she'll stay here until the wedding, or you can refuse me and she'll leave now."

Faya's father was apoplectic. "You're impert – ," he sputtered, reaching for his crutches. "I'll have you arrested."

"We'll be gone before you can pick up the telephone," he said, glancing at the bandaged stump. "And it appears that chasing us is out of the question."

"We'll be married," said Faya, descending the stairs with her suitcase, "before you can find us."

"Faya, you can't go. Who'll care for me? How will I walk?"

"We'll hire a nurse," said Faya.

"You're ungrateful," said her father. "It cuts me. It's like losing my other foot."

"So it may go," said Faya. "You know what the doctor said."

He stood beside Faya and looked down at the footless man. "You have a choice," he said.

Faya's father lifted his short leg and dropped it back on the stool. "This is blackmail," he said. "I don't have a choice."

"Of course you do. It's very simple. Either the three of us will agree on a wedding day, or Faya and I will marry this afternoon."

Faya's father agreed to two months from that moment, believing that he'd be able to change his daughter's mind or spirit her away. He was consumed, quite naturally, by a vengeful desire to prevent the marriage. He was also consumed by gangrene.

Before the nuptials, he lost his other foot. On the prescribed day, bound to a wheelchair, he found himself drugged, fevered, and disintegrating, unable to kick up dust or walk his daughter down the aisle.

Not long afterward, he put a large sum of money in an envelope and left it on the hall table. Then he died, footless and alone.

Faya found herself unable to weep. "It's revenge," she said. "My father's curse on our honeymoon."

He wrapped his arms around his wife. "Don't be angry," he said. "There's really no point. Most men plan their revenge. What happened to your father was nothing he planned."

AT THE apartment, in the silence just after the War, the knocking begins again, but this time he opens the door, his body still sharp, and sees the leather boots dropping water on the mat and the face of the landlord that flinches – a register of surprise, the shock of greeting a soldier as opposed to a woman.

"Is your mother home?" says the landlord.

"Any business you had with her," he says, "you can now take up with me."

The landlord almost smiles. "I'm afraid that won't be possible."

His military training calls for a quick, but accurate, decision. He observes the distance between the landlord's hand and shoulder. The arms of the man are thin despite his winter coat.

ALWAYS worried about Peche Island, he sets out under fair skies or, if need be, in the face of high winds and rain. He grows anxious on the way. Visiting once a month was adequate when he was a bachelor, but now, with a wife and child, he makes the run each week, anchoring in a hidden cove in the half hour before sunset.

He pulls on rubber boots and slogs ashore, a spade resting on his right shoulder like a weapon. When he reaches dry ground, he doffs the boots and hides them in a cluster of shrubs.

At this point, his routine becomes ritual; he checks and double-checks his markers to confirm that nothing's been touched. As he loses sight of the river, he turns around, watching and listening for any movement or noise. From here, it's not far. He follows a dry creek bed to a stand of scruffy trees.

He crawls behind a screen of branches, bushes, and tall grass. With the edge of his shovel, he sweeps aside twigs and leaves – debris that he'll carefully put back before he goes.

He digs until he hits the chest, keeping the soil in a neat pile. He clears only enough earth to lift the lid. Then he inspects his treasure. He often makes a deposit or a withdrawal, but what he really wants is the reassurance of seeing it.

He hopes someday to keep his fortune in a more accessible place. There's no going to it in winter. And lately he's bothered by a buzzing in his ear, the voice of Faya's dead father saying it's a fool's game to live without combinations and vaults. The words get under his skin like a sliver. He wants no financial institutions meddling with his money. He wants no unsolicited advice.

He remembers reading Emerson, the argument that society is a joint-stock company prepared to sell a man's freedom for higher dividends, for the benefit of preferred investors. I'll leave my money where it is, he thinks. I'll wait, see what comes. What I must do is all that concerns me.

STUDYING the river on clear days, searching its vague surface for new information, even the most fleeting, he pictures old pilots on the Mississippi and imagines a bend where two rivers join, where clear water mixes with brown.

He drifts and takes a few soundings on the Windsor side.

He drops the lead line at the stern. Watching it go, he thinks of Huck and Jim. He imagines them on the Detroit River, the two friends floating down from Windmill Point, resting easy in free territory, lying together on a raft beneath a blanketing sun.

He's fond of this image.

He can't explain its comfort to himself or to anyone else. It takes him back to his own youth, when all things seemed possible, when the silliest games became a hero's journey and no defeat – no competition or battle – was made up entirely of defeat.

He sees the ideal forms of Huck and Jim, their arms and legs splashing in the silver stream.

He rests his mind on this picture, a habit that shores up his strength, his substance, and provides a ready escape, at least for a moment, from the odd fear that grew in him during the War, a belief that his skin and bones were fading, turning into fog, as if his body were white vapor and nothing more.

WHY DID his mother, having lived so long in Detroit, give the landlord her trust? He blames the War. He blames himself. He could've stolen the money and figured out some way to send it back. He should've realized that a woman like his mother, so entirely alone, makes an attractive and challenging target.

The landlord owns the place. He can toss her out. He can force her to make a choice.

Without money, she has no protection.

The lesson, he thinks, is a hard one. A man's decisions must stand as a bulwark against vulnerability. There's no time for regret. The best way is to choose, pursue an available course and take it without ambivalence or shame. To do otherwise is a sad resignation, a dull surrender to forces left unchecked.

THE RADIO speaks of rain, a late spring, and now, after all the speeches and ballyhoo, the repeal of Prohibition.

The end seems entirely clear – the shipments drying up and the river less crowded than before – a new amendment, the Twenty-first, and Michigan, the Wolverine State, leading the charge for approval.

Faya rubs the stubble on his face. "Fetch your razor," she says. "I'll give you a proper shave."

"Let it be," he says. "I'm ready to grow a beard."

"At least a beard, a real beard, would be softer than this." She runs her fingers along the edge of his jaw.

"I don't care much for shaving," he says. He gazes out the kitchen window. The flower beds look bowled over, flattened by the heavy rain.

Faya removes her apron, folds it, and hangs it on the pantry door.

"It'll be finished soon," he says, leaning on the counter. "I'll be out of a job when the truckers and distributors get up to speed."

She squeezes his hand. "It isn't your fault," she says. "We'll be fine."

He turns from the window. "What will I do?" he says. "I may last the season, but after that – "

"You'll get hold of things," says Faya.

He kisses her fingers. "Yes," he says. "I'll have to."

"Are you going?" she says.

"Not tonight. The moon is up."

"I'm glad."

He won't cross anymore unless the river is black. If a strange shape rises in the dark, he cuts the engine and drifts. He keeps the bow pointed toward shore. It's there, after all, that a body stays put.

"Let's have a fire," says Faya.

"I'll tend to it," he says. "I'd like some tea."

She hums the tune playing on the radio and places the lid on the teakettle and sets the kettle on the stove. He admires her for trying to conceal her misgivings, for tending to her business as if nothing in the world had changed.

He worries and finds it difficult to sleep. He abhors lying awake on clear nights, fears the openness of solitude, so he fixes his mind on something in the room, an immediate shape, an object large enough to fill the empty space.

When he manages to sleep, he dreams of a sudden storm that rolls him over, washes him up on the Windsor shore, his boat cracking and splintering on the rocks. A crowd gathers, wringing their hands, asking for an explanation. "You ignored the warnings," he says. "You made no preparations for disaster." He grows impatient. He sees the people around him as ciphers, vessels of faith.

Waking in the night, he feels shaky, less certain of his mental and physical abilities. Growing older promises no leeway for error, no margin for infirmity or distraction, no peace.

He says nothing of this to Faya. She sleeps the sleep of the young. He wonders what he'll be after the slow disintegration of muscles and nerves – a cloud of fog, perhaps, a white vapor settling on the earth.

THE WORD on the street is that the landlord won't be trifled with. He owns the building. He plans to own most of Detroit. People say he was too old for the War, but they call him a scrapper, proud of the fact that he never backs down.

Most of the tenants won't talk. They get jumpy and close their doors when the conversation gets down to brass tacks. Others take pleasure in spilling their guts. There seems to be some agreement that the landlord thinks of his renters as property, movable parts, objects that require space and not much else.

The complaints stack up like old garbage. He listens. He digs up more whenever he can.

LIKE a soldier, he partitions his mind. He marks time on the river, floating in the shadows or visiting Peche Island when conditions allow.

Away from the water, he stays close to Faya and keeps their small house in order. They park a Ford coupe in the driveway. They own a Victrola, a collection of jazz recordings, and several pieces of fine German crystal. A mahogany table with four chairs occupies the dining room. In the bedroom is an English armoire with doors that feature hand-carved rosettes and small windows of beveled glass. At regular intervals, he polishes the wood furniture with lemon oil and beeswax.

Dorian is three years old.

Faya had wanted a second child by now, but so far she's been unlucky.

"We'll put the crib in the living room," he says. "If a baby shows."

Faya shakes her head. "Let's have the crib with us. There's more than enough space."

He smiles. He'll rearrange things and figure out the best plan.

He drags Dorian out from underneath the table and hoists him high into the air and sets him on his shoulders.

Turning the corner, seeing the lit window, the apartment where his mother sits waiting, he knows the landlord will come.

Snow's fallen steadily since morning. Detroit is a ghostly white and the streets stand empty and quiet – a hush he's hoped for since his return. In a few moments, he'll unlock the door. He'll bend and kiss his mother on the cheek. She'll ask about his day. He'll talk about being hungry or tired – something to discourage her questions. Then he'll sit with her in silence. He feels calm only when voices, when sounds of any kind, fade and disappear.

With the boat laid up early, with the roads muddy after a heavy rain, he drives his Ford coupe through Rivertown and parks at the river's edge. He walks along the seawall.

The Windsor shore looks sooty in the September light. It's used up, he thinks. He sees no place for himself in Detroit or on the other side.

Days and weeks disappear, and the boat rests in its cradle.

He spends time at home, rattling around the house like a bored retiree. He chases Dorian from the kitchen to the living room and back again.

He sits with Faya and drinks coffee. "It's a strange renaissance," he says. "The saloons in Rivertown have risen from the dead. All the signs are up and the front doors are open. They keep 'em open all night. Beer arrives by truck, and the drivers unload it in broad daylight. The cops on the waterfront are out for a stroll, for sunshine and fresh air." He pulls on his beard. "Life on the river is obsolete."

A week or two later, without much discussion or second guessing, he sells the house and the launch, collects his treasure from Peche Island, and packs Dorian, Faya, and four suitcases into the Ford.

With a hard rain slapping the windshield, they drive north. "Saginaw is a small town," he says. "My mother's family lived and died there. That's where she was born."

Faya smiles and peers out through the rain.

"We'll buy a big house," he says. "I've got plans for a new business. A clean break is lucky. It's less painful and quick to heal."

"I SHOULD'VE gone away," says his mother. "There's plenty of work in the country."

He checks the door – its brown paint peeling – to see if it's locked. "Leaving would've been suicide," he says.

His mother lets out a pent-up breath and a deep moan rises from her chest like a tree groaning.

"You had no choice," he says. "You were alone for too long. But now I'm here. I'll do the thinking for both of us. I'll decide if and when we should move."

SAGINAW lies at the crossing of four rivers, in the crook of the thumb, a once-booming lumber town now desperate for a working mill. The streets are windswept and somber, especially in November when people and storms blow through in a hurry, as if stopping or stalling runs the greater risk of fatigue and dissipation. It's a city built on salt, where a man of means can quietly take up residence, build a business or a dynasty, and go unnoticed until his efforts become visible. By then, of course, his neighbors think of him as being there from the start, a stalwart member of the community, proof of the town's miraculous potential. It makes no difference that he hailed from Detroit or that he squeezed his wealth out of a bottle.

He moves Dorian and Faya into an old house with a spiral staircase and corner towers, a structure reminiscent of a French château.

He works in Bay City, fifteen miles north on Route 13, the founder and sole proprietor of Halyard & Mast Marine Supply, a large building on the east side of the Saginaw River and close to Saginaw Bay. Finding and leasing the right space had been quick and cheap. The building came with sturdy shelves, display stands, glass counters, and cabinets for charts. It included, as well, a sizable showroom floor and a private office in the rear.

He commissions a sign and scrubs the awning and windows. He outfits the office with a mahogany desk, an executive's chair, and a brass lamp.

He orders an "insulated chest" made by the Hall Safe & Lock Company of Cincinnati, Ohio. The men who deliver the strongbox, following his instructions, slip it off the dolly and lay it down so that the door swings open toward the ceiling.

The next day he pulls up a section of the office floor, cuts away the joists, shoring up the segments that remain, and begins to dig a rectangular hole that is twelve inches deeper and sixteen inches longer and wider than the safe. In the hours that it takes him to finish the digging, he feels an unwanted movement at the bottom of his mind, a thing both familiar and unsettling. He begins to worry. He fears that something left for dead has begun to shift and there's no other course except to argue it down. He concentrates on the work at hand, wheeling the dirt out the back door and piling it in the alley.

On the third day, he dumps gravel into the hole, tamping the stone into a firm base. In the alley, he mixes cement and water in a wheelbarrow and carefully rolls the load into the office and pours it in the hole. All the while, the thing at the bottom of his mind keeps moving and demanding attention. It drops slowly into his chest and then his stomach. He works faster, striving with each breath to avert a sudden rush of nausea and weakness. He repeats the process of mixing and pouring until a thick layer of concrete covers the gravel. He smoothes the surface with long-handled tools and gives it time to dry.

Next he builds forms out of planks and two-by-fours that parallel the sides of the hole. He mixes more cement and pours it into the forms, making walls that are eight inches thick. Still, the anxiety stays with him. He wishes he'd brought a flask of whiskey from home. He feels cranky. The effort not to think has made him tired and dissatisfied. He breaks down the forms – his eyes, ears, and mouth filling with dust – and reveals a concrete rectangle that allows just enough room for the safe.

In the next week, he builds a small hoist between the strongbox and its final resting place. He checks the pulley and rope and then raises the safe and lowers it slowly, using his foot to keep it in position. Once he has it settled, he mixes more cement and uses a flat shovel to fill the thin gap between the safe and the surrounding walls, cementing the black box into the ground.

He breaks down the hoist and makes a trapdoor out of the loose floorboards. Finally, he packs his life savings into the safe and slowly closes the door so as not to let it fall and clang, steel on steel, like a church bell.

He paints the letters H.M.M.S. in gold above the dial.

He closes the trapdoor and puts a wool rug and two chairs on top of it. Now he's ready to open the store.

In the War, he learned the necessity of making careful preparations, of establishing and executing a plan with methodical precision.

It's because of this training that he follows the landlord for several weeks. He observes the man's habits, where he stops for meals and where he walks. He knows there'll be no end to the landlord's visits, the incessant knocking, and the unseemly demands. The man will have what he wants without marriage – an exercise of power – and he'll take more pleasure from that than from anything else.

He knows the landlord's routine. Now comes the waiting and watching, the cool vantage outside of time, as if time itself were indifferent.

HE RISES each day at 6:30 A.M., drinks his coffee with Faya, kisses her on the cheek, and drives from Saginaw to Bay City, opening Halyard & Mast Marine Supply at 8:00 A.M.

No customers call at that hour. No more than a dozen or two call in the first months. Except for the radio – the signal suddenly drifts, the song fading – Halyard & Mast enjoys the silence of a graveyard, the parts, equipment, and supplies waiting in mute assembly.

When the weather's warm, he keeps the front door open, allowing for an occasional sound from the street. He often jumps when the telephone rings, startled by its shrill urgency.

At 5:00 P.M., he closes the front door, straightens the papers on his desk, and leaves by way of the alley, returning home for dinner with his family.

The neighborhood perks up for an hour in the evening but then quickly settles down. At sunset, the streets and the houses are still. "Even the saloons in Saginaw are quiet," he says. "No bands. Not even a piano." He never cared much for the longhair stuff, but he'd like to hear again the quartets and sextets that kept the blind pigs lively, or the dance bands that played in the huge Detroit halls. There's no smoke or sweat, he thinks, when you crank a Victrola or listen to the radio.

WHEN Dorian's old enough, he takes the boy up to Bay City to teach him something about the store.

Dorian explores the stock, plays with anything that seems unbreakable. He likes to climb, and if there's a box filled with shackles or cleats then he usually finds it, pulls it down, and falls in an avalanche of metal to the floor.

He observes that Dorian is fond of the mailman, the only regular at Halyard & Mast, a jovial guy who hands off the bills, winks, and admires for the umpteenth time the store's magnificence. The mailman says, "It's a gold mine still sitting on its mother lode. I'm sure of it, Mr. Moore, you're bound to be rich."

"Maybe. Or maybe not," he says. "Tell me, does the post office own any boats?"

"I imagine it does," says the mailman. "But not the branch here in Bay City."

"I'm not surprised," he says. "I guess there's no hope for a fleet."

He watches the mailman go and then opens the first of three letters addressed to Halyard & Mast. He's been cagey, he knows, using the smallest part of his fortune to create a respectable inventory, purchasing equipment and supplies at cutthroat prices from men struggling and going down.

He's filled the store – the Depression be damned – with sails, spars, rigging, fittings, and tackle.

He's stocked it with mainsails, headsails, and topsails; gaffs, boomkins, and whisker poles; heaving line, stays, and shrouds; davits, bitts, binnacles, blocks, cleats, and belaying pins; and in every aisle, shelves sag and boxes burst with gadgets and gear for navigation, safety, and maintenance.

He believes that his investment will yield a significant return. He predicts revenue, success, and expansion. Everything at Halyard & Mast stands ready. But it won't work, he knows, without patience, without the capacity to hold firmly and wait.

He sits on the floor of his office rearranging the contents of his strongbox. He counts out his monthly allowance and sets it aside. Now and then, he enjoys a brief surplus of cash when a marina or a boatbuilder makes a purchase, but otherwise he uses only what he needs. "I can buy the necessary time," he whispers to himself. "I can make the store pay off."

He reaches up to close the safe, but the door slips and slams shut like a metal jaw. He sucks in a quick breath, checks the fingers on both hands. That could've been painful, he thinks.

He spins the dial and secures the trapdoor.

HE WAITS outside of time.

He hears leather boots on the wet bricks of the alley. The air is bitter cold, a night without moon or snow. He knows that patience can defeat almost anything. The cold is bad but no worse than in the trenches. The flashes of light on the horizon were no sunrise, no promise of warmth. There was nothing to do but wait. Men waited and stopped breathing. He holds his breath.

ON FRIDAYS in the summer and fall, he picks a bouquet of wildflowers for Faya, nothing fragrant or flashy, just a bundle of common blooms that grow in long stretches near the river. He yanks them up and trims the roots and wraps them in brown paper.

Faya has a vase ready when he walks through the door.

"Darling, here's a bit of color," he says.

"Thank you," she says. "They'll be lovely on the table."

"I wish I could bring you orchids," he says, "or long-stemmed roses."

All this, she knows, is part of their custom. "These are more beautiful," she says.

"Perhaps another time," he says. He kisses her, smells the fragrance of her soap, and feels the exquisite softness of her skin. "How are you today?"

"The same," she says. "No heartburn. No sickness." She fills the vase with water and tries to coax the flowers into some sort of arrangement. "The doctor said it may not happen again. I'm thinking he's right."

"How's Dorian? Was he out raising Cain?"

"Yes," she says.

"That's good."

On another afternoon, home early from Bay City, he sits at the kitchen table and watches Faya knead dough and wash vegetables. He drinks coffee and takes comfort in the economy of her movements, the lightness of her step. He says the house with her in it is a rare island. Only the water – being out on the water – promises the same magic. He guarantees Faya a ride on Saginaw Bay, on Lake Huron, though for now he has no boat.

"Stop your staring," says Faya. "You'll distract me and I'll make a mistake."

"You'll have to suffer it," he says. "Watching you calms me down. I like the hush."

"You'd think you'd be through with silence by now," she says.

"The store isn't quiet," he says. "It may often be empty, but it's not quiet."

Dorian rushes in and the screen door slams, breaking the spell.

"What's for dinner?" says Dorian.

"Biscuits and chicken soup," says Faya. "But you're a little early."

"Do I need to wash?"

"Not if you're running out again. But if you're staying in, then march to the mudroom and use plenty of hot water and soap."

Dorian downs a glass of milk and goes out the way he came in, the screen door slamming.

Faya smiles. "Time goes fast," she says.

"I can't imagine this kitchen without you," he says.

She moves away from the chopped onion, smiling, blinking back tears. "The kitchen is just the kitchen, with or without me," she says. "We're getting old. And you're getting sentimental."

HE WAITS in the shadows, in absolute silence, between a stack of crates and a large downspout. He listens for any change in the landlord's step.

He watches the man walk by, looks at the face without seeing it, and glances at the back of the head – at the hairline just above the fur collar.

He steps out of the shadows and hooks his arm around the landlord's neck.

With the accuracy of a surgeon, using a quick upward motion, he thrusts the blade of his bayonet between the top of the spine and the base of the skull. The kill is immediate and without sound.

At the height of the season, with sailboats dotting the bay, he enlists Dorian to do some dusting, sweeping, and window washing at Halyard & Mast.

An old woman and her son walk into the store not long after opening. They nose up the aisles as if they were taking inventory and then stand like sentinels in front of the cash register. They insist that the store's merchandise is the property of Uncle Sam.

"Roosevelt needs metal and rubber," says the sturdy young man. He wears a scar that starts at the corner of his eye and runs down his cheek. "You should do your part."

Glaring at the young man, he says, "I did that before you were born."

The woman grunts and takes her son's arm to steady herself and the two of them march out in a show of consternation.

That evening, having closed the store, but waiting for a truck to pick up a downstate order, he notices – and Dorian does, too – a faint scratching sound at the front door. He investigates. He expects to find a trucker waiting for a package. Instead, he catches by surprise the scar-faced young man, down on one knee, attempting to break in with a crowbar.

He curses at the young man and grabs him by the collar and yanks him into the store, the boy pulling and jerking like a snagged fish. "So you're a thief," he says, gripping the crowbar, wrenching it free, and tossing it aside. "You'd steal from me."

"It's for the war effort," says the young man, clenching his fist and swinging.

"You're no patriot – you're a punk." He catches the boy's fist in his hand and slaps him three or four times across the face.

"And you're giving aid to the enemy," says the young man, the scar on his cheek pulsing with blood. "You're a coward. You're afraid to fight."

Like a trigger, the words set off an explosion – a knocking down of partitions and doors. He squeezes the boy's hand. "There's no shame in being afraid," he scowls. Then he pummels the kid's face until the kid collapses on a coil of rope. Using the side of his foot, he kicks him once in the stomach.

The boy groans and wheezes – his windpipe closing.

Finally, in a last surge of fury, he raises the kid up from the floor and throws him belly-down into the street.

He closes and locks the door. He glares at Dorian, who hasn't moved a muscle. "Look at you," he says. "You're a pillar of salt."

Dorian is tongue-tied.

"Find your feet, boy. It's late – and your mother's waiting."

HE CHECKS the alley in both directions. Time to go, he thinks. He leaves the landlord facedown, blood flowing from his ears and nose, blood running between the bricks, trickling through the vents of a manhole cover.

The military taught him this manner of killing. They made him practice and perfect the technique using pumpkins mounted on poles. They taught other young men the same thing.

He cleans the blade. He will live outside of time until he's able to sleep, to dream, until the clock wakes him the next morning and he hears the sound of his mother making coffee.

ON THE way home, he tries to get Dorian to say something but the effort proves tiresome. They stop at the greengrocery and see nothing unusual on their way into the store, but as they depart, each carrying a full bag, they run into an unshaved man who, with a miniature flag in his left hand and a Bible in his right, appears to be preaching to patrons and passersby. "You must shun all forms of passion," says the man.

A woman in a white coat with a little boy at her side puts a coin on top of the man's Bible.

"A big stick starts early," says the man. "It breeds contempt and indifference."

From behind his bag of groceries, Dorian peeks at the man's face. No one coming or going stops to listen, but the man continues as if he were addressing a loyal congregation.

"The miseries of a lifetime live in your body," he says. "They grow, waxing and burgeoning, roiling in your guts and chest, gathering in lethal concentrations just under the skin."

The rest of the drive home is uncomfortably warm and silent. Insects splatter on the windshield. In the air is the smell of approaching rain. The transmission thumps, then the engine hesitates and whirs.

HE SEES the light in his mother's face, the rush of hope, when the landlord fails to knock at the usual hour. He watches the newspapers and listens on the street for rumors. Weeks pass and the landlord leaves no evidence of his life except a house filled with antique furniture and a closet stuffed with fine clothes.

The apartment building falls to auction and the new landlord turns out to be a woman. She often comes by for tea. A touch of confidence returns to his mother's eyes. She smiles.

IN THE newspaper is a picture of Winston Churchill drinking tea. Faya clips it out and tapes it to the icebox. Dorian seems to like it. He mentions it each time he grabs a snack.

"How Dorian goes on about Mr. Churchill," says Faya. "He thinks he's a great man."

"Dorian thinks too much. I catch him staring."

"Staring?" says Faya.

"Yes," he says. "When I catch his eye, he turns away."

"A boy studies his father," says Faya.

He agrees but neglects to mention that whenever he arrives home, even as he takes off his hat, gloves, and coat, Dorian gives him the once-over. And then it's the scraped and swollen knuckle, the split lip just under the mustache, or the bruised and puffy cheek that his son scrutinizes with particular interest. He makes excuses, blaming the injuries on clumsiness, on a box or a piece of equipment that tumbled from a dolly or the hand truck.

Dorian seems nervous and vigilant, watching for the dark expression and listening for the heavy stride.

He tries to reason with his son. "The current is changing," he says. "Business is good."

Dorian says nothing.

"There's plenty to do. Enough for both of us."

"I'm doing extra work at school."

"Fight me if you must," he says.

Dorian folds his arms. "I won't."

"It doesn't matter," he says.

Dorian wants to stay calm. "What do you mean it doesn't matter?"

"Fight or not," he says. "There's no winning."

After a long silence, he talks about Saginaw Bay and a lifetime of boats. "If you're given a gift, use it," he says. "But respect it, too. Don't trade it for something cheap." He thinks the boy should be happy, exhilarated at the prospect of inheriting a wealthy kingdom. "I built this business," he says. "I made a life for myself, and for you, too."

In time, with the first money from Halyard & Mast, he buys a summer cottage in Port Austin.

He buys a powerboat but finds it noisy and unnerving. He trades it in for his first sailboat, a sleek hull with one mast that he rigs for singlehanded racing.

When he isn't competing, he takes out Faya and Dorian. They sail beyond the bay in clear weather, the blue water of Lake Huron stretching to the horizon.

Dorian will learn to sail, he thinks. He'll see why it's necessary, as a crewman or a singlehander, to keep everything in its place.

He stares at the luminous dial.

The station he'd been listening to has drifted into silence. He reaches for the tuning knob but hesitates and changes his mind. He clicks the radio off and the dial goes dark. That's enough, he thinks, no more noise for a while.

He opens a window. The sun'll be rising soon. He starts making a list of chores but it doesn't help.

In the first turning of most days, waking from sleep, or in the last moments before closing his eyes and drifting down, he thinks of his mother, the apartment, and the battered door with the dead bolt thrown. He couldn't stay with her and at the same time live the life he'd imagined, but slipping away was impossible, unless he could guarantee her safety. His hope then was to leave her with a settled mind. He considers the problem again, the fact that he chose an available course, the only course that seemed possible. The effort now is to keep it buried. It takes discipline, a cold vigilance, to absorb and manage the cost. But he left her in the beauty of unbroken silence. Left her with the firm belief that the landlord had lost interest. At the end, she lived and died without worry. He gave her that.

chapter four

HE REMEMBERS the boat heeling, the light at Port Austin Reef, and a cold wind from the northwest making him shiver.

"There's no face," his father says again. "I'm telling you, it isn't there."

He remembers feeling sick, having turned out at midnight to set sail. He was called Jason then. He had no other name.

"Jason," says his father. "I don't want you going below. We're nearly strapped, and I need you to give a hand."

He knows that Havelock's not in the cabin. Havelock's not in his berth. No face, he thinks. How can it be that Havelock Moore has no face?

He looks up. Barely visible is a low ceiling of gray clouds. No moon. Not a single star. The sky shudders from one horizon to the other. He listens to the hull slicing the lake. On a run like this, time gets cranky. It slows down or speeds up. It ebbs and flows. The conditions – fair weather and a spanking breeze – make all the difference.

"I'm telling you," says his father, "if you found H.M. on the street, you wouldn't know it was him."

The words drift and disappear, leaving a blank space. The emptiness makes him uneasy. Wanting to fill it, he opens the floodgate, calls to mind all the old pictures and songs, the old colors and conversations – almost everything that he's seen and heard.

H.M. likes to say that there's nothing to believe in but wood. He calls a boat made of plastic a white whale. When he returns after days on Lake Huron, he speaks of being in irons, of ghosting, and of sailing free.

One story gives way to the next.

"On the lake," says Havelock, "there can be no dreaming about the man you'd like to be. Whoever you think you are, you lose." He checks the telltales. "Wind and sun'll wear you down until only the smallest part, the most essential, remains. But even that you leave behind, giving yourself to the boat – skin, hair, teeth, nails, the roots of the flesh – until the hull becomes your body."

Dorian looks out across the port bow.

Havelock tells himself to stop preaching. The boy has become a man, he thinks. He's grown up fast.

Dorian trims the main and it sets properly.

"That's fine," says Havelock. "You're a natural. We named you right – Dorian means 'from the sea.' We may not be on salt water, but this lake's as big as an ocean."

Dorian nods and manages a smile.

"All right," says Havelock. "Take the tiller."

Dorian moves into position.

"Remember, you can scuttle the boat, but a Moore never sinks."

The sails luff.

"For the love of Christ, don't be so weak in the knees. Watch what you're doing. You're spilling wind."

H.M. is too tall for the boat, thinks Dorian. He sticks up like a second mast. What keeps him planted on deck? What keeps him from going over?

Havelock leans on the taffrail. The sound of his voice follows the wind. It fills the sail's belly. "You don't know yourself or the boat until you're a single-hander," he says. "It isn't done easily, but there's freedom in it. The surface of things – wood, canvas, skin – falls away, and you can set yourself on a breeze, feel yourself moving through day and night, sound and silence. No person comes for you here. No one asks for your time or labor. You serve the boat and the weather. You choose your course or find a dark harbor. But it's your choice. As much as you'll ever have."

Dorian has stopped listening. He feels comfortable on the water. Free of hard ground, almost free of his father, he moves with an easy rhythm. He believes in the heavens, knows that the stars will make themselves apparent through the mists overhead. He finds no fear in capes or haunting inlets. He steers by clouds and the hunches of birds, every slippery, gliding, breathing thing.

His feet grip the deck and the sloop stretches and yawns beneath his hand.

Nothing suits him but the lake. At home, he feels cramped, cowed by the heaviness of his father's rooms. He hates the creaking floor and the cracked ceiling. He keeps to his bedroom and the kitchen, putters in the yard on nice days. Too long on land and he feels nauseous, a nervousness in his stomach and bowel that dissipates only when he casts off.

AT HALYARD & MAST, Dorian finds no relief. He takes inventory and prepares the store for new products, but he often fouls up, makes deliberate mistakes, a quiet protest that he hopes will disrupt business or at least break the monotony. If no mistake can be made, then he neglects his assigned duties, happy to put things off and slip away.

He follows the seawall until he has a good view of Saginaw Bay. The movement of boats and gulls calms his stomach. Still, he cannot escape the feeling that the store is built on quicksand, that the floor is dissolving, turning to fine gravel, and that the next step he makes will drag him silently down.

"Was your break long enough?" says Havelock.

Dorian doesn't answer.

Havelock checks off several items on a list. "Finish the sorting," he says.

"It's done."

"I saw it," says Havelock. "It's a mess. Hardware's spilling from one bin to the next and you left different sizes in the same bins. Most of 'em are too full."

"Do you want me to do it again?" says Dorian.

"If you're not too busy."

"Thought I'd go over and check the sloop. Clean up the topsides."

"Do it later," says Havelock.

Dorian walks down the long aisle and dumps a bin of washers on the floor. On top of that pile, he dumps a larger bin of nuts and bolts.

I'm a sailor, he thinks, and not much else. He can feel his father's contempt when they're together at Halyard & Mast. But on clear and blustery days when they leave the store behind and go sailing, he senses a change – a strange calm or satisfaction. When this happens, the preaching and the intimidation fall away. What remains is an old man talking mostly to himself. "Small craft live or die by their wits," he says. "That's our pride. The way we earn our solitude."

DORIAN notices, perhaps for the first time, the gray in Havelock's beard.

Faya rinses her hands at the sink. "It might rain," she says.

The floor creaks as Havelock leans over the counter and looks out at the sky. Something in the kitchen shifts.

The bread can't possibly rise, thinks Dorian. A hard weight, an undeniable pressure, fills the room. He imagines standing in a hole while a stranger fills it with gravel. At first, he can't move his feet, then his legs. He feels buried up to the waist when a hand drops on his shoulder.

"You okay?" says Havelock.

"Fine," says Dorian. His father's face is a cloudy and distorted mirror. He thinks of it as something quite separate from himself.

He looks forward to clear skies and the old man heading out on Lake Huron alone, disappearing for days at a time, running long races, practicing the duties, the religion, of a singlehander.

More than this, he anticipates the coming weeks when he'll drive by himself to Bay City and park in H.M.'s space. In the interest of avoiding extra work, he'll suspend all acts of sabotage and sort the mail, answer the phone, receive deliveries, and ring up customers with newfound precision. He'll take less than an hour for lunch and spend most of it at the marina talking with likely customers. But none of this will happen until his father leaves, until the singlehanded sailing begins.

Faya, still at the sink, says again that it feels like rain.

"I wish this weather would move through in a hurry," says Havelock. Nothing will calm him now except wind and sail, except running straight out from shore, alone on the water. A singlehander sleeps in short bursts, a necessity that leaves no time for dreaming, for the memories that persist in dreams.

When the time is right, he'll lock all the windows and doors, hand over the keys, and repeat his directive to keep everything closed both day and night. "Don't answer the door," he'll say. "If a stranger calls, let 'im rot." No one asks why he despises and berates solicitors, why he runs off drummers when he can, all of them terrified as they scamper down the front walk dropping brushes, hair tonic, and Bibles.

Dorian worries that H.M. will never leave, that something will occur, an accident or an injury, that'll tie his father to the house. Dorian's plan is to get a sailboat of his own. He'll go if his father stays. He'll slip out quietly with or without a fair breeze.

STANDING in the cockpit, alone on Lake Huron, Havelock feels something – a log or an old plank – bumping the port bow.

He steers into the wind and the boat stalls.

He puts on a harness. He frees a lanyard and clips one end to the harness and the other to a jackstay. Then he goes forward.

Lying on the deck, he thrusts his head and shoulders over the bow and inspects the hull for damage.

The boat bobs and swings like a cork in a rippling pond.

"She'll pitch me over," he whispers, his body beginning to slide. He grabs a stanchion.

Never forget, he thinks, harness and jack lines always serve better than a crew. And don't leave the cockpit – don't make a move – unless it's carefully planned. A singlehander's mistake is impatience, thinking a harness is too much fuss, believing a tether is foolishness, except for goons and wobbly guests.

DORIAN likes the smell of fresh biscuits. He likes talking to his mother, especially when H.M. is out of the house. He sits on the kitchen counter and watches a flurry of baking powder rise into the air.

"I saw a purple flower today," he says.

"Large or small petals?" says his mother.

"Small. Growing in a pile of rocks."

"Where was it?"

"Next to the road."

"Must be stubborn," she says.

"It looked lost," he says. "One flower with nothing around it. Just rocks and gravel in all directions. Why would it grow there?"

"Why doesn't matter," she says. "It's something beautiful."

"It's not pretty," he says. "I wanted to pull it up."

"Did you?"

"No. I left it."

"Good. Better it should fend for itself."

"But it can't fend for itself."

"It's there, isn't it? Who are you to decide?"

"It's just a flower," he says. He slips off the counter, opens the refrigerator, and takes out a pitcher of iced tea.

"Pour me a glass, too," says his mother.

He fills two glasses and cuts a lemon. "I bet it won't last long," he says.

THE STORE is almost tolerable, he thinks, with Benny Goodman on the radio and the morning sun, hard and flat, filling the street. The cash in the register drawer matches the receipts.

He cleans the display cases and sweeps. He raises a few windows, opens the front and back doors and the door to his father's office. A breeze comes up from the bay. It moves through the aisles like a mountain stream.

Into the store walks a tall young woman with auburn hair. She glances down the aisles but takes no interest in the merchandise.

"Can I help you?" he says.

"Not really," she says. "I'm waiting for my family to finish breakfast. I saw the open door. It looked cool and peaceful in here. The air is lovely."

"It's a fair breeze," he says.

"My name is Meredith," she says. "Is this your place?"

Dorian almost laughs and shakes his head. "My father owns it."

"I see. So you're the manager?"

"No. He's the man in charge."

"Is he here?"

"He's out sailing."

"You're the boss, then. At least for now."

"I suppose."

"Sounds to me like you should be sailing, too."

"Sure."

"Do you ever go with him?"

"Sometimes. Mostly he's a singlehander."

Meredith looks surprised. "Is that possible?"

"Of course."

"I don't know anything about boats or bays or the Great Lakes."

"There's a lot to know."

"Is there?"

He moves a stack of paper on the counter and, seeing the balance sheet, starts going over a few figures.

"I'm sorry," she says. "You're busy. I'm taking too much of your time."

"There's always work to do," he says.

Meredith leans on the counter. "But the work bothers you."

The words catch him off guard. "Is that a question?"

"It's in your face," she says. "You look gloomy."

"What are you doing for lunch?" he says.

She smiles. "I just ate. I don't think I'll be hungry by noon."

"I could take a late lunch – get some work done before we go."

"But you don't like the work."

"I know."

"It's sad. You're the boss, but you don't like it."

"Maybe you should take over," he says.

"If your father offered me the job, I'd accept."

He looks around the store and then at Meredith. "Fine with me," he says.

"I could do it," she says.

"I imagine so."

"Will you tell him I can do it?"

"Sure."

"Why do you dislike him?" says Meredith.

" – I don't."

"That's not true," she says.

"It's not that exactly," he says.

"What is it then?"

"He makes me nervous. I'm under his thumb."

"When will he be back?" she says.

"It depends."

"On what?"

"Wind. Weather."

She nods.

He looks at the curve of her neck and the perfect line of her shoulders. "Where are you from?"

"Bloomfield Hills," she says. "I'm only here for the weekend."

"Are you free for lunch?" he says.

"There's a customer," she says. "Ask him what he wants."

IT's GOOD wood, thinks Havelock. No damage.

He stands and feels the tether pulling on his harness.

Almost smiling, he remembers the last time he fell overboard. He'd somehow managed to ignore a frayed painter, lowering a dinghy into the current. Snap went the line and he plunged into port, the water closing over. But a Moore never sinks.

He kicked to the surface, saw the clouds making way for sunbeams, the water in all directions glinting like a field of diamonds. How could he drown surrounded by such beauty? How could he give up? He felt no urgency, despite wet gear and heavy shoes, to lift his body out of the bay. Instead, he floated and breathed steadily. He accepted his fall as a matter of hard use, as something unavoidable.

DORIAN sits at the kitchen table and makes a drawing of the sailboat that he'll someday own. It's a cutter. It looks like his father's sloop, but in addition to the main and jib, it carries a forestaysail, and the mast is stepped more amidships. He gives the vessel a wide beam, a full-length keel, and a dramatic bowsprit. He glances at two or three of his earlier drawings. This is the best version so far, with the freeboard and keel in correct proportion, the stays and shrouds fully delineated, a samson post on the foredeck, and visible chocks on the stern and bow. The cabin house shows a hatch cover and four portholes.

His mother comes in and puts on her apron and peeks over his shoulder. "Big dreams," she says.

"It's easy on paper."

She takes a closer look. "I didn't tell you, but I made a boat the other day." He smirks.

"The tub was full so I folded some newspaper. I did it exactly the way your father used to do it when you were a boy. I christened it *Faya the First*."

"How'd it turn out?"

"It sank." She gazes at the drawing. "What would you call her?"

"I don't know. A good name is hard to find."

"I'd call her *Blue Morning*."

He lets it sink in. "Not bad," he says. "You should use it."

"For what?"

"I don't know. A new boat, maybe."

She laughs. "If you like it, keep it. I think it suits you. You'll be a sailor just like your father."

"I don't think so."

"Why not? He says you're better than him already."

"He does?"

"All the time."

He looks at the boat he's put on paper. "Would you like to go out sometime soon?" he says.

She smiles. "We were out just a few days ago."

"I know. But would you go only with me?"

"Of course," she says. "I'd consider it an honor."

He packs up his drawings and slides them carefully into a folder. He picks up his pencils and eraser and wipes down the table. Before he leaves the kitchen, he turns to see whether he's left anything behind. He grabs the pencil sharpener and puts it in his shirt pocket.

ALONE on Lake Huron, Havelock toys with the idea that he'll keep going, sail in a straight line as far as the wind will take him.

He pictures a town on the far northeastern shore, a quiet harbor with an old marina and fishing boats. If such a place were real, he'd go there now. But then he remembers that nothing's ideal – not the unmopped deck, motoring out, not the stretched mainsail or the worn, tangled line.

On fair days, he thinks the lake is constant, less treacherous than the land. He sees the water's long reach meeting the sky, the fish and the birds eyeing each other on the horizon's blue line.

But finally, as if commanded by instinct, he looks over his shoulder. He slows the boat and finds himself plotting, figuring his position, preparing to come about.

NEXT to the phone is an old list of chores. Faya considers the possibility of throwing it away.

It occurs to her that she had uncovered, not long ago, on the table next to the big reading chair, a stack of lists concerning the basement, the boiler, appliances, cars, boats, banking, gardening, and tools. Some of the lists were at least five or six years old.

On the day she went with Dorian to Halyard & Mast, she noticed lists of merchandise covering the desk and the office walls.

And when she last sailed on the ketch, she discovered in the galley drawer, much to her dismay, a list of things that inevitably return: hunger, loneliness, nightmares, cracks like spider veins on a plaster ceiling, a dripping faucet, dry rot in the hull or keel.

Now, with Dorian finished and out of the kitchen, she glances again at the phone, at the wrinkled and soiled list. She puts the dinner plates in the sink, plugs the drain, and runs the hot water.

A ragged squirrel stares at her through the closed window. In the next instant, something spooks the animal and it darts down the fence.

She checks the yard. She sees a bird taking flight and a branch swaying. Then her husband comes through the gate.

He knocks on the back door. She throws open the dead bolt and greets him with a long embrace.

He sets a trophy on the table. It bears his name in capital letters. "I won," he says, "and I wrote it all down." He conjures a piece of paper out of thin air. "A Moore never sinks," he says. "And now, dear Faya, I can tell you why. It's all here."

"Another list?" she says. "Don't we have enough?"

She finds it odd, almost embarrassing, that taped to the bathroom tile above his straight razor, scissors, and brush is a list of general procedures for hygiene and grooming: wash face and hands; clean and clip fingernails; trim nose hair, eyebrows, and beard; brush teeth and massage gums; rinse with mouthwash; apply salve to dry skin; powder feet; check for fungus.

"Sit," she says. "You must be hungry."

She rubs his shoulders but can't put out of her mind the list on his dresser: ring, wallet, watch, pocketknife, and hat.

She watches him pull out his notepad and pencil. She observes how he draws his eyebrows together, his effort to concentrate, and then the movement of his hand as it slides across the paper, the lead scratching and tapping.

"Why so many lists?" she says. "Your memory's better than mine."

"It's important to stay organized," he says.

Away from the sloop, between racing and repairs, Havelock keeps to his office and goes over orders and receipts.

He listens to Dorian helping a customer, explaining why it would be to the gentleman's advantage to spend a little more on heavier tackle, especially for cruises and stretches of foul weather.

Later, after walking the aisles, he says, "Everything's in good order." He says it in a loud voice, but Dorian's not around to hear it.

Havelock checks a list and crosses off several items and looks up at the ceiling and thinks about stacking things higher. On some days, the windows and doors seem to bulge, as if the store, growing too fast, runs the risk of bursting. He feels a dull pain, sometimes a pressure, in his head. He pulls out a fresh notepad and starts another list.

He wonders how much more he can manage. He cleans the wide counter next to the register, rubbing the glass until it sparkles. He questions the wisdom of owning a second boat, a ketch, a stately vessel that he thought would be important for a growing family. He told Faya, who needed some convincing, that the ketch would carry a crowd. "It'll hold all of us together," he said. "It's not an extravagance. It's a steady boat. It lends itself to relaxation and peace." He saw that nothing would persuade her. "The sloop is narrow and made for speed," he said, trying to put an end to the conversation. "It isn't a boat for picnics."

He leans on the counter. He remembers buying the ketch and going out for a shakedown with a paid hand. They'd cleared the mouth of Saginaw Bay, the wind up and the boat leaning, when the main halyard gave way. After a brief discussion about motoring back, he climbed the mast, the paid sailor watching from the cockpit. He went up slowly, glancing at the horizon, pausing at the spreader and then rising again to the masthead. By then, the sparkling blue water and the back and forth motion of the mast had lulled him into a calm reverie. Waves and thoughts became one movement, and every half-seen, gliding, beautiful thing, every dimly discovered, uprising fin seemed to him the substance of a bottomless soul. He might have stayed in that moment forever, suspended between lake and sky, happy to sleep or dream, but then his hand slipped, or almost slipped, and a jolt of adrenaline shocked him into consciousness. Suddenly, he understood his position. He looked down and recognized the deep water for what it was – what it is – something hard and unforgiving. He wrapped his arm around the mast, cleared his mind, and made the repair.

A man drifts into the store, leans on the largest display case, and peers at a gimballed compass. After a minute or two, he leaves.

Havelock switches on the radio.

He hears the voice of the Lone Ranger, a burst of gunfire, and the approach of a galloping horse. The Masked Man considers the situation and asks for Tonto's advice. "You're right," says the Lone Ranger. "We're surrounded. But at least, my friend, we'll die together."

Havelock smiles. He'd rather listen to music. He reaches for the tuning knob.

"Hi-yo, Silver!" says Dorian, having returned with coffee and sandwiches.

"I think it's near the end," says Havelock. "Should I leave it on?"

"No," says Dorian. "It doesn't matter."

They eat lunch and begin checking inventory, the front door locked for the afternoon.

Havelock can't find the sales tally for the last two weeks. "Where would it be?" he says. "Where in the Sam Hill would you put a thing like that?"

"I'll look again," says Dorian.

"Look lively," says Havelock. "We need it now, not next year."

The telephone rings and Havelock answers. He listens for a moment and nods. "It's for you," he says. "A woman. Says her name is Meredith."

The conversation is very one-sided.

After a while, Dorian says, "Don't worry. I'll check that and call you as soon as I can." He hangs up.

"New customer?" says Havelock.

Dorian nods.

"What's the story?"

"A spinnaker. A birthday present, I think."

"Why didn't you check the order while you had her on the phone?"

"I'm not sure where the paperwork is."

Havelock rolls his eyes. "Maybe it's with the sales tally."

"I'm not like you," says Dorian. "I always lose track of things. I don't mean to, but I do."

"It takes discipline," says Havelock. "Get yourself a notepad and start making a list!"

DORIAN misses the deadline for college admission, a ritual that he's repeated each year since high school. He explains to his mother that he can't find the time, that the paperwork alone is too much. She asks him whether or not he's using his time wisely, especially at Halyard & Mast. He doesn't argue. Time is solid or liquid, he thinks. It drags or runs like water. Either way, it's difficult to keep straight.

To offset his failure, he reads the classifieds twice a month, circles one or two possibilities, and plans to write letters of application. In the end, he loses interest.

On sunny days in Bay City, he walks around the marinas and checks the sailboats that have been put up for sale. Now and then he inquires about a boat's specifications and history. When he finds an interesting possibility, he contacts the owner and makes arrangements to go aboard. These are the only appointments he keeps.

He doesn't travel or stay out late, though he does drive to Bloomfield Hills, to Meredith, as often as he can, sometimes on a weekend, her mother making supper and offering the guest room, or sometimes during the week when, if he's lucky, difficult orders or late shipments send him on errands to Pontiac or Detroit.

Whenever he drives out of Bay City or Saginaw, he pretends that he'll never return. I'll head south, he thinks. I'll keep going until I hit the Gulf of Mexico.

He dreams of designing and building boats. Perhaps H.M. would approve, but the risk of mentioning it is too great. A boat is a living thing. Making the claim that he can build one strikes him as foolhardy, prideful, too dangerous. H.M., knowing what's at stake, may not believe it's possible. Building a useless boat, a boat no one recognizes as living, would be tragic.

After three days away, on a hot morning that promises brisk business, he arrives at Halyard & Mast and finds the store open and H.M. sitting in his office.

He knocks on the open door. "I thought you were heading out today."

"I was. But there's a raft of work right here." His father scribbles on a notepad. "Don't stand there like a statue," he says. "Come in. I have something to show you."

Despite the brightness of the day, the office looks shadowy, something close to twilight, the dark blinds like bars on the window. He watches as his father moves the chairs and pulls up the rug and raises the trapdoor. For the very first time, he sees the black box in the ground, the letters H.M.M.S. painted in gold above the dial.

"This is how we stayed alive. Everything you ate or wore as a child, the roof over your head, came out of this safe."

He hears his father reciting the combination and understands the moment as a rite of passage. He knows that learning the numbers will open the door, and he knows that in that instant all other doors will close. He imagines a mason pushing a wheelbarrow down a long corridor. The mason stops at a door, checks to see if it's locked, and then, without hesitation, walls it over with bricks and mortar.

Havelock also feels the weight, the importance, of this moment. "We're launching a new store," he says. "I decided right off that it should be a distance from Bay City – on Lake Huron rather than the bay. What would you say is the best location?"

"Port Austin."

"It's the obvious choice," says Havelock, his face filling with satisfaction. "It'll be your store. And you'll have the cottage to live in."

"When do we open?"

"In the spring." Havelock adds something to a list. "It's time, too, that you have your own boat. I'm moving the ketch to Port Austin – the slips are cheaper there – but she's too much for a young man. Anyway, you'll want your own."

"I'll find one."

"First," says Havelock, "mind the store."

FOR THE rest of the season, showing up every day at Halyard & Mast, Dorian answers the phone, takes orders, and rings up purchases both large and small. He stocks and straightens the shelves, wipes the finger-marked display cases, files the charts by letter and number, and keeps the books and manuals in alphabetical order. He checks the hardware for oxidation and watches the canvas and line for fraying or discoloration. He studies the ledgers, talks to the store's accountant, and takes a salesman or two out to lunch.

He ranges over the length and breadth of his father's kingdom.

He stops making mistakes.

MEREDITH visits more often after haul-out.

Over the summer, on days with warm, southerly winds, Havelock had tried twice but failed to get her out on the water. He'd found her resistance puzzling but attractive, listening with amusement to her complicated excuses and assuming that she'd go out only with Dorian. Now he wants to hear the whole story.

"So how is she?" says Havelock.

"Fine," says Dorian.

"By Christ, I don't mean how is she today. How is she on deck?"

"She's good."

"I guessed it," says Havelock. "You can see she has the legs for it – the hips, too."

"She's strong," says Dorian.

"Does she take to it like a Moore?"

"Almost."

"You'll bring her around," says Havelock. "You've got time."

"Plenty of time," says Dorian.

"When did it happen?" says Havelock. "Did you run out when I wasn't looking?"

"No," says Dorian. "It was a boat I'm thinking to buy." He's glad to have said it. Now they'll stop talking about Meredith.

"A shakedown?"

"Call it that if you want."

"Takes gumption – a new woman and a strange boat." Havelock pulls on his beard. "Listen, don't make an offer before I see it."

Dorian waves off the advice. "I'm not buying it," he says. "She seemed unhappy in the water."

"Was she cranky or stiff?"

"A little of both."

"You gotta wait for the right one," says Havelock.

"I know."

Dorian remembers how the owner, watching from the dock, seemed wary. He'd tossed off the line and tried to reassure him. "Don't worry," he said. "I can handle the boat by myself."

He motored out hoping for a steady wind, but even before he raised the main, the boat felt dull and clumsy, a disappointment after he'd seen the smooth fiberglass hull and believed that it would outdo his father's sloop. Even the rudder felt sluggish, as if the boat were moving through oatmeal instead of water.

It's dead, he thought, just like H.M. says. Maybe he's right. Maybe a boat, when it isn't built of wood, is a dead thing. I can't be entirely sure. This one, at least, should be put out of its misery.

AT THE new store, hypnotized by monotony, oblivious to the bare trees and the snow falling, Dorian unpacks boxes and sorts merchandise. He works slowly, methodically, designing the floor plan, building shelves, installing counters and display cases – and then driving to Saginaw or Bloomfield Hills when the small summer cottage, chilly in winter, seems too quiet and too lonely.

In the dead of January, he travels through the dark and arrives at Meredith's door feeling shaky, the journey having been treacherous, slowed by whiteouts and sudden drifts.

He rings the bell. He sees a neat row of jackets hanging on pegs in the front hall. He keeps ringing the bell and Meredith, wearing only a blue towel, finally answers the door.

She sweeps her wet hair to one side. "Nobody's home but me."

He glances over her shoulder and into the dark house. "There's hardly a soul in Port Austin," he says. "I think you'd like it."

Meredith agrees.

In the morning, before rising from bed, she suggests a possible date for the wedding.

He smiles. He pictures her standing at the door wrapped in the blue towel. It occurs to him that he'd meant to propose and that Meredith had accepted. "You choose the day," he says.

THEY exchange vows in the summer with Meredith showing – but taking no pains to hide it – and with the minister dripping sweat on her white gown.

Havelock drinks too much at the reception.

Behaving like a well-mannered thief, he cuts in on Meredith's dance with her father. "Stop your stumbling," says Havelock, nudging the man aside.

He takes hold of Meredith and they turn and counter-turn, the guests looking on, some of them shaking their heads.

Faya grabs Dorian and they waltz onto the floor. "Reclaim your bride," she says.

Before Dorian can find an opening, Meredith's father taps Havelock on the shoulder. Havelock ignores him, beaming with pride, moving off with Meredith in the opposite direction.

Undeterred, Meredith's father waits and taps again.

This time Havelock turns and takes the man's hand and grabs his waist and the two of them start dancing, whirling across the floor, faster and faster, until Havelock, leading through a broad turn, sends his tuxedoed partner careening toward a table.

A circle of guests fly from their chairs and scatter. In the next instant, Meredith's father, his coattails flapping, lands on a steaming plate of spaghetti, the wineglasses spilling and shattering on the floor.

The episode clears the hall.

Dorian makes apologies while Meredith rocks back and forth between laughing and crying. They say their good-byes and drive through a gentle rain to Port Austin.

On the following Monday, they unlock the store and put a bright banner in the window. It says GRAND OPENING.

ALL DAY in a good wind, Dorian watches the gulls drift and climb, down-curving at last to the water's deep mirror. He wonders why one bird searches for a partner while another won't. Is it accidental or entirely by design?

Two sloops had followed him out, and the three of them, in their heeling moment, entering the vast body of Lake Huron, shadowed each other for a time. They made a small but impressive symmetry. But then, as time passed, they seemed to think of why they'd come or, as it happened, where they were going, and finally they took up new headings, the first boat falling away to the south.

He aimed his boat higher, to the southeast, dreaming of an up-bound cruise, remembering a trip with his father to the northern reaches of Lake Huron, passing the De Tour Light, a squat white tower, where freighters make the turn toward Drummond, past De Tour Village. They sailed though the turn and spent the night in St. Martin Bay.

Now, with the sun fading, he aims for home, thinking of the Straits of Mackinac, regretting how, in foul weather, they'd made the decision to turn back.

He swears that someday he'll climb Lake Huron again, that when he does he'll turn toward Drummond, ascend through the locks at Sault Ste. Marie, and then rush into Whitefish Bay, looking ahead, waiting for the blue of Superior to spread out before him like an endless sky.

HAVELOCK and Faya sign over the deed to the summer cottage, a last gift to the newlyweds.

Havelock also sends a crew to Port Austin with plans to build an addition, a nursery, nothing too large or fancy, just a simple room suitable for his grandson. He tells the contractor to paint the walls light blue.

Faya scolds him for being presumptuous. "What if it's a girl," she says. "You shouldn't paint until the baby arrives."

Havelock listens but goes ahead with his plan, and Meredith, exactly three and a half months to the day of her wedding, gives birth to a boy.

Dorian hangs a mobile of red, yellow, and blue sailboats over the crib.

"I like the boy's calling card," says Havelock. "Jason. Jason Moore makes a fine sound. It's one hell of a name."

WHEN the cottage feels cramped, Dorian goes to his new boat and keeps busy with maintenance and minor repairs. Meredith stops by only out of necessity. Upon arrival, she waves, puts her left foot on the dock, and then freezes.

They'd started this routine from the very first when she stood on the dock's threshold and he shouted from the cockpit vouching for the boat's safety and comfort, trying to convince her that she needn't be afraid.

"Jason's too little," she said. "Maybe when he's older." She pulled back her foot. "You can always make a trip with Havelock. I'm sure he's dying to go."

"H.M.'s angry," he said. "I didn't ask for his advice or approval."

"Call him," she said. "He can't stay away forever."

Quietly, without invitation or warning, Havelock finally turned up. "Does your wife like it?" he said. "How does she look standing on the bow? She'd certainly be an improvement. A plastic bobber needs something to dress it up."

"It's fiberglass, not plastic."

"I know. The wave of the future. At least Meredith is beautiful."

"I can't argue with that," he said, mindful of the old man's preoccupations and the secret of his wife's fear, her trembling at the sight of water.

He thinks now that if she wore a bathing suit and sunned herself on the foredeck, if she came up the companionway carrying drinks, he'd adore her completely. He'd call her the Lady of the Lake. He'd drop anchor in an unknown bay and they'd go below.

But she stays at home or in the store.

He works on the boat and in the summer he eats dinner there.

After dark, he goes home and lies down beside her, the room quiet and cool and her face peaceful, the lines of her body quite visible beneath a thin cotton sheet.

"Jason," says H.M., "you spoke your first words on the water – you'll be a natural."

He smiles at the old man. He's heard this before. He's also been told that he learned to walk on the ketch, his feet following the toe rail, his pudgy hands gripping the lifeline.

He's tried to learn the boat's language but he always forgets the words, distracted by sounds and rhythms – the sibilance of wind pouring over sails, the water when it laps the hull or rushes past with a sigh, the surf's rise and fall, the lake breathing.

A sharp command brings him back and sets him in motion, but he drifts before long and forgets the order and leaves the job incomplete.

"Show me your hands," says his grandfather.

He holds out his hands, palms up.

"That's what I thought. Better for work that's delicate."

His father nods, "Your name has a story, too."

Then they wave at H.M., who stands like a post on the seawall and grows smaller as they move away from shore.

"It kills me," says his father, "when H.M. goes off about fiberglass. According to him, new boats – each and every one of them – come decked out in lies. 'No maintenance! No worries! That's how they're sold,' he says. 'Why believe it when you know it's not true?'"

The wind picks up and the boat heels.

"But H.M. goes sour – you can see it on his face – when the wind's thin and his boat refuses to point high, the hull designed to an old rule, too much underbody and too much keel."

He watches as his father trims the main. "Are you and H.M. fighting?" he says.

"No," says his father. "I like wood, too. It gives a boat character, a solid foundation, or, as your grandfather would say, a place in the long history of trees."

"When I was out with Grandpa, we saw a big sailboat that he said was made of wood – but I didn't think so."

"Was the hull perfect and a blinding white?"

"I had to squint."

"Then you were probably right."

He likes the sound of his father's words. "Grandpa wouldn't listen," he says.

Now, with the shore disappearing and the wind even stronger than before, he imitates his father and looks up at the wind vane, a buffeted black arrow, and checks the forward edge of the jib. He feels the boat gaining, gliding, skimming across the water like a perfect stone.

"Jason," says H.M., "I need you to give a hand."

He helps his grandfather pull and then listens to the gulls and pretends that he's a bird migrating from one summer to the next – flying through seasons and school years, watching almost everything in the world, except the huge lake, disappear beneath him in a blur.

He hears everyone talk about time. His dad worries about how much of it gets spent at the store as opposed to sailing. His mom looks forward to the day when they'll leave their small house forever. "Sometime soon," she says. And Grandma and Grandpa talk about time running out, as if tomorrow they'd cease to exist.

He feels his stomach drop when the boat heels, then he watches for the light at Port Austin Reef, the one marker he recognizes from a distance.

Floating in the water is a large bird, not a seagull, with its wings stretched out and unmoving like the arms of a crucified man.

"Did it drown?" he says.

"Probably not," says his grandfather.

"Then how did it die?"

"A broken wing, maybe. Or a sickness. Maybe it was old."

"Why do things stop when they're old?"

"Things run down. They get tired."

"What makes them?" he says, turning away from the bird.

"A lot of things or nothing. It isn't easy to say. All right, Jason, prepare to come about."

"Will you run down?"

"Yes. We all do."

"I'll never run down."

"You've got a long time to go, that's true. It must seem like forever."

"Can we stay on the boat forever?"

"We can if the weather holds. We can stay as long as you want."

HE'S BEEN told that his grandmother feels weak. She's been confined to her bed in the house with the spiral staircase. She rarely ventures downstairs. The family doctor can't find a thing that's wrong, but the fatigue, the tiredness, won't go away.

Time drags or runs like water.

Now, more often than before, he visits with his mom and dad. They bring flowers and fresh bread.

His grandmother puts on a good face, tries rising to the occasion, but she looks entirely wrung out by the time the visit is over and they close the bedroom door.

The frequent trips are monotonous. He complains about always having to go. Now that he's older, he wants to stay home on his own. He needs to practice. He'd rather hang out and play records or make a few bucks cutting grass.

To tell the truth, he likes staying in Port Austin because it's the place where his grandfather keeps the ketch. He feels good being near the big boat. He rides his bike to the water and sits with the ketch when H.M. isn't there. He knows that smaller boats, the ones with single masts, the ones good for racing and sailing alone, get old and worn-out. He's seen snapshots of the boats that aren't around anymore. But the ketch is tireless. He believes it'll never wear out. "It's built of wood," says his grandfather. "It takes hard work to keep her Bristol, but with foresight and care she'll last a lifetime."

H.M. doesn't believe in new boats. "Your dad's sloop, I'm telling you, is a plastic tub. It's a white whale."

He wonders what his grandfather means. "But both the ketch and the sloop are white," he says.

"It's a matter of substance," says H.M. "A boat is a living thing because it's made of living things. There's no life in plastic. It's empty. It's blank – like a white whale."

SCHOOLMATES in bright white T-shirts come tearing down the street shouting and laughing. He can feel them gaining and knows that if he looks over his shoulder he'll lose speed, but he can't resist and his head begins turning and he sees a boy almost at his heels. He rounds the corner and spots the familiar fence and jumps over the closed gate but catches his foot and goes sprawling on the tiny front lawn – on the thick grass that should've been cut before now except that the rain made it impossible. He starts to get up when a boy pounces on his back and holds his face to the ground, cursing in his ear. He hears the voices of the other boys closing in and they fall on him, too, their fists pounding his rib cage and the back of his head, and all the boys yelling or screaming, "Nigger pile. Nigger pile."

At the bottom, he can't breathe, already breathless from running, and he believes that he'll suffocate, drown in the watery grass, and he feels a hot pressure building behind his eyes, his arms and legs pinned to the ground, when suddenly a tremendous blast, an explosion, blows everything into silence.

He looks up. The weight rolls off his body. On the porch steps is Otis with a shotgun aimed at heaven.

"You boys got no business here," he says. "You best run on home before I come down there and get mean."

Like ghosts disappearing on the air, the boys scatter and slip away.

"I'm sorry, Mr. Young." He manages to pick himself up. "I looked back and really didn't think – "

"There you go again with your Mr. Young," says Otis. "What else are you sorry for?"

"I don't know," he says. "I didn't mean to start something."

"Well, we already have. You see, everybody's left their dinner on the table. They don't care if it gets cold." Otis smiles at the scared faces. "It's all right," he says. "Nobody's been shot."

The woman next door says to her husband, "That's the white boy who always comes 'round – I think his name's Jason."

He hears the edge in her voice and brushes himself off and starts for the gate.

"Slow down," says Otis. "You got somewhere to be?"

He shakes his head.

"Then get yourself in here. We'll have some lemonade."

He walks slowly toward the house and, climbing the four porch steps, notices that his knees are weak, that his whole body feels shaky.

After they're inside, Otis tucks the shotgun under his arm, opens the breech, and removes the spent shell. "Take my reading chair. It's more comfortable than the front lawn."

He falls into the chair and sinks into the soft cushion, his heart still pounding. He suddenly feels heavy and wants to sleep for a long time.

Otis goes into the kitchen and soon returns with two lemonades. "Try some of this," he says, handing off the glass.

"Thanks." He wraps his fingers around the drink but can't keep his hand from shaking. He spills lemonade on his shirt before he can get the glass to his lips.

"Careful," says Otis. "I was thinking we could have your lesson today, now that you're here and all, but – "

"I didn't bring my guitar," he says.

"I realize that," says Otis. "I figured you could use mine, but with hands like that, there's no use." He sips his lemonade. "What did those boys want with you anyway?"

"They don't like me."

"Really?"

"Something happened at school."

"You mean those boys got after you on the playground and then chased you all the way out here?"

He nods.

"Did you sock one of 'em in the eye?"

He shakes his head.

"Did you call 'em names?"

"No." He raises the glass of lemonade to his lips and this time he doesn't spill, though his hand is still trembling.

"Let me guess," says Otis. "Those boys don't like the fact that I pay you to cut my grass. They don't like the fact that you come here for lessons. They're scared that you know something they don't."

He'd been trying not to cry since he sat down but now he can't help it. He starts to sob and spills more lemonade as he sets the glass on the table beside the chair.

"It's all right," says Otis. "But you should've told me."

"I thought you'd get mad," he says, trying to breathe.

"So what? What if I did get mad? What if it hurt my feelings? Do you think you're old enough and wise enough and powerful enough to protect me?"

"No."

"Then you should've just told me. Told me flat out."

He nods, wiping away tears with the back of his hand.

"I've seen some things," says Otis. "You will, too. Things you shouldn't keep to yourself." Otis grinds an ice cube between his teeth. "I've gotta make some calls and pay a few bills. You can stay here as long as you want. I'll be out back if you need me."

He sees Otis pick up a stack of envelopes and an address book and then hears him go down the hall and out the back door. He settles deeper into the chair and closes his eyes.

He remembers that when he finally woke up the room was dusky and silent. After a while, he heard a clock ticking, its white face glowing through the shadows, and knew that his parents, if they hadn't already, would soon call the police. He decided it didn't matter. The chair felt better than his bed at home and the sweet smell of the leather made him feel safe. He thinks now that he slept there, that somehow he never left.

"Faya's much worse," says a doctor. "Bed rest by itself isn't working."

These words, spoken with routine precision, give way to a hospital, a white gown, and a team of well-meaning specialists. Despite the nurses and the additional care, she gradually declines, baffling the physicians who order test after test but fail to put forward a convincing theory. Eventually, they abandon all hope for a diagnosis.

Time drags or runs like water.

It's repeated in whispers that the old man abhors his helplessness. He speaks to no one – no one will know his story for now – and he tries to ignore a new worry, a cramp in his abdomen, a sensation that grows from bothersome to chronic to debilitating in a period of weeks.

When the pain makes him sweat, he tells a young doctor, who performs an examination and wants him admitted without delay. He says he'll give himself up, but only if the hospital agrees to put him nowhere near Faya.

The young doctor makes a swift and precise diagnosis, cancer of the spleen.

For several days, Havelock occupies a private room on the second floor. When visiting hours begin, he removes his robe and puts on his suit and tie, descends by elevator to the lobby gift shop, buys a bouquet of flowers, nothing extravagant, and then takes the elevator up to the fourth floor and sits with Faya, as if he'd just arrived from home.

Eventually, a surgeon stops by and prods him and decides quickly, having already studied the X-rays, that the cancer is inoperable.

"There's no other course?" says Havelock.

"No," says the surgeon. "No other course."

Havelock looks in the mirror. His gray beard is bushy. He sees weathered skin and dark recesses under his eyes. He lifts both hands and touches his face. "I can't feel it," he says.

He turns and glances around the room. The surgeon is gone. He rubs his hands as if his fingers were cold. He touches his face and again feels nothing. "I'll be damned," he says.

THE YOUNG doctor processes Havelock's discharge, walks the old man to the front door, and hands him a bottle of painkillers.

There's relief in the smell of fresh air. He'd like to go out on Lake Huron, run with the singlehanders for the last time. Instead, he continues his routine, visiting Faya each day, always dressed in his suit and tie, stopping first at the lobby gift shop for flowers.

Through the end of winter and into the spring, the young doctor, in awe of

Havelock's constitution, rewrites the prescription again and again, increasing both strength and dosage over time.

Havelock swallows the pills. He checks the wind and sky each morning but keeps himself close to home and steers clear of Saginaw Bay. Lake Huron falls away like a broken dream.

On a morning in late June, just before sunrise, Faya stops breathing.

When the nurse arrives with Faya's pills, she finds Havelock dressed in his suit and tie sitting near the bed, a small bouquet of flowers in his hand.

He signs the necessary papers and pays the bill.

After that, he drives to Port Austin. He makes one turn after another until the old summer cottage comes into view. He stops at the curb, staying a safe distance away, and sees a line of fresh linens in the midmorning sun, the bedsheets billowing in the wind like sails.

He parks his car near the water and walks down to the ketch, his eyes tracing the lovely lines of her hull. He boards and goes below.

He opens a locked storage compartment and takes out a sawed-off shotgun, a souvenir from his days in bootlegging. He opens the breech, tucks the gun under his left arm, and reaches for a shell. The warning on the thin cardboard box is faded. He shoves in the shell and locks the breech. He puts the muzzle under his chin and fires.

"Jason," says his father, "stay close."

They push their way through a small gathering of gawkers, gossips, and policemen.

His father boards and goes below while an officer waits on deck. He emerges a minute or two later, visibly shaken, unable to step off the ketch without assistance.

"Your grandfather's not there," he says.

"Where is he then?"

His father looks back at the ketch. "Down below. But you can't go aboard."

"If he's there, then I want to see him."

"You can't. It's not possible."

He feels the grip of his father's hands. "Why not? Why can't I see him?"

"There's nothing to see."

He tries to twist out of his father's arms. "Let me go," he says. "Did he say he won't see me? Why won't you let me – ?"

"I'm telling you, there's nothing to see. There's no face. Your grandfather has no face."

chapter five

THE BOAT rests easy in its cradle. Humbug Marina, thawing in the April sun, smells like a spring meadow, a second chance, as if the brittle ground, despite wood shavings and rusty debris, had opened itself like a flower. Now, thinks Coleman, I'll make a go of it. She'll be ready by June. I'll take her upriver, through the narrows, to sail on an inland sea, the clouds swelling in the sky like waves.

A breeze comes up from the water. He feels light on his feet, almost buoyant. He breathes.

The scent of damp soil carries him back to a waning spring, to warm nights thick with humidity, the fast but narrow roads between Detroit and Port Austin, sad songs on the radio, the darkness of Lake Huron on one side and a blur of trees on the other.

"A full-throttle weekend," says a voice over the airwaves. And so he goes, anxious for the end of high school, driving with the windows open and the radio turned up, hoping to see Otis and the light at Port Austin Reef. Needling him is the inescapable fact that he's in his father's car. He fiddles with the tuning knob, annoyed by static and the fading signal.

He glances in the rearview mirror, feels a shot of adrenaline. "You made the decision. And you finished it," he says, seeing his father in the backseat. "You tore the guts out of Halyard & Mast. We'd barely gotten H.M. over the side and already the plan was in motion."

He looks again but there's no one there.

Never once did he question his father's course. Never once did he get in the way. He punches the accelerator and the engine unwinds. But how do you stop a thing like that? He was too young. He barely made a sound in his father's world. Even so, he blames himself for being a willing accomplice, for working closely with his father, cleaning and repairing the ketch, making it Bristol, and then standing by in silence while his father, without hesitation, turned the ketch over to a collector of fine antiques, a trophy hunter, a man with no interest in sailing.

"You must be crazy," says Otis, "driving up here in the dark like a bat out of hell."

"I would've waited till tomorrow," he says, "but I saw the light on – "

"It's nearly midnight," says Otis. "Suppose you'd rung at the wrong moment? What then?"

He checks Otis's collar for lipstick. "You'd ignore it, I guess."

"Is that what you guess?" Otis chuckles. "All right, Jason, get your sorry ass in here. I just brewed a fresh pot. I guess I can spare a cup."

He steps through the door and picks up the scent of coffee and old leather. "A couple of weeks," he says, "and I'll be finished with school." He follows Otis into the kitchen.

"What's your plan?" says Otis.

"Boston College," he says. "They gave me a scholarship."

"Then you're not really done with school."

"I meant high school. I'm gonna buy a used car and drive to the coast."

"Guitar going with you?"

"Naturally."

"You want cream and sugar?"

"Black," he says.

After handing off the first cup, Otis pours one for himself and stirs in two teaspoons of sugar and a lot of cream. "You swing by the old store?"

He shakes his head. "I came straight here."

"It's still boarded up," says Otis. "No businessman wants it. It's a sorry sight. I wish your old man was still there."

"You teaching?"

"Off and on," says Otis. "Every so often I get a boy who reminds me of you, but it doesn't pan out. Port Austin is a small town. Folks just pick up and leave." He takes a slow sip of his coffee. "How's Detroit?"

"It's big," he says. "I didn't know how big till I started driving."

"You get downtown much?"

"Sure," he says. "All the time."

"But now you're heading for Boston."

"As soon as I can."

"That's how it goes," says Otis.

He looks at Otis looking at his coffee. "How what goes?"

"You just got off Gross Ile and into Detroit and already you're planning to leave."

"Wayne State is too close to home," he says.

"That's true," says Otis. "But there's more to it than that. Like me and everybody else – you get tired of the people you're with. You like to imagine yourself in a neighborhood that's different from the one you're in. The whole thing makes me irritable."

"But they're offering me a free ride."

"That's not what I mean. I'm talking about staying with a place. When people pick up and leave, it breaks things up. It changes the landscape."

"You left Detroit and New York."

Otis nods. "I did." He walks over to the sink and rinses his cup. "In any case, you're too young to settle down. You're right. You go to school. If Boston turns out to be your place, then stay there. You want more coffee?"

"No thanks," he says. "I gotta use the can."

"You got a room somewhere?" says Otis.

"No. I brought a sleeping bag. I'll go down to the lake."

"Looks like rain," says Otis.

"You think so?"

"The sofa's free. You better sleep here. It'll rain for sure if you don't."

COLEMAN carries a five-gallon bucket. In it are rags, paper towels, oil, regular and waterproof grease, wrenches, screwdrivers, hose clamps, a wire brush, and a flashlight. He shifts the bucket from one hand to the other when he feels a cramp.

Sitting on blocks near the fence is a giant cruiser, a Chris-Craft, with a rotting hull. He's never seen anyone go near it. The local philosopher, a gaunt alcoholic, calls it a ghost ship – the yard's monument to damage and disrepair. Next to the cruiser is another wooden boat that looks brand-new. The river sparkles beyond the docks.

He keeps walking and takes a deep breath and tries to keep himself steady. Lately, when he leaves work, his clothes, even his hands, smell like beer. There's plenty of daylight left, he thinks. Humbug is better in the daylight. Loads of fresh air – and enough dreams and defeats to go around.

He stops at the *Pequod*, the smooth fiberglass hull curving away from him toward the bow. He bends and sets his bucket on the ground next to the ladder. I'll open the cabin, he thinks. I'll let out everything that's stale.

He pulls a slip of yellow paper out of his shirt pocket. He checks the list of jobs that need to be done. He knows the work is critical for both safety and comfort, but most of the repairs are more than he can do. Spring commissioning, or so H.M. liked to say, involves know-how, keen observation, and planning. "But it takes more than that," he mumbles, realizing that in the yard, with the boat cradled and dry, it's easy to drift off, sink into currents of sanguine reverie, evade or somehow deny the fact that there's no real hope at Humbug, no chance, without talent, money, and time.

He looks around. No one else is out this early, he thinks. A jump on the season should count for something.

Even with the snow almost gone and the sun shining, Humbug offers little more than gray, silver, and white. He tells himself that Jen would plant flowers here. He remembers in the darkest months how she often came home with bouquets for the kitchen and bedroom, with French soap, honeysuckle or lavender, for the dish on the pedestal sink.

In Tobermory, the houses on the harbor are red, yellow, and blue – a line from a letter long ago, and now he repeats it like the chorus of a song. "In Tobermory," he says out loud, "the houses on the harbor are red, yellow, and blue."

He thinks of the call from Cape Hurd and the journey to salvage his father's boat, the trip unfolding in the last spring of the millennium, the scent of warm earth rising around him like fog. The long drive made him feel cramped and stiff, a bit older than forty-five, as he sped across the Ambassador Bridge and passed through Windsor in a flash, traveling north through Ontario and up the Bruce Peninsula to arrive unannounced at Jennifer's door.

She didn't seem flustered, not even surprised. She brewed tea, Darjeeling, and talked as if there were no time or distance between them, as if the long years of his marriage had somehow been forgotten.

They sat at the kitchen table. "Welcome to Tobermory," she said.

The word flowed from her like music, a sound quite different from the one he'd known as a boy, the sailors on Lake Huron dividing the word into stiff Midwestern syllables. He basked in the comfort of her voice. Did it flow like water the first time? Or was it later, when she whispered Tobermory in a dream?

As far back as Boston, the stories began, with Jen going on about her grand-mother's house and the summers she spent there as a girl, about Big Tub Harbour and its century-old shipwrecks. He listened, taking in as much as he could, building a picture of Tobermory in his mind, making it the town they'd run to if need be, a refuge he thought of as perfect, knowing then that to go there and actually see it would destroy the possibility.

"When Granny died," said Jen, "she left me the house. I was settled in Boulder, thought I'd stay there forever, so it wasn't simple coming back." She poured a second cup of tea and described how the journey had filled her with misgivings, but then, magically, arriving by water, she'd felt the tension in her shoulders give way, glad that Bay Street, the seawall, and the fishing boats, all washed by the late afternoon light, looked exactly the same. A hush fell over her mind, a serenity she'd known only in her grandmother's house, the story-book house that might've been built in Edinburgh or Amsterdam, the house that she finally claimed and where, like her grandmother, she now lived alone.

He raised his cup and remembered their days together in college, sleeping late under thick blankets, holding her close when she woke startled from a dream. "All that I wanted then is forgotten now, but you," he began to say, but his voice sounded strange, almost absurd, so he stopped after the third word and helped himself to another biscuit.

She'd never been far from his mind. Her face was there, he sat thinking, and the days we lived without worry or plans, walking endless streets, going home to sleep in rented rooms, then lost each other somewhere, now unclear, except for the orchard and the October light.

She'd said, "Come back or not. You won't find me." But from the day he married Maureen to the day they split their property, even on the day Heather was born, he'd always known where Jennifer was. He might've gone to her hoping to win her love back. Instead, he waited until tragedy forced his hand, until news of his father came from Cape Hurd. Then he drove straightaway to Tobermory.

He made no expression of regret or hope. He chose only to drink tea, play the part of an old and tired friend, a man who'd come to visit for no other reason than the fact of business nearby.

Jen took his nonchalance in stride. "When they found your father's boat," she said, "I wanted to call you. I always thought Dorian was a little like me." She looked into her empty cup. "But then I made up my mind that you'd come. And here you are."

"I have to haul it back," he said.

"When will you do that?"

"I have to hire someone – a trailer and truck."

"Will you sell it?"

"Store it," he said. "At least for now. Probably Humbug."

"What's Humbug?" she said.

"A marina. He kept it at the Ford Yacht Club. But Humbug's closer."

She took the cold teapot to the sink and rinsed it. "And you're sure?"

"About what?" he said.

"That it was no accident," said Jen.

"No. No accident. He knew how to read the sky. The storm was huge. Every inch of canvas was up when they found the boat." He wanted to tell her how lovely she was, that it was good to see her again. He complimented the house. "It's exactly as you described it," he said.

"It's my home," she said, sitting down, brushing crumbs from the table.

He nodded. "I don't see that you're like him at all."

She took a minute before she answered. "Maybe it wasn't the right thing to say. It just seems to me now, thinking of him again, that he was always on the water, always slipping out. After Halyard & Mast went to pieces – "

"He killed it, you know. He brought the place down like – "

"I know," she broke in, "that's what you always said. But he seemed chained to it even after it was gone. He was never free of it. He wanted to be, but he never figured out a way."

He sat back in his chair. "And what about you?" he said. "What are you chained to?"

"Nothing," she said. "So maybe you're right. We're not the least bit the same."

THE MUSIC of her voice is always with him, the round vowels and soft consonants, even now, having come here in the April thaw to make the boat ready, to wax the faded gel coat, check it for crazing, a sign of uneven stress, and look for deeper cracks, making sure the laminate underneath is still sound.

He sets the wax and mildew remover on the ground next to the bucket. Since the close of Halyard & Mast, every marine supply he's been in seems small, a sorry excuse for a store, a bad imitation. It chills him to think of Halyard & Mast's surrender, the fits and starts of its sudden death.

He remembers the first sign of its passing: his father's nameplate, DORIAN MOORE, black letters on gold, half buried in a mountain of coffee grounds in the Dumpster behind the Port Austin store.

My old man made a killing, he thinks, standing next to his father's boat. In his quiet and steady way, he liquidated H&M's stock. He reordered nothing. He let the shelves and the display stands fall into disarray. He stopped answering the phone, fired the bookkeeper, and gave the cashiers and the manager time off to look for other work. He took offers from wholesalers and scavengers buying inventory on the cheap. He did all this after the suicide, after cleaning, repairing, and putting the ketch up for auction.

He checks the ladder for stability, rests his left foot on the bottom rung. He remembers, on his sixteenth birthday, his father boarding up the stores in Bay City and Port Austin, dismantling in three years what took more than thirty years to build. He can hear his father saying, "Your grandfather was Halyard & Mast. Not me. He's dead now. So's the business."

Back then, the disposal of H&M felt like a killing. He still thinks of it this way and wonders why it stays with him. It's true that he'd always loved the water and the boats, the quiet movement, but he lacked his father's talent. He cared more for a landlocked dream. So why should it bother him now? Suppose he'd been the favored son in full possession of the family gift. Would it have made any difference? His father, after all, threw in the towel, chose to give it up. He wonders what it means to kill something inanimate, a dream or an idea. But then he returns to the matter at hand. He knows it's the nature of things to be seen only once. Everything must die for a while before it can be remembered with affection.

My father, he thinks, lived with blood on his hands. That's what made him move. A man can't live where he's committed a crime. And Saginaw was too close, even Port Huron or Algonac. So he hauled us downriver. He drove fast.

"Too easy," said his father, looking at the small towns along the way. But no one knew to whom he was speaking or what he meant. He only said, "We won't go as far as Ohio."

As it turned out, they settled on an island, Grosse Ile, part of a small archipelago in the southern reaches of the Detroit River, not far from Lake Erie. He thinks now that he said to his father – after they'd crossed the bridge, the new house almost in sight – "Mom's the one it won't be easy for – there's water on all sides."

THROWING back the boom tent and opening the cabin, the April air rushing in as if he'd opened a crypt, he thinks about the years in Boston and then Chicago, trying to capture the flow of those days, the first tours with big-name players, and the endless stream of cities and hotels. No time, he recalls, to write songs or do sessions, feeling always under the gun, always late, but enough time nonetheless to disband the trio, to cut the cord between himself and Brian James.

Then his thoughts drift again to an autumn day in an orchard of old trees, with branches that form a low canopy, a dark tunnel, where he leaves Jennifer without turning or glancing back. Stepping out of the orchard, he shields his eyes against the hard afternoon light. He squints, keeping his head down, one foot following the other, listening to the crunch of gravel as he hurries up the road.

The next morning, having returned to Wrigleyville, bending over a suitcase half filled with stage clothes, toiletries, and staff paper, he jumped, his heart pounding, when a loud knock broke the silence. Jen might've lost her key, he thought. He opened the door and expected to see her but instead found Brian with a bottle of vodka tucked under his arm.

Brian smiled and handed him the bottle – around the neck was a bow of blue ribbon.

"Thanks," he said. "I'll pack it right now."

"Where's Jen?" said Brian, stopping in the hall and looking at the photographs.

"I'm not sure," he said. He didn't feel like going into it. "I came back alone."

"You left her there?"

"I didn't plan to."

"Did she go all right?"

"I guess."

"Have a scene?"

"I guess." He wanted to explain but knew that he'd feel silly and selfish if he tried to talk about what happened.

Brian leaned on the doorjamb. "You letting the place go?"

"Not now." He pulled the zipper on the suitcase. It stuck. "Not right away."

"Good," said Brian. "Last night, I dreamt that I came over and all the windows were boarded up."

He yanked on the zipper. "What a cheap-shit bag."

Brian had picked up a framed photograph. "This is at the Mill," he said. "And we all look good, especially Jen."

"Take it."

"You don't want it?"

"There's more than one."

"You sure?"

"Pretty sure."

"You should pack it," said Brian. "You might get tired of the people you're with. You might miss it."

"I've got plenty."

"Do you think it's the only one?"

"Can't be." He grabbed the suitcase, glanced around the room, and caught a glimpse of himself in the mirror. His worried expression bothered him. "I guess that's it," he said. "Keep Chicago like I left it."

"I can't," said Brian.

He looked at the picture in Brian's hand. "It's not easy to go," he said.

"But you passed the audition," said Brian. "You always do."

He wanted Brian to block the door. He wanted to say things that never come easily. Instead, the silence grew deeper.

Brian slid the picture inside his jacket. "Good luck, Cole. Call me when you get a chance."

"I will."

He slips in and out – O'Hare to the apartment and back again – but he calls no one while he's in town. He blames it on fatigue, the demands of touring. He sees Brian less and less, and the things that belong to Jen eventually disappear. The lease expires but he continues to pay the rent. He likes the fact of having a place that's familiar. It's good, he thinks, to hold it in reserve, especially if the course he's chosen leads nowhere.

As it turns out, he keeps the apartment for two years. He never lives there or sleeps in the unmade bed. Instead, he visits for an hour or two whenever he can. He checks the mailbox. He walks through the unfilled rooms, turns on the faucets until the water runs clear. Sometimes he brings a bottle, sits at the kitchen table, and pours himself a drink. He listens to the refrigerator, the clicking and groaning. He ignores the thickening dust. He tells himself that there's nothing unusual about hanging on to the place, that it's no different than clinging to an old coat or a favorite pair of shoes. Finally, the landlord calls him crazy. "I don't like ghosts in the building," he says. "If you send another check, I'll tear it up. And I'm fixing it so your old key won't work."

After being locked out of the apartment, he takes more bookings, more time on the road. He lives like a man without a country. Mail rarely finds him, not even warnings from the IRS.

From one motel room to the next, he watches old movies and short bursts of MTV. He eats carryout. He tries to write but finds no inspiration in the stolid routine. Managers and promoters come to the clubs and shake their heads. They make excuses or deliver proclamations. "Jazz is dead," they say. "We thought it was dead years ago, but that was a false alarm. This time we're sure."

Jazz is dead. He remembers first hearing the idea from Otis, who liked to go off on philosophers and critics who were in the business of declaring this or that thing deceased, particularly music, books, theater, small towns, newspapers, public education, motherhood, empathy, justice, hope, even God. "Tell me this," said Otis. "When I pick up my guitar and play, even if I'm alone in my house, is jazz dead?"

Given the opportunity, Otis would riff on what he called "premature burials." He'd point at a headline and say, "There they go again, ready to stack bodies in the street. What they're really up to is killing dreams, any dream, especially if it's one they don't quite understand. Sometimes they succeed, of course. Sometimes they have to go so far as to commit murder, maybe an accident or an assassination, but then sometimes the whole thing backfires and the dream gets bigger."

Otis often talked with his guitar in hand and played licks between the words. It came off as some sort of musical essay, an extemporaneous lecture with a soundtrack. "Those boys who chase you around," he said, pausing to play a short run, "they won't come back, now that they know I've got a gun. Nobody in this town sanctions a black man with firearms, especially foul-mouthed white boys." He stopped and played another phrase. "They see their fathers with rifles resting on their laps, serious men trying to keep the rust off their weapons – each of them rubbing a dark barrel with a white cloth. And the boys think of the day when they'll own their own guns and do with them whatever it is they like."

When Otis ran out of things to say, he'd return to the notes and phrases that he'd left hanging in the air, and he'd start to collect them and string them together, searching for a new idea. He could go on for hours like that. It was easy to listen to.

He tried to remember what Otis played and what he said, the patterns and the lectures, but as time passed it became more and more difficult to keep everything straight. In the days after Chicago, exhausted by travel, he felt the weight of his loneliness and doubt and wondered if he should ditch the whole game, walk away from performing, stop in some out-of-the-way city and open a guitar shop or a record store. Drinking too much, he told himself that he needed a break. And when a long national tour finally fell apart, he decided to quit, fed up with cancellations, thin crowds, and humiliating pay. Whatever Otis had taught him about commitment didn't seem to matter. He told the faithful, "Playing guitar is a job like any other. Music is ungrateful. It's no better than a pimp."

Off the road, he found himself south of Detroit, flipping channels on a black-and-white TV, sleeping in his old room in the house on Grosse Ile. On the first morning of his visit, his mother put English muffins in the toaster. "The tulips are late," she said. His father shook his hand and went off to the yacht club. He watched him drive away.

He took pity on the dog that seemed a bit senile after a long and brutal winter. Walking the animal for the third time in one day, he met a tall and commanding redhead, Maureen, who said she was house-sitting and managing her brother's rottweiler.

He hated music when he met her, hated the managers, the club owners, and the record execs, hated that he had no choice but to continue playing. Maureen started with a couple of questions. He answered briefly. Then he asked a few things about her. The dogs raised their tails and sniffed. Maureen showed no curiosity about music or his life as a musician. He fell in love with her lack of interest, with the possibility of change.

He stands in the cockpit, massages the pain in his hand, and tries to decide what to do next. He smiles about the dogs and his conviction to give up music. He smiles about the honeymoon.

The infatuation, he remembers, went on for almost a year, but then he sensed from Maureen a growing boredom, a frustration with his hopes and desires, his apparent lack of practicality. At that moment, the phone rang. A voice offered a gig and good money. It seemed that doing the road again might shore up his sinking marriage, but the notion was dishonest, a denial of everything he knew about touring. He accepted the offer and, as Maureen had suspected, it made matters worse.

He soon found it easier, less painful, to stay out several weeks at a time. He even missed the birth of his daughter, calling Maureen from a club in Pittsburgh, using a pay phone near the bathrooms, a crush of voices echoing in the narrow hall.

He pictures himself on stage tuning his guitar while a woman sitting down in front and wearing an open blouse leans forward to hand the waitress some money. The woman smiles.

"Don't be messin' with that," says a voice from behind the piano. "You gotta keep yourself occupied."

He shifts his gaze. Sitting next to the woman is a man with thin arms and drooping shoulders. He looks again at the open blouse.

He rubs his left hand.

He stays occupied these days driving a truck, negotiating the stiff clutch and the creaking transmission, the wide turns and the low-hanging wires. Going back and forth across the Detroit River, hauling Canadian beer from Windsor to Detroit, he feels at times like the ghost of H.M., though he works regular hours – no midnight runs. If the police stop him, it's usually for a burned-out brake light. The owners of liquor stores and convenience stores never say much when he makes a delivery. He discourages what little conversation they offer and collects the necessary signature and leaves a copy of the invoice.

Making deliveries, particularly in winter, takes a toll on his back. He wears a brace and never hurries, even when he's running late. He drives a straight diesel with a hydraulic lift. He uses a heavy-duty hand truck with oversize wheels.

Each day that he drives, he thinks about how he got here, about the fat man who examined his application and his license, offered him the job with a reluctant handshake, and then died of obesity a year or two later. "You're old," the fat man said, smiling an unfriendly smile. "Why should I hire an old guy with banged-up hands?"

"My hands'll be okay, I swear."

"Make sure of it," said the fat man.

He chooses the bridge or the tunnel depending on the time of day. He wonders what H.M. would say about his truck, about carrying beer that's legal. A road, like a river, provides direction – destination. Maybe that's why H.M. left the river, he thinks. It was the lake he wanted, the promise of unfettered movement. He pictures H.M. on the shores of Lake Huron, a blue infinity, face-to-face with absolute freedom, ready to strike out without worry or fear. It's better driving a truck, he thinks. I know the roads. New routes aren't much of a problem. It's a matter of staying alert, watching the turns so you can find your way back.

He knows his truck and listens for anything odd. He keeps a close eye on the dashboard gauges and the dummy lights. If necessary, he fills out a maintenance order at the end of the day. He wishes he could do the same for the boat, just report what ails her to someone at Humbug. He thinks of spring commissioning and his father's excitement, all the fuss and expense, the tedious list of chores.

HE CHECKS the masthead fittings and spreaders, finds some minor crazing on the cabin house and a shallow groove in the gel coat, as if someone had scored the surface with a box cutter. He remembers seeing a can opener in the galley. If it isn't rusty, he can use it to begin the repair, widen the groove and bevel the edges, following his father's example, before taping it off and patching it.

He goes belowdecks. He forgot to buy bilge cleaner and a new brush, although both are on his list of supplies. He'll do the scrubbing and flushing next time, and then he'll test the bilge pump and the float switch. For now, he opens and closes each seacock, lubricating the ones that seem stiff. He hooks up the water hoses, connects the freshwater pump, and fills the tank. The pump cycles on and off. Must be a leak, he thinks. Nothing's open, but I can hear the damn thing running.

He pokes around in the galley drawer. The can opener looks brand-new – no corrosion. He struggles to pull it out and it slips away like a wet fish. He can't pick it up. He can't close the fingers of his left hand. There was a time, he says to himself, when I didn't have to think to make it happen, when barre chords and big grips required no particular effort.

He hears the pump running, a white noise, almost a comfort. He admits that bringing the boat back had more to do with Jennifer than anything else. It now seems ironic and tightfisted, using his father's death as the impetus, substituting one grief for another.

TOBERMORY, still a fishing village after 150 years, lies at the tip of the Bruce Peninsula at the mouth of Georgian Bay. He marks its position as less than five miles from Cape Hurd, from the point where his father's boat washed up without a trace of its captain.

It's lovely, he thinks. It's the place I always imagined, a storybook of old houses. It's slow, as if the town and everyone in it were outside of time.

He walks toward his car, his body leaning into a stiff wind. He hears the thump of shutters. He's drunk enough tea for two men. He turns and goes back through the gate and up the walk to Jennifer's door. He knocks.

Jen tries not to smile. "That was quick."

"I forgot to use the bathroom," he says.

She laughs and directs him down the hall.

He sits on the toilet and takes more time than usual to get started. His bladder's too full. It's painful. When he finishes, he lets out a deep breath. He washes his hands and looks at his face in the mirror. His beard needs a trim. There's gray around his temples, more than he ever noticed. He checks to see if his hair is thinning.

He walks into the living room with his jacket over his arm. Jen is sitting on the sofa. "Thanks," he says.

"So I'll see you tomorrow?" she says.

"Sure." He hesitates. "You busy now?"

"No," she says. "Not now."

"Can I stay a little longer?"

"If you like."

He drops his coat in a chair and sits on the edge of the sofa. "It's early. I saw a lot of vacancy signs on the way in. I shouldn't have trouble getting a room."

"I doubt it."

"Do you have plans for dinner?"

"I made soup yesterday. But I need bread."

"We could go out."

"If you like."

The wind whistles in the chimney. Something bangs and clangs on the side drive. "Garbage can," says Jen. She gets up and walks down the hall and out the back door. He follows.

She wedges the can between the garden hose and bag of peat moss. She puts the lid on tight. He steps inside and a gust of wind slams the door behind him. He winces. He turns and opens the door.

"You okay?" she says.

"Of course."

"You look like you saw a ghost."

"Just startled," he says. He could tell her the truth. He could say that the sound of a door closing is more than he can bear.

"Noise always bothered you," she says, rinsing her hands at the sink.

He nods.

"You got that from Meredith. I remember the time in Chicago when the guy upstairs started rearranging his furniture in the middle of the night."

He laughs. "She wanted me to call the police."

"She started packing her bag," says Jen. "She said she'd find a quiet hotel."

He looks at her profile and sees a passing smile. "She's gone," he says.

Jen shuts off the water and dries her hands. "When?"

"Two years ago."

"But she wasn't old."

"Sixty-seven."

"Was she sick?"

"No. She went out for a walk and her heart stopped. She left just before noon. I was working. Dad was out on Lake Erie."

Jen leans on the counter as if to steady herself.

"A little girl selling magazines found her. Someone called 911, but it was too late."

"Seems wrong," says Jen, "for a woman like Meredith to die that way."

"I suppose so."

"She was elegant, graceful."

"More than most."

"And now Dorian," she says.

"Yes," he says. "Her dying like that is how the boat got here."

She waits.

"He wasn't there when she died. She was already on a slab when he got to the hospital."

"You sound surprised."

"Do I?" He hears the wind rushing against the window. "After the funeral, he left the boat in its slip. He gave up the water for two seasons."

"He didn't sail?"

"That's right."

"Then how did he – I mean, how did the boat get here?"

"He decided he'd had enough. Disappeared three or four weeks ago. After a couple of days, I drove over to the yacht club to check the slip. It was empty. After ten days, I suspected he'd gone north."

"Just like that," she says, "without so much as a word. You always said – "

"But I could've stopped him."

"Do you really think so?"

"Maybe not. But there was a moment. I had my chance."

KNEELING on the cabin house, using the tip of the can opener, he widens the groove in the gel coat. He pictures his father showing him the steps for repairing a crack: the preparation, the taping, and the patching. He uses less pressure and begins to bevel the edges. The laminate underneath is fine. This may not be the case near the samson post where he's found a deeper crack, where the stress and crazing have made the laminate vulnerable, open to damage.

His father rarely talked about how to do things; he preferred, instead, to offer demonstrations, walking people through the skills and the necessary steps.

He rubs his hand and thinks of the day that he stopped at his father's house and discovered that the brass clock and the gimballed lamp were gone. Then he drove to the yacht club and found the *Pequod* stripped of its boom tent and covers, and his father scrubbing the deck. The trees whispered in the breeze.

"Heading out?"

"Tomorrow," said his father.

"Where to?"

"Out. Just out."

"Is she ready?"

"Enough so."

"Need help?"

"No."

"I got some Ketel One," he said. "Stop by tonight and we'll have a drink."

"If there's time."

He put one foot on the gunwale, preparing to step off, but then he turned and faced his father. "It's been quite a while," he said.

"It's all right," said his father.

"I know," he said. "Your name is your ticket. You can always go back."

Standing in the cockpit, he felt the impulse to embrace his father, but he turned the urge away, believing at that moment that his father would slip through his arms like fog. He stepped off the boat, his legs suddenly unsteady. He paused at the end of the dock and looked back, but his father had gone below.

He watched for his father past midnight, left the glasses and the bottle on the counter, the ice melting. After another hour or two, he locked the door and turned off the lights. Probably an overnight on Lake Erie, he thought. He's old. But he knows the water. It never occurred to him that his father, as if he were a young man, would journey upriver, slipping past Algonac and beyond the Blue Water Bridge, to sail on Lake Huron again.

Later, driving to the beach to recover the stranded sloop, the coast guard official, fond of facts and formalities, kept repeating the one thing he'd been told: "Mr. Moore was last seen in Port Elgin, where he'd found safe harbor the night before the storm."

The weather, of course, was no mystery. He knew that his father could sense a furious blow long before it arrived. With the coast guard official still talking, he closed his eyes and imagined how it began, how sheet metal and cinder block droned, how the boats at Port Elgin made a steady and dissonant music, shafts and crosstrees keening, stays and shrouds whining, the slapping of loose lines. And then, as if he were there, he saw his father, waterborne and well prepared, slipping out under a press of sail, the storm clouds gathering to the west.

The white hull stranded on Cape Hurd looked like a beached whale. He left the coast guard official behind and approached his father's boat, wondering what was left of the keel. He pulled himself up, his left hand throbbing, and climbed over the transom. It's ghostly, he thought. A grounded ship with all its gear in place is unbearable. It's barely alive.

HE ADDS a few drops of catalyst and begins stirring. His hand seizes up. He bangs it on his leg, but it won't work. It's frozen in the shape of a hook, a useless claw. Now the mixed gel coat'll go off, and he'll have to try again tomorrow or next weekend. This is too much trouble, he thinks, for a small repair.

He swears he'll hire someone, but then he considers the bill for hauling the *Pequod* from Cape Hurd to the cradle at Humbug. He recounts the charges for fixing the keel, not to mention the propeller shaft, the prop, and the rudder. He hears Maureen fretting about child support and telling him to scrap the boat. It isn't something he asked for. He admits it's an albatross. There's no way around its crazed hull – or his crippled hands – but, for now, he can't let it go.

THE WIND dies off and then comes again in a sudden gust. It pushes against the house.

"I'm tired of the kitchen," says Jen.

Taking the lead, he floats down the narrow hall. He hears her footsteps and the floor creaking. They return to the sofa. He leans back and rests his head, and she sits sideways and closer than before, one leg folded beneath her.

"Are you hungry?" he says.

"Not really."

He arches his back and lets out a pent-up breath.

"Something wrong?" she says.

He shakes his head. "Too much driving. That's all."

"I'm sorry."

"It's okay."

"No. Not your back."

"I don't follow."

"I'm sorry."

"About what?"

She shrugs. "Nothing and everything. The past, maybe."

"It was me," he says. "It was always about me."

"Listen," says Jen. "The wind's gone."

"You called my bluff," he says. "I never imagined that you wouldn't be there. Then I stopped and turned and you were nowhere in sight."

She reaches over and turns on the lamp. "We don't have to go through it again."

"But you said you were sorry."

"I am."

"Well there's no reason – "

"I know that."

The lamp illuminates one of her photographs, a detail of the Wrigley Building.

"Are you taking pictures?" he says.

"Not so much. Not seriously. I gave it up before I left Boulder."

"Is it as lovely there as they say?"

"Yes," she says. "Perfect light."

"Then why did you quit?"

"It was the teaching – all that history in Chicago and then photography in Boulder. I taught everything out of me. If I had any vision or inspiration or ambition, I taught it all away."

"Your students were lucky to have you."

"Maybe." She looks past him into the shadows. "In the other room are folders filled with images – huge trees, rock formations, the Rocky Mountains. The older ones are in black-and-white and the later ones are in color. And then that was all."

"Did you teach after that?"

"For a while. But I came here to stop. I knew that Canadian schools wouldn't hire me."

"And you don't miss it?"

She shakes her head. "I manage well enough. I make the quilts and tapestries in the winter and two of the shops in town sell them to tourists in the summer. The house is mine so I don't need much."

"And what about photography?"

"My camera's obsolete. No one sells film anymore."

"That's not true."

"Making pictures with an old camera feels slow and out of step."

"What's wrong with being old-fashioned?"

She smiles. "You were old-fashioned when you were twenty."

"That's a kind way to put it." He looks again at the photograph. "I remember all the shots of me and Brian, of the three of us – "

"Have you seen him?"

"Not for a long time. You?"

She shakes her head. "Not since Chicago."

He wants to touch her hair, still long and dark. "I went back," he says. "I stayed with Brian for a while."

She looks startled. "When?"

"When Maureen and I were breaking up." He thinks of those days, the gray overcast like concrete and the effort it took just to move, to get around. "I couldn't go home," he says. "Brian put me back together."

"I miss the music," she says. She tilts her head as if she were listening. "I miss it more than seems possible."

He feels his hand throbbing.

"Are you still playing?" she says.

"Barely."

"That's cruel."

"If you say so."

"I do. It's a bad joke. You can't throw me over and then give it up. It isn't fair."

"No," he says. "It's not fair."

"You play now and then, don't you?"

"When I can," he says.

"Let's talk about something else," she says.

"If it's a good day, I sometimes – "

"Don't," she says. "I don't want you to explain."

"It's not – "

"I'll get my jacket."

He grabs her arm. "It's my hands," he says. "It's because of my hands."

The words fill the room like a broken melody, like an echo that overlaps and multiplies, refusing to fade. He leans forward, perched on the edge of the sofa, and sees objects and furniture, the lamp, photograph, and table, beginning to move. Everything turns and slides away until nothing remains but a floor of cracked asphalt.

In front of him, as if he were on his hands and knees, as if he were crawling or being dragged, is a flash of black steel. He feels a warm grip on his forearm, picks up the scent of well-barbered men. And then he sees her, the woman whose name he's forgotten, standing off to the side, wearing what she's worn all night, a tight, thin, and sleeveless shirt with a low neckline. His eyes follow her arms and shoulders. He likes the lean definition. He wants to trace with his tongue the texture and shadings of her middle-aged skin – the lovely imperfections of experience. It's unnatural, he thinks. I've lost my hands and feet, but I can't refuse this obsession.

It's late and the air is cool. Her hard nipples press against the shirt. There's a gray shadow where her face should be. What color were her eyes? What shape were her lips? His mind is a blank, though he'd flirted with her for hours, working hard to attract and then keep her attention, her gaze. He thinks he'll lift his hands and rest them on her breasts, but he can't move.

He hears the dull sound of a latch closing or opening, perhaps a dead bolt being thrown. In the smooth expanse of black steel is a sudden void, a gap that widens like a mouth yawning. A man in a dark suit and a red tie steps in front of the woman.

He'll fill the gap and close it.

HE OPENS his eyes to a room without black steel. He sees no woman in a sleeveless shirt. Jen is the only one with him now. She looks like a friend in mourning; her gestures are careful and tentative, almost ceremonial. She holds his right hand and examines the swollen joints. "Your fingers used to be long and straight and lovely," she says. "I didn't realize. I didn't see – "

He tries to slip his hands beneath his legs, but she won't let him.

"Is it arthritis?" says Jen.

"Something like that," he says.

"What is it then? What do the doctors say?"

"They say it's unfortunate."

She lifts his left hand and turns it over. She rubs. She tries to smooth and straighten his bones.

"Is there pain?"

"Most of the time. I take pills."

"When did it start?"

"It didn't start," he says. "Not in the way you're thinking. It just happened."

"What do you mean?"

"Nothing," he says. "It just happened."

chapter six

AT THE old Detroit club, guests in loud colors drift in after nightfall. They slowly turn black, white, silver, and gray. A man wearing a pinstripe suit but no tie emerges from the dark recesses of the stage. Holding a vintage guitar, he takes a few tentative steps, casts about like a lost child, and then nods and comes to rest on a high wooden stool.

He plays "Do Nothin' Till You Hear from Me," the bald crown of his head and his round Calabrian face floating in the spotlight like a pale moon. Despite the steady illumination, half his countenance is dark, a pool of deep shadow formed by the heavy brow, large nose, and thick mustache. In the corner of his mouth is a stocky cigar that somehow stays lit from one song to the next. Every now and then a wisp of smoke curls upward and dances above his ear.

Coleman sips his martini. He feels good. His tailored suit wears like a pair of jeans and a casual shirt. At the next table, a woman in a formal white dress and a cropped evening jacket turns her head at regular intervals and glances in the direction of the door. Her long straight hair is black, swept to one side, and secured with a silver clip.

"Are you expecting someone?" says the woman. "A friend, maybe, or a lover."

He recognizes the rising and falling of her words, the round vowels and soft consonants. "I'm waiting for Bogart," he says.

"Funny," she says. "I'm waiting for him, too."

The music of her voice makes her all the more captivating. He wants to say something funny and profound, a line that she'll consider unexpected, altogether fresh and flattering. Instead, a waiter shows up, hovering above the tables like a devoted genie.

"Again," he says, handing the waiter his glass. "And a champagne cocktail for the lady."

The waiter disappears.

The woman tilts her head toward the stage. Her face is round. The olive perfection of her skin seems smoother and darker in the club's soft light. "It's a lovely guitar," she says.

He nods. "It's a Gibson L5. I believe it's the same one he played back in '74."

"I meant the music," the woman says.

He rubs the knotty fingers of his left hand. "Joe plays like no one else."

Beginning with her hips, the woman slides her small but perfect hands down her thighs, smoothing, as it appears, the folds of her dress. "You must know him then. You're on a first-name basis."

"Not really. I crossed his path a few times. That's all."

Her dark eyes return to the stage. "He's uncanny," she says. "And with such short fingers."

"Short but quick," he says.

She smiles. "It's all a blur."

The tablecloth beneath his elbow is bunched up and creased. He fusses with it, trying to work out the wrinkles. "I can't remember how he looked the last time I saw him. It's been a while."

"At least ten years," says the woman.

"At least that," he says.

The waiter seems to rise up from between the tables. "One vodka martini with olives," he says. "And one champagne cocktail."

Joe plays the last notes of "Do Nothin' Till You Hear from Me," and the club rumbles with applause. He gets up to leave, but the MC, speaking from somewhere above the stage, calls him back. "Let's hear it for Joe Pass," says the MC's voice.

"Thanks," says Joe. He takes the cigar out of his mouth. "I'm happy to be here." He smiles. He has the look of a man who's just finished a fine Italian meal. He starts playing. The tune is "Sophisticated Lady."

"That's lovely," says the woman. "Such grace."

"I saw Joe in Philly," he says. "He played 'How High the Moon' all by himself. No bass. No drums. He played it fast. And he didn't cut corners. He was probably forty or forty-five in those days. I was just a kid."

The woman smiles. "It makes me crazy when I see someone doing a thing that's impossible."

"Why?" he says.

"I lose my grip. I think I can do it, too."

"What's wrong with that?"

"It's not for everyone, you know."

"Of course not."

"In the end, it may be the province of one person – perhaps only two or three."

"I suppose."

"So, where does that leave the rest of us?"

Too much talking, he thinks. I'm missing the song.

"There are limits," says the woman. "Throwing yourself against them is crazy. And when you find there's no greatness, only tricks and imitation, then you punish yourself – or someone else."

He scratches his neck. He feels perspiration inside the collar of his shirt. He excuses himself and walks through the sea of small tables, up three steps, and past the bar.

The men's room smells like citrus. He loosens his tie and splashes water on his face. He combs his hair straight back and checks the lines of his beard. Maybe she'll leave, he thinks. But that's not really the thing he wants. He likes having someone to talk to. He tries to button his collar but his hands won't cooperate. He stretches his fingers and tries again. It's no use. He leaves his shirt open and takes off the tie.

He passes the bar, looks over at his table and then at the stage. He observes the empty stool and the Gibson L5 bathed in soft light. He hears the calm murmur of voices, an occasional wave of laughter. He sees that the woman has rearranged things to make room for a visitor, a man with a high forehead and dark hair. They give the impression, sitting in apparent silence, of being together, as if they were old and respectful lovers.

He envies the white dinner jacket and the black bow tie. Taking the long way around, he can't discern the man's face from across the room, too much shadow and smoke.

"Pleased to meet you?" he says, glancing at the woman, his manner both cautious and proprietary.

The visitor gets up and offers his hand. "Likewise."

He can't return the man's grip, but he's glad to discover that this lothario, putting aside the forehead and, perhaps, the eyebrows, isn't Bogart at all.

"You look relieved," says the man.

"Sorry," he says. "I thought you were someone else."

"He's a composer," says the woman, "a songwriter."

He takes in the man's full measure. "Interesting," he says.

The songwriter nods. He looks cool and composed, entirely suave, but then he orders another bourbon and the dam breaks. "Okay," he says, lighting a cigarette. "I'll come clean and tell you I'm more a lyricist, a poet, than anything else, but I find melodies up here, too." He taps the side of his head. "It's hard to do words and music. There isn't a single rhyme in "Moonlight in Vermont." You ever notice that? You think it rhymes because of the music, but it's all tennis without a net because the net's no longer important. You can't separate the music from the words or the words from the music – and that, my friend, is sublime." He takes a deep drag on his cigarette. "Let's talk tunesmiths. Some guys write catchy. Others write schmaltz. A few go for a song that's smart. But then there's a handful – the top-hat class – that set out for the sublime. Jerry Kern's in that territory, and Irving Berlin. Hoagy Carmichael and Billy Strayhorn, of course. And who can touch Gershwin or Ellington? You can't always hear where they're going, so it's better just to close your eyes and hang on for the ride."

The woman sips her champagne cocktail. "What territory are you in?" she says.

"I don't know," says the songwriter. "But I know where I'd like to be. Sometimes my own stuff sounds like Strayhorn or Kern. I worry about it. But, like I said, I'm better at words than music. My motto is, 'Immature poets imitate; mature poets steal.'"

"I'd rather talk music than poetry," says the woman. "It keeps a respectful distance. I've never understood those big bullish writers who go around explaining how they write poems. It's like going around and explaining how you sleep with your wife."

The songwriter rubs his high forehead and says, "I've tried a lot of things.

You have to make a living; you have to matter in the world before anyone takes you seriously." He slips his hand beneath the lapel of his dinner jacket, reaching for the inside breast pocket, and pulls out a seed packet. "Let me tell you about my little business. It's called 'Please Plant This Song.'" He reaches into more pockets and winds up with eight seed packets on the table. He turns over the seed packet for sunflowers. "Printed on the back of each packet," he says, "are the lyrics to a song. For a long time, I took all eight and stacked them up and tied them with a ribbon and sold them as a set. Each song – or I should say poem – has something to do with the flowers that grow from the seeds. I've got more poems than I can use: lyrics about Van Gogh, Custer, the *Titanic*, Golgotha, karma, winos, the Hindenburg, John Donne, Ulysses, oranges, Jesus, Baudelaire, the New York Yankees, Captain Ahab, Kafka, and Sidney Greenstreet." He pauses to catch his breath. "I've got plans, you see, for a second set of eight. But these'll do for now." He regards the products of his labor, and, for a moment, his face fills with wonder. "In this set, for example, Van Gogh goes with sunflowers, John Donne with bluebells, and Ahab with white peonies. The whole thing works like this: You buy the packets and you plant the seeds in the ground and you read the poems and plant the ideas in your mind and before long you're growing your own songs like flowers."

The woman's hand reaches across the table and settles on the packet bearing a giant blue hydrangea. She picks it up. She turns it over and reads. "This is wonderful," she says.

"It can't be," he says, spinning the olive in his drink. "Read it out loud."

She leans forward. "'The Sidney Greenstreet Blues,'" she says. "'I think something beautiful . . .'" But then she breaks off. "I can't do it. Here. Read it yourself."

He takes the packet and sets it on the table. "I'm glad it's short," he says. "My eyes and this light aren't made for an epic." He leans back in his chair until the words come into focus.

The Sidney Greenstreet Blues

I think something beautiful
and amusing is gained
by remembering Sidney Greenstreet,
but it is a fragile thing.

The hand picks up a glass.
The eye looks at the glass
and then hand, glass and eye
      fall away.

"I'm surprised," he says, looking at the woman and then at the songwriter. "I like it. It has a quality I like."

"Thank you," says the songwriter. He picks up his glass and finishes his bourbon in one swallow. "I gotta hit the road," he says.

"Yes," says the woman. "It's time for me as well."

He doesn't want them to go. "Let me buy another round," he says.

"I appreciate it," says the songwriter. "But I've already been here too long."

"Stay," he says, catching the woman's eyes. "We can listen to the next set."

"She listens like no one else I know," says the songwriter.

"I should go," she says.

"We'll take my car," says the songwriter, gathering and stacking his seed packets.

Coleman pushes across the table "The Sidney Greenstreet Blues."

The songwriter gestures for him to stop. "You can keep it, my friend. It's yours."

He puts the seed packet in his breast pocket and stands as the woman and the songwriter prepare to leave. She turns and says good-bye. He holds her perfect fingers and raises her hand to his lips. "Another time, then," he says.

"Yes," she says. "Another time."

The songwriter cocks his head. "Please plant that song," he says.

He watches the woman and the songwriter disappear beyond the bar and then orders another martini. The stage is quiet and the crowd thins. All the nearby tables go dark. He observes a middle-aged man and a boyish man as they talk and smoke. He toys with the idea of playing guitar, but there's no audience now except for the two men. Still, he finds it difficult to leave. He yearns for a time and place he's never been. Something about the club gives him hope, lets him believe that grace and passion were once possible and could be again. He lifts his drink, feels the cold bite on his tongue. Yes, this room is lovely, he thinks. Even now, with only the three of us, it's lovely.

ON MONDAY morning, the sky overcast, gears grinding, he drives through farmland and small towns, down narrow and half-deserted streets, the full load making his truck less squirrelly in the turns. He listens to the news. He stares at the road and the sky beyond the trees. He double-parks in front of the Flat Rock liquor store. He slides out of the cab and walks to the rear of the truck. It's early and the street's gray, but the air is already thick with humidity. He lowers the hydraulic gate. He wishes that small stores had concrete loading docks like the grocery chains. The height of the truck's bed is made for that kind of delivery. Convenience stores force him to do more maneuvering, more ups and downs. He steps onto the lift, hits the switch, and the platform jerks him skyward. He unlocks the roll-up door and raises it. He stacks cases and twelve-packs on the hand truck, tips the load, and swings it toward the lift.

On most mornings, he moves with rehearsed precision, but on this day, with the truck filled to capacity, he tips and swings but misjudges the distance, crushing his fingers between the hand truck and a wall of beer. His arm recoils. He staggers, cursing the cargo and his clumsy move. He rubs his left hand and feels pity for its helplessness, its growing deformity. He holds it in front of his face like an object that has no relation to his body, and he hears Heather's voice telling him to wear his gloves, the heavy ones, the pair that he always keeps in the truck but then leaves on the dashboard beneath his newspaper and cap.

He rolls the beer onto the lift. His hand throbs. His fingers feel heavy and his knuckles weep, the skin scraped and torn. He looks out at the street and the asphalt moves. He reaches for the switch to lower the lift, but he can't find it. The neon letters that spell LIQUOR float in circles around his head. He grabs the hand truck to steady himself. He glances down, takes a deep breath, and feels his heart racing. He breathes again.

After a while, the beer, truck, storefront, and street stop spinning. When he regains control, he sees that his right foot is close to the edge. Another step and he might've gone over. He pictures the accident he just missed. Short of falling and breaking his neck, he would've dropped his foot into thin air and snagged his trousers, tearing the inseam of his pant leg from ankle to thigh and leaving thin peels of skin on the edge of the lift.

He teeters on the brink. It's often like this when he stands on a dock or a seawall. But the habit started long ago, somewhere on the road – perhaps in Montreal, in a small theater on a proscenium stage. The acoustics impressed him as the show continued, so he ignored the roadies and the union rules and kept the place going until midnight. He listened to the music and the measured silence; both came to his ear without flaws, without a crackle or screech, without the distant drone of voices. Then his vigilance gave way and he played without thinking. During Brian's solo, feeling a new impulse, he adjusted his strap and stood up, squinting at the footlights. He closed his eyes and drifted to the edge of the stage until Tom hit a rimshot that startled him and brought him back. The next step would have found him in the laps of two women sitting in the first row.

"I was swept up in a transcendental moment," he said. "The music suddenly made sense, complete and absolute sense."

"That's right," said Tom, wanting credit for preventing a disaster. "I saw you stepping off, landing facedown on your axe, your cord snapping and trailing behind you. That's pure transcendence."

He wheels the beer into the store and goes directly to the freezer. He takes a bag of ice and drops it on the floor, kicks it a few times until the frozen mass breaks into pieces. Then he rips open the plastic and thrusts his hand into the cold.

"You got a problem?" says the owner.

"Yeah," he says. "An accident."

"You bleedin'?"

"Not much. Maybe a little."

"You bleedin', you bought it."

"Okay. Put it on my tab."

"What tab? You ain't got no tab."

"Jesus," he says. "Must be one hell of a margin on ice."

The owner swats a fly with a rolled-up magazine. "Fuck the margin. It's three bucks."

"I don't have it."

"Don't shit with me."

"I don't have it. Like it says on the truck, drivers don't carry cash."

"Even a bum carries three bucks. What about lunch? You do pay for lunch, don't ya?"

"I've got a credit card, that's all."

"Plastic man. That figures." The owner swats another fly. "Gimme the card."

He takes out his wallet and fumbles the handoff and the card falls behind the counter.

"I suppose you want me to find it," says the owner.

"I can cancel it," he says.

"Maybe you should do that. Call the bank right now, cuz I'm lookin' hard and I don't see it."

He glares at the owner and feels the muscles in his right arm tighten. He wants to knock the man's head off with a roundhouse punch. Instead, he sets the ice on top of the beer, tips the hand truck, and starts for the door.

"Where you goin' with those suds?" says the owner.

"I lost your invoice," he says. "Can't deliver without the paperwork."

The owner pulls a handgun from beneath the counter. "I'd stop right there if I was you."

"You gonna shoot me?" he says. He points at the camera in the corner near the ceiling. "You gonna kill me on closed-circuit TV?"

The owner lowers the gun. "All right, plastic man. You win. Just leave the beer."

"I'll take a trade," he says.

The owner bends down and picks up the card. He slides it through the slot on his register.

"You can cancel that transaction. I want the card *and* the ice."

The owner hits a button and puts the card on the counter. He smiles – a front tooth missing and a gold cap.

A light in the ceiling flashes and pops.

He slides the hand truck out from under the load. "I'll leave the beer right here," he says. "I'm sure you can manage."

"You can't leave it in the door."

"It's not in the door." He grabs his credit card and the bag of ice. "See. I can get out. No problem."

He hustles back to the truck, buttons up the rear, and raises the lift. He keeps an eye on the side-view mirrors while he starts the engine. He rolls off using his right hand to shift and steer. His left hand is pleasantly numb, resting in the ice like a dead fish.

THE NEXT delivery takes more time. He gripes out loud about the market being run-down, about its thick stoop and heavy door, its narrow and cluttered aisles. Looking inside, he sees the wholesome young woman who works the counter two or three mornings a week. She looks over the shoulder of the customer counting his change and waves.

Pulling with one hand, he gets stuck at the stoop. His second attempt fails. A man wanting to get through the door plants a heavy boot on the bottom of the hand truck and gives him a boost.

"Thanks," he says.

The man grunts and brushes past him toward the magazine stand.

He wheels the load to the rear of the store and leaves the beer stacked against the wall. He waits until the customers have gone.

"You okay?" says the young woman, her face filled with concern.

"Got a bum hand," he says.

"Sorry," she says. "You should've taken the day off."

"Just happened," he says. "Here's the bad news for the beer. I need you to sign this one."

She initials the paper. He breathes in her scent. "Is that shampoo or perfume, or what?"

She smiles. "I don't know. I don't wear perfume."

"It's nice." He stares at her initials. "Where's Frank?"

"He's in back. You need to see him?"

He looks up. "No. Just tell him I said hello." He wants very much to reach across the counter and touch her. He hates it that his hand is throbbing. "I'd rather see you than him," he says, "but don't tell Frank I said that. He'd only feel bad."

She smiles again. "Are you flirting with me?"

"No," he says, backing away from the counter, feeling a sudden pinch in his gut. "I hope not."

"I'm sorry," she says, the blood rising in her cheeks. "I didn't mean anything."

"I didn't either," he says. He stuffs the paper in his shirt. "You're nice. It's nice to see you."

He heads for the door and pushes the hand truck over the stoop. He stops and turns. He lifts his arm and tries to wave but his swollen hand floats in the air like an inflated rubber glove. He feels silly and self-conscious. I'm a clown, he says to himself. A damn fool.

AT THE Black & White Club, he sips his drink and looks closely at the woman who appears to be sitting with him at the table. She wears a hat with a large white brim and a veil. Because of the hat, the dim light, and the cigarette smoke, he finds it impossible to see her face. He follows the outline of her cheeks and chin but all the other details elude him. In sharp contrast, her arms and shoulders, accentuated by a tight, thin, sleeveless dress, reveal a tempting symmetry, a curve and slope so enticing that he wants to brush his lips across her skin. It's cooler than usual in the club. He notices the slight rising and falling of her chest.

"You okay?" he says.

The veil trembles with the give and take of her breathing.

He rubs his knuckles. "Something wrong?"

"What makes you ask?" says the woman.

"Since we got here," he says, "you haven't said a word."

"When did we get here?"

"I'm not sure. Later than usual."

"We missed Django," she says.

"We did?"

"That's right. Django was here. But we were late."

He glances at the stage. "I didn't know."

"It doesn't matter," she says. She sits with her forearms on the table, her right hand resting on top of her left. "You're a fool," she says. "What did you see in me?"

"I'm not sure," he says. "Nothing was clear – the lights, the smoke – "

"That's not how it seemed."

"No," he says. "I suppose not."

"If you couldn't see, why did you do it?"

"I was bored."

"That's not a pretty thing to say."

"All right," he says. "Some things I could see."

"Yes," she says. "I know."

He spins his drink on a ring of condensation. "I wanted what I saw. It was that – and the boredom."

"Whenever I heard you play," she says, "I thought you were playing for me, just me."

With a steady gaze, he tries to penetrate her veil.

"It was difficult for me to sit with another man and listen to you."

He wonders if she's telling the truth. "Music is like that," he says.

"But you did it," she says. "You made it that way."

"Yes."

"You used your guitar for me?"

"Yes. At the end."

"You're unlucky," she says.

"I've heard that before. But I'm not so sure. I have a history."

"That sounds mysterious," she says. "Are you from another country? Did you kill a man?"

"No, not me."

"Then you're unlucky."

"I believe in pattern and symmetry," he says. "Like a song. Like the curve of your neck and the slope of your shoulders."

"Yes," she says. "But you're still unlucky."

He downs the rest of his drink. "Say a man commits murder and gets away with it. Will another man pay for the crime?"

"Why should he?" says the woman. "There's no justice in that."

"Justice is hardly the point," he says. "Symmetry is the point."

The woman laughs. "I see. God keeps a ledger, a sheet with long columns, and He keeps it balanced any way He can. Is that what you believe?"

"Why not?"

"You're trying too hard," she says. "You're trying to explain things."

"Maybe so. But when enough water builds up behind a dam – maybe it's a natural disaster, or man-made, if you like – the dam breaks so the water can even out." He stops. He wonders what would happen if he reached over and lifted the veil. "Innocent people get swept away."

"I'm tired of this," says the woman. She turns toward the couple at the next table.

He looks over and sees a young woman with red hair. She raises her drink and throws it in the face of the older man sitting across from her. A waiter appears with a fresh cocktail and a towel. The man wipes his face. "I hope that satisfies you," he says. She leans back in her chair and smiles. "Oh, darling," she says. "I'll never be satisfied." The waiter hovers over the man and dabs at his suit with the dry corner of a towel. "Bravo," says a voice from somewhere in the room. "Well done," says another.

Concerned about the tiff, the manager of the club comes over and says a few inaudible words to the couple. He offers an apology to those sitting nearby.

A girl carrying a tray and wearing a jacket and short skirt follows the manager. "Cigars, cigarettes, chocolate," she says.

"Swiss chocolate?" says Coleman.

"No. Nothin' fancy," says the girl. "Unless you want an imported cigar."

"No thanks," he says.

"Nice hat," says the girl. "It's classy, with the veil and all."

"Thank you," says the woman. "Do you have chocolate mints?"

"Sorry," says the girl. "Straight chocolate is all I got."

"I'll take a rose," he says.

"Dark or light?" says the girl.

"Dark."

The girl lays a long-stemmed rose on the table and then takes her tray elsewhere.

"That's a sad but lovely rose," says the woman.

"Then it's perfect," he says.

"What are you trying to do? Are you trying to make things pretty?"

"That hardly seems possible."

"Do you still want me?"

He gazes at her arms and shoulders. He sees the shadow between her breasts. "Yes," he says. "That never changes."

"You can say that?" she says. "Even after what happened?"

"Of course. What happened had nothing to do with you."

"You're a fool. An unlucky fool."

"You've said that."

"I have guilt, you know. I should've said or done something."

"There was nothing you could've done."

"You're kind to say it." She reaches for his hand but draws back before touching his crooked fingers.

"There was nothing," he says.

"Are you sure?"

"Yes."

"And you want me?"

"Yes. It's always the same."

The woman stands. Her hand picks up the rose. She looks at the rose and then, with great care, lays it on the table. She walks off without saying good-bye. She goes to the bar, greets a steel-jawed man wearing a dark suit and tie. In the next moment, she lifts her veil and removes her hat. She dips and shakes her head and her hair falls around her shoulders.

He cranes his neck, trying to catch a glimpse of her face. But it's no use. The room is too crowded. It's filled with smoke and flickering light.

He knocks off early and pulls into his driveway before six. The wind is up out of the northwest. He sees the day's overcast making way for black and purple clouds. He goes in through the garage, finds the house dark and stuffy. He opens the front and back doors and the windows that aren't painted shut. Cool air rushes in with the scent of damp soil. His hand throbs. He takes a double dose of pills. He shuffles to the freezer, dumps three trays of ice into a bucket, and buries his hand in the cubes.

He walks into the living room and sees a station wagon pull up at the curb. With his hand deep in the ice, he watches as the landlord slides out of her car, lowers the tailgate, and pulls out a stack of red pails. She hurries up the walk, her breasts nearly visible beneath a thin cotton shirt, her cutoffs revealing the broad curve of her hips and the firmness of her thighs. She lets herself in.

"Big rain on the way," she says. "Looks like I'm just in time." She points a finger at the ceiling. "I'm worried about that old roof. If she starts to leak, you can set these pails in the attic – head off some of the damage."

"Is there a problem?" he says. His eyes do a once-over of the ceiling and then settle on her. "Looks fine to me."

"Can't be careful enough," says the landlord. "Once I went to Sacramento to visit a friend and got caught in a three-day blow. The windows rattled and the roof leaked like a sieve. The whole place looked to be made of cardboard. My friend kept apologizing. He said, 'Everything in California is built like a shoe box.' He thought the paper walls were on account of the weather. But I knew better. There's no fear of God in California. If they had any respect, they'd put up stuff strong enough to take a beating. You gotta be prepared, I say. So I'll leave you these, just in case."

She puts the stack of pails on the floor. "If you need a few more, let me know." She turns and looks up through the dirty screen. "Seems like God's a little pissed off today." Then the screen door slams and she's gone.

He hears thunder groaning in the distance. The sound strikes him now like the murmur of troubled voices, a kind of warning, though this time the storm approaches, as opposed to an earlier time, a different night, when a woman in a sleeveless shirt with a low neckline stood in the parking lot, almost empty, puddles like small mirrors catching her in fragments, while the thunder moved away, the flashes of light over her bare shoulder growing dim. He can't see her face. It's as if she'd arrived wearing a gray veil and then never took it off.

He takes a handful of ice and drops it in a glass. He fills the glass with vodka. He picks up the drink and wraps his arm around the bucket and walks into the living room. Through the window he sees the trees in the front yard bending. He hears the sound of rushing water. He sits on the couch and rests his hand on the ice. He sips his drink. The room is darker now than when he came home. Better to leave it dark, he thinks. He likes the cool wind and the scent of damp soil.

He closes his eyes and hears the thunder as if it were a fading sound. He thinks of the woman without a name or face and the rain-washed parking lot glistening under the streetlights. He wonders if the pills will let him sleep. Should he take more? How many does he need? He feels uneasy, despite the distance and the years, knowing that the parking lot in question is still in Chicago behind the Green Mill. He'd been playing there for two weeks, sitting in as a guest or a substitute with different groups, trying to keep himself on the road, putting off his inevitable return to Michigan, Maureen, and his four-year-old daughter.

He sits on the couch drinking vodka. The living room flickers, a flash of lightning, and then thunder rolls from the west, growing louder as it comes, cracking and rumbling beyond the line of bowing trees. He wants to keep his mind occupied, pack his brain in the bucket of ice. But the sounds and smells of the storm, the vodka and the pills, and his hand, almost numb, make him unsteady and vulnerable, open like an upturned palm, unable to shut out his final days – his final minutes – at the Green Mill, that old and familiar club where, in the end, not a single friend or acquaintance came to hear him play.

It is 1992, the year that is perpetually with him, the year that will not let him rest.

An older woman with dark hair sits near the edge of the stage. He sees her for the first time over the tip of his shoe. Formal for the Mill, she wears a tight blue dress with spaghetti straps. He savors her arms and shoulders. He likes the look of her skin, the uneven shadings of experience. From where he stands, the lines and symmetry of her body achieve a stunning perfection.

Sitting with her is a serious man in a dark suit and a stylish red tie. This man goes unseen the first night and for several nights thereafter. The only thing visible is the woman: her blue dress or, later, her blouse with the plunging neckline; her green skirt, amazingly short; her boots and her leather pants.

He barely thinks of what he's playing. He stays focused on the woman, holding her gaze through the rising and falling of old ballads. A voice in his ear admonishes him, tells him to use his talent for its own sake. Don't make it a job. Don't use it for this. But it's been twelve years since he performed with the trio, with Brian James, four or more since he played with anyone who mattered. He's turned music into a reason, an excuse for staying away from home, from Maureen and his daughter. He plays with uninspired precision. The woman leans on the edge of the stage. Making a request, she extends her arm and hands him a paper napkin.

He remembers that she arrived early each night and chose the table that stood in his direct line of vision. He saw her willingness and her cool determination, her gutsy and provocative confidence – an exhibitionist at the top of her form. But all this drove him to distraction. She obscured everyone around her, including her companion, a well-built man, entirely ageless, wearing a midnight jacket, a vibrant but elegant tie, and a face of black steel – smooth, cold, unchanging.

He should've seen the man's expression, the black skin drawn tight around the eyes and mouth. The threat should've been clear. But he gave himself to the excitement, the obsession, squandering songs and solos, spending everything he had, an offering to destiny that he might not remember the thing most worth remembering: the Mill with Jennifer in it, her head tilted to one side as she listened with unabashed joy.

Outside, the mounting storm offers its own excitement: a lightning flash, a clap of thunder, the wind buffeting the house. But now nothing will let him forget, not even the sound of white water or the black and purple sky. The back door slams. He jerks like a man touching a live wire, feels his hand throbbing as if he'd somehow smashed it again.

He cannot quiet his brain. He replays the moment when he opened the napkin. He sees the title of a song and a short list of directions, a summons. He plays the tune but pays no attention to the quality of his performance, and he packs up in a hurry after the last set, anxious for his meeting, for a room in a downtown hotel, a view of Lake Michigan – the dark water of her face.

He kisses the curve of her neck, traces the slope of her shoulder with his tongue. He loosens his grip. His fingers are keenly alive, sensing the nuances of her skin, the lean definition of her arms.

She comes to the Green Mill on the following Wednesday, and again on Thursday and Friday. But on Saturday she arrives with an entourage, a group of black men, handsome and serious, more than can fit at her table. When he catches her eye, she hides her face.

Someone in the audience calls out a request and a voice from the bar says, "You need a different band for that one."

He glances at the woman. She turns to the man she's with, a shadow – his tie like a red vein. It doesn't matter, he thinks. Tonight's the end of it. I'm flying out tomorrow.

In the last set, he plays "Black Orpheus," and for a moment his phrasing and tone cast a mesmerizing spell, something fragile and almost forgotten. Gradually, the room falls into a churchlike silence. Each player, bathed in blue light, listens. The old man at the piano looks up.

When it's over, he puts his guitar in its case, collects his money, and goes out the front door. He checks the traffic on Broadway; a few cars make a sizzling sound on the wet pavement. A storm has passed. He hears distant thunder, sees a soft flash of light. He walks to the corner and turns.

His body convulses, folding over a fist that robs him of his breath. He feels like a drowning man. He gasps. The street and the buildings begin tumbling with stars. His arms are pinned to his sides. His legs buckle and give out. He can't lift his feet; they drag behind him like stone blocks.

Everywhere is the scent of well-barbered men. In an instant, the ground is no longer a sidewalk. Beneath him is darkness like the night sky, a field of asphalt made slick by the rain. Just ahead is the glint of a polished door.

He breathes and the world stops spinning. He finds himself in the parking lot behind the Green Mill. He's wedged between the shoulders of giant men. He's close to a sleek limousine, its engine running. Into his line of vision steps the man with the face of black steel, and then he sees her, standing off to the side, the woman whose name he's forgotten, wearing what she's worn all night, a tight, thin, and sleeveless shirt with a low neckline. He looks again at her arms and shoulders. Her nipples press against the shirt.

"So, what to do with an entertainer?" says the man.

Without answering this question, the giants crank up the pressure like a vice. He feels his stomach rising to his throat, his head ready to burst.

The man adjusts his red tie. "You want him to perform?" he says, turning to the woman. "Is there something you'd like to hear?"

She doesn't move or speak.

He'd watched her from the stage, her moves and her expressions, but now there's a gray shadow covering her face. What color were her eyes? What shape were her lips? He wants to lift his hands and rest them on her breasts, but he can't move. He regards the limousine, the long body like a panther stretching toward the street.

"I'm told," says the man, "that a guitar has a neck. A body. That a musician holds it and plays it like a precious thing." The man offers his hand to the woman. She comes closer. He stands behind her and runs his index finger down the slope of her shoulder. "So I'm curious," he says. "Did she play for you? Did she make the sounds you wanted?"

He can't make out the woman's face. "I wouldn't have – " But one of the giants cuts off his air.

The man brushes the woman aside. "I'm a person of means, of property," he says. "You owe me for unauthorized use."

The giants drag him forward and the door of the limousine opens. The polished steel catches the street lamp and flashes. He looks down at the asphalt and sees the woman in fragments, the puddles like shards of glass reflecting her thighs, her hips, her dark hair. The opening door creates a breach, a gap that widens like a mouth yawning. He wants to crawl into the limousine. Instead, a dead weight falls on his shoulders and drives him to his knees.

He struggles against the cold grip just below his wrists. He watches his hands being forced into the breach. The woman shrieks. In the next breath, the door slams. The bones in his hands shatter.

The parking lot pitches and slides away. He drifts. He feels the first fire of unending pain. He sees his guitar jammed beneath a tire, its black case like a coffin waiting nearby. Slowly, the door of the limousine opens as wide as it will go. Then, without conscience, it slams again.

chapter seven

HEATHER looks taller in her cap and gown. She must be wearing high heels, thinks Coleman. He hugs her and whispers in her ear, "You better walk like a girl in finishing school. It's a long way down from those shoes."

She smiles with old friends and poses with the new guy who took her to the prom. A quick inspection of the boy, his face in Coleman's viewfinder, reveals a tight smile, a smartly trimmed goatee, and a rhinestone stud in the auricle of his left ear. His thin arms and narrow shoulders barely support his gown. Alongside Heather, the kid looks like a beanpole, a stick figure wrapped in a bedsheet.

A light wind moves through the trees making the sound of water. Heather gazes at the blue sky stretching to the horizon. "There's your invitation," he says. "You need to get this done and go."

He braces himself for the speeches. He knows exactly what to expect, particularly from the principal and the assistant principal. They'll swear like men under oath that this graduating class represents a new hope for America, a treasure trove of diversity and talent.

He imagines school officials all over the country testifying in the same way, creating the illusion, for parents, grandparents, and teachers, that these graduates are somehow different – fresher, stronger, and smarter – than the kids who walked the boards last year or the year before. It's the hype, he says to himself. It starts early. It's like selling a record.

The crowd moves from the parking lot into the auditorium. The stage lights illuminate a podium, a microphone, and several rows of brown folding chairs. Near the podium and at the corners of the stage, clusters of mums and carnations, purple and white, the school's traditional colors, stand at crisp attention.

He sees Maureen sitting up front with a group of old neighbors and decides to sit toward the back where it's darker and less crowded. Despite the day's low humidity, the air in the auditorium feels sticky.

At three o'clock, faculty and staff walk down the side aisles and take their seats. Then "Pomp and Circumstance" comes through the PA system. The melody wavers. It groans and for a moment goes flat. A worn-out cassette, he thinks. I need to make a donation. I'll buy the school a CD player. I'll even buy the CD.

The doors for the center aisle swing open, and the class president, the valedictorian, and the salutatorian lead the procession. In their academic robes, the kids look like members of a religious sect. The uniformity grows hypnotic, so much so that his mind begins to drift. He dreams of an orchestra playing in perfect tune, celli and violins filling his ears with a silken whisper. He almost misses his daughter when she steps through the door, her hair tucked under her cap and her tassel on the wrong side.

He considers the fact that more than thirty years have gone by since he last attended a commencement. He pictures his father seated in the first row look-ing proud but distracted. His mother struggles with a package of film. She opens the camera and loads it.

He remembers that the class of '73 seemed clumsy, too large for its own good. Even when a fourth of the students turned out to be no-shows, those waiting for their diplomas numbered six hundred. The missing seniors repre-sented a protest, a boycott. They refused to be questioned and searched, frisked by security guards trying to confiscate dope and booze. This new policy came from the desk of Truant Officer Baines. The graduates, by his design, were forced to arrive two hours early. They formed a line so that men equipped with Mace and handcuffs could pat them down. One of the boys got slapped. "Any higher," he'd said to the guard, "and you'll be yankin' my balls."

A rising squeal of feedback causes everyone to clutch their heads, and then Principal Trip covers the microphone with his hand and makes it worse. It finally ends with a screech and a sonic boom.

"Testing," says Principal Trip. "Testing one, two, three – " He looks heavier under the lights. His pudgy hand clutches a hankie for mopping his forehead and chin. "Parents, family, friends, and graduates, welcome . . ."

I shouldn't have said it, he thinks, that remark about finishing school. She's not a girl anymore. She never acts like a teenager. In two months, she'll be packed and gone. She'll find a more hospitable climate, a place that becomes her. I love the tilt of her head and the electricity of her smile. She's like my mother, the way she glides into a room. But she's fearless. There's not one thing she's afraid of.

Principal Trip introduces the valedictorian. "She'll be attending the Uni-versity of Chicago," he says. He delivers this news with considerable glee, with the élan of a game-show host announcing the grand prize.

The valedictorian begins her speech, but the words pile up like water behind a dam. Rising around him, swiftly and without compassion, is a flood of ghosts. He stares at his crooked hands and remembers the dark mahogany in the Green Mill. His mind dwells on the black limousine, on the window at Northwestern Memorial framing the gray expanse of Lake Michigan.

Brian collected him when he was discharged. "Where to now? You can't drive with those hands."

He'd thought about going back to Gibraltar and finding a place close to Heather and Maureen. "I'll catch a plane to Detroit," he said, "or maybe a train." But even as he said it, he realized he wouldn't go.

Michigan, he knew, offered no refuge. His old house, a small colonial with a view of the Trenton Channel, was no longer his home. He thought of it now as belonging only to Maureen – a payment, reparation for his long habit of infidelity. But he wanted Maureen to have the house, if not for herself then for Heather.

Leaving the hospital, he found it difficult, even infuriating, to manage the simplest moves – opening the car door, buckling his seat belt, rubbing his eyes – so he leaned on Brian and stayed in Chicago. He can't say now whether he moved in for three years or four. Brian never asked him for money or raised the question of when he might leave. They ate dinners together, went to movies, and shared the same bathroom. He learned another man's habits like he once knew Jennifer's and Maureen's.

Always in those days the doctor kept repeating himself like a broken record. "It'll take time," he said. "Rehabilitation is a tricky thing. It'll take a lot more time than you think."

After that, he lived with the dull weight of plaster, surfaces of pure white that gradually showed crazing, soil, and stains. As the casts became smaller, he picked and scratched, the sloughed yellow skin falling to the floor like wood shavings.

The months piled up and he passed to the next level: braces made of plastic and steel; physical therapy three times a week. When the braces came off for good, he kept his withered hands out of sight. He took them out only when necessary.

In the apartment was a battered, unstrung guitar. After a while, in moments of guaranteed privacy, he'd test his resolve by lifting the soundless antique from its half-hidden place. At first, he could barely hold it, but then, with each new effort, he found himself hanging on a bit longer, his body rocking, his hands grateful for the warp of old wood.

On bad days, lacking energy and resolve, he'd think of the shanty in Port Austin and his keen interest in Otis's black guitar, the Gibson ES-355, the sister of Lucille, and the thrill he felt when he got the nod from Otis and touched the neck for the first time, trying to keep his head, acting as if he knew all about Lucille so that Otis wouldn't think he was green. He took the guitar out of its stand, held it like a sacred object, like something brought back from a dream, and then rested the thin body on his leg and said, "So you're Lucille's sister. My name's Jason. Good to meet you." And Otis laughed.

He supported the neck and tucked the body beneath his arm.

"That's good," said Otis. "You shouldn't squeeze her too hard." The old man stepped across the room and picked up a songbook and began reading and turning pages like someone engrossed in a novel. Against a backdrop of framed photographs, dressed in black pants and a crisp white shirt, he seemed altogether wise and serene, a figure frozen in time, his head bowed in meditation. After a long silence, he looked up and said, "A guitar should feel just like your girlfriend."

"I don't have a girlfriend."

Otis put down the book. "Then imagine what one would feel like."

He wondered if a girl would be as heavy as this. The thought sidetracked him until Otis grabbed the fingers of his left hand and positioned them on the neck in a way that felt relaxed and natural. "Now strum," said Otis.

The guitar wasn't plugged in but he could hear the chord, a cluster of notes that together made a perfect harmony.

"That's G," said Otis.

The fact that he'd made any sound at all amazed him, distracted him again, until Otis plugged in the guitar and turned on the amplifier and took hold of his fingers and bunched them together on the first three strings. "Go ahead," he said.

This time the sound was louder and fuller, more beautiful than before.

"That's D," said Otis. "Now go back to the first position."

He moved his fingers but couldn't remember the exact configuration. Otis set him up once more and this time when he played the note on the lowest string he felt the vibration in his chest. He giggled and almost stopped but then made the change to the D chord.

"Good," said Otis. "And you're not getting tangled up and I don't hear any buzzing. Maybe the guitar suits you."

Now, HEARING the voice of the valedictorian, the long cadences of her speech, he thinks of Lucille's sister and the unstrung guitar in Brian's apartment. He remembers Brian coming home with a black Les Paul.

"I like the neck," says Brian. "It's narrow, tighter than what you're used to. I figure it'll be easier on your hands."

He stares at the guitar, afraid to pick it up.

Brian lifts the Les Paul out of its case and hands it over. "Just hold it," he says. "I know it's heavy." He opens the storage compartment in the case and takes out a cord. "I'll get an amp. We'll practice."

He folds his arm around the Les Paul and supports the neck. He hears Brian's voice calling from the other room.

He looks up and sees unblemished students sitting in perfect rows. Most of them have straight teeth. He'd like to be disparaging but admits as well that he envies their good looks and their view from the stage. They can't conceive of his long struggle, the starting over and the wasted time – repeating old lessons and rebuilding skills like a man recovering from a stroke – but for him there's no forgetting, even in the light of commencement, because the only thing he's able to see, beyond their bright eyes and shining faces, is the time they have, and he knows he'd steal from them if he could.

He remembers plugging the Les Paul into a small amplifier and tuning to Brian's bass. He opens and closes his left hand and then positions his thumb on the back of the neck behind his first and second fingers. He checks the action and makes sure that his palm stays clear of the neck. He plays a few chords, C, D, and G, in first position. His fingers feel stiff but workable.

He begins with scales and simple tunes, trying to find flashes of his lost dexterity and speed, his shattered technique.

He hangs back while Brian starts a walking figure in A. They keep it slow and he moves through the pattern without much trouble. They slip into the relative minor and he plays a large barre chord, F#-minor, pressing all six strings at the second fret with his first finger. The position hurts. He plays a B-minor chord after that and it forces him to stop.

He asks Brian what he paid for the Les Paul, for the case and the small amplifier. He worries that all of Brian's time and trouble will make no difference in the end. He massages his hand and thinks of the pain as something insidious and purposeful, a cruel force making its way like water.

When necessary, he visits the doctor and complains about his range of motion. "Accept it," says the physician. "Your hands are now twice your age."

He carps at the receptionist and demands an apology. He announces to everyone in the office that he can't pay, says he'd refuse even if he could. He walks out. Part of him wants to slam the door but the sudden twist in his gut makes him hold off. His left hand throbs like a hammered thumb.

"SOUNDS okay," says Brian.

He shakes his head. "No. It's stiff. It sounds like a march."

"You're right. But for two or three measures, I felt it swing. How's the pain?"

"Okay. The pills help."

"You been stretching?"

"Sure. My right hand's better than the left."

Brian raises his hand, palm out and fingers wide apart. "Here," he says. "Push."

As best he can, he tries to match the spread of Brian's fingers, but nothing quite lines up. He pushes and a wave of fire moves through his wrist and up his arm.

"C'mon, Cole. I don't feel it. You had more strength a couple of days ago."

He puts some weight behind it but he's afraid of the pain. He shakes out his hand like a dust rag. He plays a G chord, then D and E-minor. He plays a B-minor and winces. Barre chords make him crazy.

He rubs his hand. "You hungry?" he says.

"You're on your own," says Brian. "I got a gig."

"You didn't mention it."

"I'm sitting in for Bob Birch at the Showcase. You should come over and listen."

"No," he says. "Next time."

"Sure," says Brian. "Leftovers are in the fridge."

Alone for the evening, he decides to straighten up the apartment – a contribution to the domestic effort, a ritual which gives him a small measure of self-respect.

When he was a boy, his mother had to stay after him to keep things organized and clean up his room. If she could see this, he thinks, she'd finally be happy. He pictures his old room, the books, papers, and dirty clothes littering the floor, the unmade bed, and the bulging closet. He also sees the one immaculate corner reserved for his guitar, amplifier, wooden stool, and music stand – a clean, well-lighted space, orderly and uncluttered.

"It's hard coming in here," says his mother. She makes her way across the room, her long legs stepping over obstacles both large and small. "Why can't you keep all of it lovely like this corner? Look. Even your sheet music is stacked perfectly."

He shrugs.

"Over here, you've made a shrine. But the rest," she says with a sweeping gesture, "looks like a bad accident."

He laughs.

"Why cordon things off? Think bigger. You could make your entire kingdom a shrine."

He hears the back door open. "Meredith," says his father. "You home?"

"Well, Jason, maybe for Mother's Day you could make me a room that's immaculate." On her way out, she straightens the framed black-and-white photo of Wes Montgomery, a gift from Otis, which hangs between the bookcase and the door.

He recalls now that a year or so later, for her birthday, he managed to put the whole place in order. He forced her to wear a blindfold and then led her into the room and spun her around two or three times just for fun. She pretended to be stunned and amazed when she uncovered her eyes. "You see," she said. "Your life would be so much prettier if you did everything the way you do music."

A LOUD wave of applause carries the valedictorian to her chair. Principal Trip finds his way to the podium. He seems wetter than before. He says, "Our next speaker – "

His introduction gets cut off by a commotion in the audience. Four or five people are up on their feet and looking down at a gasping man. "Someone call an ambulance! Call 911," says an old woman. Her reedy voice cuts across the murmuring crowd.

Principal Trip confers with two or three teachers. Then, squinting up into the lights, he says into the microphone, "Can we have some music, please?"

"Pomp and Circumstance" begins again. It wavers and groans while the teachers try to help. They pull the stricken man out of his seat. With the football coach on one side and the basketball coach on the other, the man floats up the aisle and out into the lobby.

It takes a few minutes for the audience to quiet down.

Principal Trip foregoes the introduction and a young man walks to the podium.

"'The Road Not Taken,'" he says, "by Robert Frost."

"I THOUGHT you'd be asleep by now," says Brian, short of breath, having climbed the stairs with his bass in tow.

"I couldn't sleep if I wanted to. Need a drink?"

"No thanks. I've had more than my share."

"How'd it go?"

"Good. Almost a full house." Brian takes off his sport coat. "My amp pissed me off."

"Muddy?"

"No. Too much humming and buzzing."

"Is that right?" he says. "I can't believe it."

"Eat shit and die," says Brian.

"I knew the noise would finally get to you."

"Did you do any more practicing?" says Brian.

"About an hour."

"What else you been up to?"

He picks up a thin book. "Poetry," he says. He holds it up so that Brian can read the cover.

"Where'd you find that?" says Brian.

"Right here on the shelf. You recognize it, don't you? The name should ring a bell."

Brian takes a second look. He shakes his head.

"It's the old poet we backed at the Francis Parker School."

"That benefit?" says Brian. "That's ancient history. Jesus, was it '80 or '81?"

"I'm not sure."

"It must've been February," says Brian. "They covered the poster with hearts and cupids."

"You're right," he says. "It was Valentine's Day."

He can still see the old poet standing in the wings, flirting with high-school girls, waiting for CBT to finish its set. Then he comes out and sits on a stool at the center of the stage. Brian begins a twelve-bar blues in A. They keep it slow, leaving plenty of space, and the old poet recites lines in time to the music.

"The guy was great," says Brian. "But then he started that riff, 'I'm gonna roll a rug and smoke it. I'm gonna roll a rug and smoke it.'"

"That's right. That's what the old poet said. And he really dug it. He loved it so much he couldn't let it go. He stayed with it – "

Brian, laughing, cuts him off. "Until that horsey woman with the bulging eyes ran up and ripped the microphone out of his hand."

"But the old poet kept going," he says. "Even though the kids couldn't hear him. Then that guy in the tuxedo – he must've been an investment banker – came up and thanked the woman for saving the student body from corruption."

"It was a good gig," says Brian.

"Yes, it was." He remembers that his fingers were straight and fast.

"How's the book?"

"It's okay." He flips a few pages. "Listen to this one."

I Looked Up

It was just last night when

John Barley climbed the steps
to my studio apartment and threw
his sax on my desk sayin'
he'd lost the use of his hands.
Not arthritis. Not rheumatism.
Just fingers can't find the keys.
I was busy writing at the time
and told him
                    take
your funky, old horn
                              off
the finished part of my manuscript.
John didn't apologize.
He just moved the case and said,
"Man, it's over. My lady
won't sound like she use' to.
Look at you typin' –
you know where everything is.
Typewriter's growin' off your hands!"
I think I smiled.
"But my lady's makin' noise
like she don't even know me."
As I recall,
        John Barley
cleared his throat,
                    left

his beat saxophone on my desk,
and, under the steps
to my studio apartment,
hanged himself
before I looked up
from my typewriter.

He doesn't say anything after the last line. Neither does Brian. They let the poem settle. They sit in silence for a long time.

Now, having heard himself read, he has second thoughts about the poem and wishes he could take it back. He doesn't want Brian to think he's feeling sorry for himself. He tosses the book aside. He worries that self-pity, like chronic pain, will always be with him; there was too much at the beginning, more than anyone could use.

When he left the hospital, he felt like a man whose hands had been amputated. He struggled with everything, particularly in the first months when his fingers were immobile, locked in concrete gloves, his arms like stone posts hanging at his sides.

He relied on Brian to pour his drinks, to set up his coffee, juice, or vodka with a plastic straw, and in the early days he depended on Brian to feed him his meals, slicing his roast beef, bringing forkfuls of meat and potatoes to his lips, and wiping his mouth with a napkin.

In time, he learned to hold silverware between his casts, but the effort to eat, twisting his forearms and dipping his head, remained an exhausting and often embarrassing routine.

Everyday items and activities – doors, telephones, remotes, appliances, driving – were impossible or nearly so. He gave up shaving and brushing his teeth. Blowing his nose meant going outside and leaning over a hedge of stout junipers to empty one nostril at a time.

He wore shirts without buttons and pants without zippers. He hated the fact that he couldn't tie his shoes.

Most of all, he hated the bathroom, the daily humiliation. A hired woman, a retired nurse, wiped him after defecating. She ran the water in the shower and soaped him and helped him dry. He stood like a passive child in the presence of this woman. He answered her questions but never made eye contact. He allowed no real conversation. He let Brian settle her fee and the extent of her duties.

During this time, peeking around corners or the edge of a door, the people in Brian's building kept watch. They made it their business to know everyone who came or went. Finally, someone complained to the landlord. Brian received a letter and a copy of the lease with the rules for subletting highlighted in yellow. He explained that he wasn't renting a room, that the man living in his apartment was a houseguest.

"How long does he plan on staying?" said the landlord.

"As long as he needs to," said Brian.

"Houseguests stay for a week or two. They don't stay for a year."

"Then call him a roommate," said Brian. "The guy's down on his luck."

"I don't care what you call him," said the landlord. "I'm getting complaints."

"What kind of complaints? We don't make any noise. We play a little music, but it's never loud and it's never late at night."

"It's not the music."

"What is it then?"

"It's not my place to say. But if you hear something, just remember that it wasn't me who said it."

COLEMAN walks down the aisle. He passes Maureen's row and tries not to notice that she's flanked by two men, either of whom could be her escort.

Approaching the stage, he raises his camera. He wants a close-up of Heather before she stands and receives her diploma. He zooms in and starts to focus, but his eyes fill and the image blurs. I'm being foolish, he says to himself.

Heather looks down from the stage and the flash fires. He tries to step back and turn away, but he thinks only of the days when he was barely with her, the sporadic visits after the divorce, after losing his hands, the weekends when she came like a sprite to Brian's apartment, having arrived by train with her mother, and they ate pizza and played games, making up stories about a lovely and benevolent world, a place that someday they would go. Finally, at the end of those years, with his hands gaining strength, he could play a song without pain, a slow but happy tune that made his little girl smile.

Now his memories go unchecked, and he sees Heather in a high chair, his perfect fingers moving toward her and holding a plastic spoon filled with applesauce. Taking the sweetness between her lips, she slaps the tray in front of her and laughs.

Then he finds himself at Brian's apartment, at the kitchen table, his hands encased in plaster, and he watches the slow stirring and sees black fingers lifting toward his mouth a spoonful of yogurt. The movement is languid, mesmerizing – a kind of dance that fills him with comfort and shame.

It wasn't long after Brian spoke with the landlord that one of the neighbors left a message, black letters on white, taped to Brian's mailbox. It said: "Take your gay miscegenation elsewhere."

He remembers now that Brian came in and slammed the door and pinned the note to the corkboard near the phone. "What's that?" he said, seeing the stiffness in Brian's shoulders.

"Mail," said Brian.

He read the words and realized their brutality and suddenly felt slapped in the face. "What the fuck?"

"That's what they think," said Brian.

He stayed in the kitchen after Brian stormed off and stared at the note and poured some vodka in a glass. He heard Brian running water and opening and closing drawers. Then the commotion died down. Finally, Brian came back and said, "That's some ugly shit."

"Look, Brian, maybe I should leave. I've taken advantage of the situation. I've stayed longer than I should have."

"Leave because you want to," said Brian. "But don't leave because of that."

"I should go. It'll be easier for you – "

"Don't," said Brian, cutting him off. He ripped the white paper off the board. "Don't you dare feel sorry for me. Not for this."

"I'm sorry."

"Sorry for what? What are you apologizing for?"

"I've made you angry."

"You're damn right I'm angry. I'm always angry. But you hardly notice."

"If I leave, they'll forget I was here."

"You don't get it, do you? You've been trying to be black for as long as I've known you, but you still don't get it. It's easy for you. It's easy to *say* they'll forget. You get to play both sides of the street. I don't."

Unable to look at Brian, he turned and dragged himself out of the kitchen.

"And don't walk out," said Brian. "You're the best when it comes to walking. You played the guitar. You were in love with a great woman. But then you split for something better. It's easy for you to move. You can go anywhere. It's just that wherever you go, nothing stays whole."

He rubbed his left hand and straightened a pile of magazines. "You want me to leave?"

"I told you. Go if you want to. But don't go because it's difficult for me."

"I could talk to the landlord," he said. "I could canvas the building, leave a few notes of my own."

Brian shook his head. "What in the hell are you saying?"

"I'm saying I could help."

Brian threw up his hands. "I see. If you can't be black, then you'll be the savior – is that it? Listen, I don't need saving."

He sits in the auditorium thinking about redemption. He wants to tell Brian that being part of the trio was more than an act of ego or pride, more than usurpation or theft. It came from a bottomless need, a yearning to be someone other – someone that didn't look, act, or feel like himself. Why should he be lumped together with his grandfather and father? To be seen like them – or understood like them – was anathema to him. And now the thing he finds frightening, the thing driving his bitterness, is the possibility of being judged like them, of facing reparations, a day of reckoning that will hold him account-able for the lives and money they stole. He can't deny that one man took up cruelty and the other indifference or that both were selfish, possessed by a singular vision, so much so that everyone around them was made to live in the margins. But redemption, he thinks, isn't the answer. The important thing is to show the world a face of his own – a face not inscribed by history.

He's come late to this understanding, though not so late, he thinks, as to his knowledge of the family crime. Had he known the truth and so the entire scope of his character, he might've explained, to Brian or to anyone else, his desire – his need – to be someone other. But he'd been deprived of the full story. He had to wait until his father's boat, salvaged from Cape Hurd, offered up its unquiet ghost.

He towed it back to Michigan, set it on a cradle, and opened its compart-ments to the light. In the cabin, he discovered books and charts, a photograph of the old house in Saginaw; when he pulled the stuff from hiding, an envelope slipped out, fluttering through the air like a falling bird. He might have thrown it in the trash except that the envelope bore his father's name in a heavy and formal script, an immediately recognizable hand. Knowing it to be from his grandfather, from the pirate Havelock Moore, he raised the flap and removed the letter. He unfolded two sheets of water-stained paper. *To my dear son, Dorian*, it began.

It should've been simple, he thinks. A suicide note should offer a reason, a profession of love, an appeal for mercy. But the letter caught him off guard. Rather than providing comfort, it made a confession, a declaration of guilt. It spoke of winter in old Detroit, an alley in Rivertown, and a landlord with a slit at the base of his skull.

It was the business of war that taught me the method, wrote Havelock. *And the business of war is godless. They make it that way, despite their encomiums and prayers, so that soldiers can kill without sin. Being young, I believed them. I took them at their word.*

He remembers squinting in the semigloom of the cabin, his eyes drawn several times to the date at the top of the letter, *June 22, 1968*, the day of his grandfather's death.

Havelock explained that a world without God was conducive to the business of war, to the pursuits of power and wealth. *But after the War*, he wrote, *after survival and success, after marriage and a child, I found myself betrayed. I wasn't allowed a godless world. Someone had called for a restoration. Someone had resurrected God and guilt and eternal damnation.*

It could've ended right there, he thinks, picturing the letter tucked away in the top drawer of his dresser. He saw it today looking for a tie clasp – the one Heather gave him for his birthday. He never intended to memorize the letter, but somehow the words stay with him. In the last lines, just above the signature, Havelock wrote: *God ruins our happiness like a harvester ruins the mouse's nest. He is arbitrary. He has no sense of proportion.*

HE FEELS a tap on his shoulder. A father with a camera squeezes by and takes a picture of his son, a cherubic boy who snatches a diploma from the hand of Principal Trip. It'll be Heather's turn before long.

He loosens his tie. He wishes he could turn and find Jen standing beside him. He'd like to see her moving through the aisles and taking photographs, recording the day's key moments.

"Heather Maureen Moore" rings through the auditorium, and he watches his daughter stand and walk gracefully across the stage. She shakes the hand of Principal Trip and accepts her diploma with a smile. She looks down at her mother and then at him – her proud father. He snaps a picture.

Now she has her ticket, he thinks. She'll stay out late tonight, despite Maureen's curfew and my advice, and when she finally comes home she'll no longer feel the weight of our demands. She'll pull the big suitcase and the duffel bag out of her closet and begin planning her move, deciding what she'll need and what she won't be taking. She'll quit the Lighthouse Diner and visit Humbug once or twice before she leaves. At first, she'll call all the time, but then, with homework and new friends, she'll wait for a Sunday afternoon or evening. Finally, the weekends will be too full, and she'll call once a month, usually late at night, laughing or holding back tears.

He turns to walk up the aisle. He glances at Maureen. She clutches the thick arm of the man on her left and smiles and dabs at the tears running down her cheeks, her face glowing with contentment. He pauses for a moment, hoping that she'll notice him, but she seems oblivious to the people around her. Gazing up at the stage, she gives the impression of being softer somehow, less defensive. She looks the same as she did on Grosse Ile, on the day they met walking the dogs, when her boredom with music felt to him like a breath of fresh air.

At the start, she was patient and loving, but his habits and disposition wore her down, particularly those things that were careless, even reckless, and that fell, he believed, within the province of an artist's life. When he went back on the road, she urged him not to go. When he came home and women from far-away cities called in the middle of the night, she pretended to be asleep. When he left the water running and the kitchen sink overflowed, damaging the countertop and the cabinetry below, she reset the tile and refinished the wood doors without complaining. When she found a small stash of pornographic films, she feigned interest. When he misplaced the car, his wallet, and then his keys, she left the front door open. And when a teenage girl wanted private lessons and came to the house in the middle of winter wearing a tiny plaid skirt and a bikini top, Maureen slammed the door and saved him from jail. In these ways, he used up whatever patience she had. He used it up so completely that going home with broken hands seemed presumptuous, utterly ridiculous, a burden he couldn't ask her to bear.

The assistant principal reads another name, and several guys in the audience break into applause. They keep it going, whistling and cheering, while a young woman with a movie star face struts across the stage. She turns and waves and the boys fire up their enthusiasm.

Back at his seat, he takes off his jacket. All morning he's been uncomfortably warm, a condition that he can't explain given the weather. Heather, of course, appears cool and relaxed, entirely comfortable, even though she's been under the lights for more than an hour. He thinks of women, at least those in his life, as remarkably composed, more resilient when subjected to pressure, whether gradual or sudden. Some have a high tolerance for pain. Others can hear the snapping of a bone without flinching.

He wipes his forehead with his sleeve and thinks about the weekend stretching out before him, the reception later this evening at the old house – Maureen's house – and then Sunday, a day of work at Humbug followed by cooking and eating alone. He hopes the dry Canadian air sticks around through the start of the week. High humidity makes it difficult to breathe.

HE KNEW that the bartender would crank up the air as the Green Mill filled with people. He wiped the sweat from his temple and felt happy to be in a darkened room, not only because the last three days had been humid but also because Jen, a worshipper of heat, oblivious to the ovenlike atmosphere of the apartment, had ignored his fuming and his threats and reset the thermostat whenever he turned the other way.

Brian and Tom were already in back and he was tuning again, dissatisfied with the new strings he'd put on the day before. As a purist, he'd been resisting the lure of an electronic tuner, but lately his ears weren't working and the frustration made him wonder if he shouldn't give in.

When he sat down, he thought he saw someone familiar out of the corner of his eye, but when he scanned the crowd there was no one he recognized, and so he busied himself with the tuning, though the feeling stayed with him, as if a person he knew were watching from a shadowy corner. A few minutes later, feeling entirely ill at ease, he got up, looked around, and stumbled, catching himself at the edge of the stage, staggered by the figure of Otis sitting alone in one of the small booths against the wall.

"My God, Otis," he said, rushing over and shaking the man's hand until Otis told him to sit down. "What are you doing here? You never leave Port Austin."

Otis centered his drink on the small white napkin. "I decided to make an exception." He gave the impression of a man sitting in church, rather calm, almost solemn, with one arm held tightly against his side. "I don't hear anything. I don't get any news. What's a man to do?"

"I'm sorry. Jen always asks about you. We talk about coming to Port Austin."

"You do? You only brought her around once. I can't remember what she looks like."

"She's gorgeous."

"That's good," said Otis.

"So how long are you in town? Where are you staying?"

"Slow down," said Otis, shaking his head. "I see you're still in a hurry. Let's get through the first set, shall we?"

He flagged the waitress and glanced at Otis's black jacket and white button-down shirt, an outfit that was too nice for the Mill and too heavy for the weather. "Another for my friend," he said. "And I'll have a vodka on the rocks."

The waitress walked away and Otis watched her go. He shivered. "I gotta get out more."

"You okay?"

"It's chilly in here," said Otis, sitting perfectly still.

Suddenly, as if the bartender had turned up the lights, he saw that Otis's face was drawn, thinner than he remembered, and the shoulders seemed less substantial, pinched or crumbling, beneath the fine tailored coat. He lowered his voice and said, "It's not the chill, is it?"

Otis sipped his drink with measured dignity and then set the glass down on the napkin. "I've come to hear you play. That's all."

"What's bothering you?" he said.

A man walked up to the table. "You're Otis Young, aren't you? If I'm not imposing too much, would you mind signing an autograph?"

Otis winced and wrote his name on a scrap of paper and kept his other arm pressed against his side.

"Thank you," said the man. He bowed and walked away.

"C'mon, Otis. What's the story?"

"All right," he said, sitting flawlessly upright with one hand resting on the table. "This is my last wish. Will you grant me my last wish?"

Later, somewhere in the first set, trying to play for Otis, wanting more than anything to do him justice, he felt himself losing control, filling up with the grief of time passing, of long summers and tired dreams, a flood of memory, hope, and desire rising in him until the song and his playing became prayer, a tribute to the man who'd given him meaning, who'd shown him the possibility, if only in brief flashes, of a rare and elemental sound that could live forever against time, and so he played without thinking or knowing and finally looked up, the lights low and the room drained of color, and saw that Otis was composed and seemingly without pain, his body leaning toward the music.

AFTER the applause, the soloist leaves the stage and some of the graduates use the moment to shift in their chairs and take a deep breath. Then Principal Trip returns to the podium. "Now we'll hear from the chorus," he says.

A group of seniors comes forward and members of the sophomore and junior classes join them on the stage. The director looks like a descendant of Ichabod Crane and bows deeply before turning to the singers. Snapping his fingers, he counts off a quick tempo, and the kids leap into a song, a spiritual, a celebration of deliverance and freedom. In a flash, the auditorium feels like church.

Fanning himself with a program, he listens to the voices and imagines a preacher rising above the chorus, the students in their purple gowns – bathed in bright light – waiting for redemption.

"I'd say kids these days could use more religion." He wishes the words weren't so fresh in his mind. His landlord had made the remark when she saw prints of Heather's senior portrait – wallet size to 8" x 10" – spread out on the kitchen table. As a committed overseer, she'd come by before work and caught him in his bathrobe making coffee.

"I've been trying to reach you," she said, running her hand through her short wet hair. "But your answering machine never seems to work."

"What's the problem?" he said.

"No problem. The city needs to redo the sewer lines, so the street'll be torn up soon and there may be a time when the toilet won't flush."

"Thanks for letting me know," he said.

"That your daughter?" said the landlord.

"Yes."

"Pretty girl."

He nods.

"Pretty girls need to be careful. They grow up fast. Kids these days could use more religion."

On stage, the singers smile and sway. He taps his foot and listens to the harmony. It doesn't work, he thinks. If high school is slavery, what comes next?

Struck by the song's hope for heavenly reward, he imagines the parking lot behind the Green Mill and transforms the scene into a dark church and considers whether or not the sacrifice of his hands served as some sort of redemption, a strange rite of passage – a fated balancing of the scales. He sees himself kneeling on the asphalt waiting for the service to begin.

A choir would've been just the thing, he thinks, the ceremony could've used a song, an upbeat score. Had a priest been standing nearby, I would've confessed, admitted to sloth, pride, envy, and lust. My guilt was certain beyond a reasonable doubt. As it happened, though, no priest was available, and I had yet to discover the full extent of my sins, the crimes of my family, my history, but there's no salvation in pleading ignorance.

I've made discoveries, of course. I'm in possession of more knowledge, some might even say truth, but it makes no difference. When people are punished, when they're pushed into a corner, pinned or driven to their knees, they lack objectivity. They lack perspective. Taking a broad view of things seems ludicrous.

I've paid for more than my crimes. And no schedule of penance will restore my hands; no regimen of pills will stop the pain. I should take a broader view, but these days I side with H.M. God is unjust. He has no sense of proportion.

THE RECESSIONAL music begins to wobble and go flat. The graduates laugh and some break formation, skipping and running out of the auditorium.

He stands in the parking lot, shields his eyes, and feels the heat of the afternoon rising from the blacktop. Maureen walks out with the thick guy who'd been on her left, her arm around his waist, her red hair sparkling in the sun. She looks enticing in her summer dress. He spots Heather – all smiles and laughter as she moves through the crowd. A circle of girls pull her in for a photo.

The beanpole who took her to the prom walks up from behind and taps her on the shoulder. He whispers in her ear. Heather smiles and shakes her head. She floats over to the other side of the circle and the boy follows. When she turns and sees him, she attempts to step farther away, but he grabs her gown and pulls it toward him.

Without thinking, he feels his weight leaning toward his daughter. It strikes him that she's no longer happy. He sees the guy grab her with his other hand, and then Heather tries to twist out of his grasp.

I'll walk over, he thinks, and say it's time to go, though the prearranged plan calls for Heather to leave with her mother, to have dinner with Maureen and her sizable friend before the evening reception.

As he approaches, he hears snickering and broken laughter.

"I'm good for the prom but not for tonight?" says the boy.

"You're drunk," says Heather.

"I'm not drunk," he says.

"I can smell it."

"I've had a drink. But I'm not drunk."

He can almost smell the liquor on the boy's breath. He walks through the parting circle but stops when Heather waves him off.

"Go home and I'll call you tomorrow," says Heather.

"You must think I'm stupid," says the boy. "You won't call."

"Why wouldn't I?" says Heather.

"You'll be too busy."

"I don't have any plans," says Heather.

"That's not what I mean."

"Watch it," says a tough-looking girl. "Heather's with me. And you better not be spittin' in her direction."

The boy spits. "I get it. I'm a one-time fuck. I'm the after-prom special."

Coleman grabs the kid's gown. "That's enough," he says.

"And what the fuck do you want?"

Using his forearm and elbow, he checks the boy – a sharp jab to the stomach. Heather sucks in a short breath.

The boy doubles over, his mortarboard and tassel flying.

He hooks his arm around the kid's neck and puts him in a headlock. "When you can breathe," he says, "I think you should apologize."

Before long, he senses the quiet that surrounds him. He looks up and sees Heather, Maureen, and most of the people in the parking lot frozen in place, their faces aghast, watching him choke a skinny high-school graduate.

He lets the boy go and a couple of friends help him scamper away. Slowly, the crowd comes back to life.

"Bravo," says Maureen.

Heather hurries off with her mother. He sees her getting into the backseat and closing the door. He wants to explain himself, make some sort of excuse – a reflex, lack of sleep, a sad effort to protect her reputation – but he doesn't move. His feet feel heavy, glued to the warm asphalt. Heather stares at him through the closed window as the car speeds out of the parking lot.

chapter eight

JENNIFER reaches up and closes her fingers around a large Red Delicious. She pulls but the stem refuses to give way. The branch bends, leaves trembling, until she rotates the fruit and breaks it free. She holds the apple as if it were a precious stone, polishing it with her shirttail. A voice in her ear tells her to give it away, but now the orchard, despite the brilliant October day, stands empty.

It is 1982.

Before picking the apple, she watched him go, his body becoming smaller, drifting through the corridor of dark shade, the old trees forming a low canopy. She saw him stumble into the light, where, in a moment of indecision, he glanced back.

Jennifer crouches and sets the apple in a basket. She takes care not to bruise it. A breeze touches her face and the leaves begin sighing. The air tastes sweet, a slight consolation. She'd like to step out of the orchard and find herself in another country, in a busy café, away from the trio of birds that move with her from tree to tree, away from Michigan, having traveled here to visit his family and friends, to fulfill obligations. Today, they'd driven to Blake's Orchard, speeding northeast from Grosse Ile to a town called Romeo, because he wanted a shaded place, a place without people, to say all the things he'd said before.

At first, they walked without speaking, listening to the orchard. Then, breaking the spell, he said, "Let's leave tomorrow. We've been here long enough."

"You haven't picked any apples," she said, swinging the empty basket.

"What about you?"

"I'm searching for just the right one."

"Forget the apples," he said. "Are you ready to leave?"

"Yes. I've been ready since we got here."

"Too much for you, is that it?"

"Let's not start – "

He narrowed his eyes. "I didn't choose the place I came from."

She stopped and put down the basket. She looked at the long row of trees and then at Coleman. "What are we doing here?"

"I needed some air."

"Is that all?"

"All right," he said. "I'm going on the winter tour."

"You say it as if you're unhappy." She felt the chill of the afternoon on her bare shoulders. "Are you starting today?" she said, rubbing her arms. "Am I driving home alone?"

"I fly out of O'Hare on Monday."

"Go now," she said.

"What do you mean?"

"Go. Take the car. I'll stay a little longer."

"That's crazy," he said. "You don't know anyone here."

"It's no different than being on tour. I'll try it. Maybe I'll like it."

"I think you should come home," he said. "With me."

"What for? To keep you company until you leave?"

"There's more to it than that."

"It's your choice, Cole. It's always been your choice."

"That's true. But it hasn't been easy."

"I never – "

"You're perfect," he said. "Too perfect. You care too much. It makes me hate myself."

"You're right," she said. "You need someone else. Someone less perfect."

He rubbed his forehead. "I need to do this on my own."

"Is that what you want?"

"I don't know."

"And the rest doesn't matter?"

"No," he said, unable to hold her gaze.

"Go," she said. "Take the car. I'll be fine."

"I'll be back in a few months."

"Come back or not," she said. "You won't find me."

He began to turn and then stopped.

Beyond him, looking down the long tunnel of trees, she glimpsed a small circle of daylight. "It happened too fast," she said, wiping her eyes. "For a while, everything was whole. Remember that."

The orchard grows still, no breeze, not even the birds. She admires the apple resting in the basket and touches its cool skin. It's perfect, she thinks. The kind you see on a teacher's desk or in a painting. It's large enough to be a meal in itself.

THE APPLE reminds her, quite unexpectedly, of a prayer, *Hail Mary, full of grace* . . . She remembers sitting on a plastic chair and the prayer rising on her breath, nearly two years ago – the rules concerning payment tacked to the wall, the carpet threadbare and soiled. *Blessed art thou among women, and blessed is the fruit of thy womb* . . . Women come here bearing fruit, she thinks. We're stuffed birds bloated with bread and giblets. The *Ave Maria* keeps repeating itself like a broken record. She sees with the clarity of a picture the sliding glass window, thin and smudged, that separates her from women wearing white uniforms and white shoes. She'd come directly from the station, afraid to go home, afraid of losing her nerve, after a moment of foolishness when she followed him onto the bus, having rehearsed her speech in front of a mirror – *blessed is the fruit of thy womb* . . . But she knew too well how his face would look, pale with incomprehension, the fear gradually changing to contempt, and although he'd suffer guilt, she knew where he'd place the blame. There'd be no accusation, no epithet, but he'd think of her as solely responsible. She knew all this because he'd shown his true colors more than once. In the odd weeks when she was late, rare occasions by any count, she'd lived with his misery. She'd seen just how desperate he could be, given to mania and panic, rattling around the apartment at night, unable to sleep, going on about his weakness, his unborn talent, predicting the slow death of everything he held dear.

SHE HADN'T seen these things in Boston, in the beginning, when he parked his rusty Dodge at the curb and pulled his guitar and suitcase out of the trunk. In the orchard now, without birds, with only the company of trees, she tries not to remember, tries to keep herself exactly where she is, but it takes too much effort.

She steps through the door with a bag of groceries, unpacks the fruit and vegetables, and puts a box of oatmeal on the shelf over the sink. The tiny room, a studio with a single bed, feels cramped. Sometime soon they'll find a new apartment. She sets a bottle of vodka on the table. He pours a shot and raises the glass.

"Thanks for going out," he says. "It's cold today."

On the table she sees a letter bearing the insignia of Boston College. "What's that?"

"A warning from the dean. Says if I slip much further, they'll review my scholarship."

"Are you slipping?"

"No. It's just routine."

"I don't understand," she says, holding the letter closer to the light. "Who's Jason Moore?"

"That's me."

"It is?" She looks at him as if for the first time. "Then who are you? A CIA operative? A British agent?"

"I'm sorry," he says. "I should've told you before this. My stage name is Coleman."

"Your stage name?"

"That's right. A bar owner christened me Coleman last summer."

"What's wrong with Jason?"

"It's boring."

"No, it's not."

"Well, it isn't particularly musical."

"That's silly."

"Jason's my name because I was supposed to be just like my father."

"In what way?"

"A sailor."

"Navy?"

Coleman laughs. "No. My grandfather sailed the Great Lakes. He ran singlehander races from Port Huron to Mackinac Island. My father inherited the gift."

"But not you."

"No. Not me."

"I couldn't possibly change my name," she says.

"Why not?"

"I couldn't answer to anything else." She fills the teapot and sets it on the stove. "Anyway, my mother would disown me."

Later, sipping tea, she listens to his guitar and watches the movement of his hands, his fingers, the careful pressing and plucking of strings. On some days the music carries him to a world all his own, a place swayed by technical expertise, by speed and virtuosity, but she soon realizes, as the chords and melodies build, that he's playing himself into a corner, a dark recess that for all its impressive and intimidating skill feels lonely and confined. On other days his playing strikes her as passionate, often tender, a kind of meditation or prayer. In such moments, with the music like water, she forgets the small apartment and goes her own way, gives herself to an impulse, the childlike urge to splash and float, her feet kicking free without fear, her body turning in the swells, rising on sudden waves, striking out farther and farther from shore, from recognizable ground, until she feels nothing but hunger.

SHE HEARS no music in the room where women bearing fruit, sitting in plastic chairs, fill out forms and wait. She sees the face of a teenage singer on a dog-eared magazine: the famous mouth wears lipstick the color of cotton candy; the famous breasts, standing at attention, create a dark canyon of cleavage. The words next to the singer's face declare her need, her absolute desire, for a baby. *Hail Mary, full of grace* . . . A nurse opens the door next to the sliding glass window. She steps into the room of weary and nauseated women, her white shoes catching the light. The nurse calls a name. A girl without lipstick or visible breasts picks up her coat and purse. She follows the nurse and the door closes behind her. Another magazine bears the face of a man, the only man in sight. The article says he's earned millions in advertising, mostly women's lingerie and beauty products. "It's a delicate art," he says. "We must make women want the things they need." More photographs show him sitting behind a sleek desk or looking out over a vast cityscape. *Pray for us . . . Pray for us . . . now and at the hour of our death.* She puts down the magazine. This is a room without music, she thinks. Women come here after the fat lady sings.

SHE ALWAYS returns to the good years in Chicago, after college, when Coleman found work at the Green Mill, when Brian and Tom turned up and the CBT Trio started playing around town. The flat in Wrigleyville, a charmer with high ceilings and a bank of southern-facing windows, overflowed with light. She loved teaching history and felt grateful that her job was close to home. She explored the neighborhoods and shot roll after roll of film. After a while, she converted the flat's extra bedroom into a darkroom. Her sister lived in Evanston and often came down on a southbound train, getting off near the ballpark, and they walked and shopped and ate lunch on Addison. "It isn't the same as Boston," she said to her sister. "Here I can breathe. The streets and the sky seem wider, less cramped."

And then she thinks of the road trips from Chicago to Detroit, the Michigan weekends, which seem to her now no more than daydreams, brief scenes filled with light and water. Dorian offers his hand and she steps onto the boat. Coleman stands on the dock holding a bowline and waiting while the motor warms up. The Ford Yacht Club feels friendly, more so than Coleman had led her to believe. The boat slips out of its berth and points toward open water.

"This is the Trenton Channel," says Dorian. "We're heading south to where the river meets Lake Erie. The island to port is called Celeron. East of that – and Grosse Ile, too – is the Livingstone Channel. In that one, if we're lucky, we'll see a big ship, a southbound freighter. Farther east is an island with an amusement park, Bob-Lo. Jason went there as a boy. They've had their problems. Early this summer two girls fell from a cable car. Only cuts and bruises but it isn't helping ticket sales. Between Bob-Lo and Canada is the Amherstburg Channel. The northbound freighters use that one."

Sailing with Dorian feels to her like waltzing with an experienced and graceful partner. Every action is well-timed and economical, nothing flashy or ill-prepared, and so the movement – the sails filling and the boat picking up speed – appears to be effortless, soothing, quite magical.

She sees Dorian checking the wind vane on the top of the mast. He looks out to starboard and then at her. He glances at her camera. "Jason tells me you take pictures."

"All the time," she says.

"Maybe you'll spot something out here."

"There's so much," she says. "I may miss the thing I'm looking for."

"What's that?"

"I don't know." She watches Coleman go forward. He sits on the cabin house with his back to the cockpit. "It's the same teaching history," she says. "There's too much. It's easy to leave out what's important."

"I suppose so," says Dorian.

"But the kids are all right," she says. "For them, it all comes down to one question. What's on the test?"

Dorian squints at the horizon.

In the room with women and plastic chairs, she waits. Words from the *Ave Maria* flash in front of her eyes like roadside billboards. She looks at the woman with black hair and bronze skin sitting two chairs over who can't seem to stop coughing. She watches the woman cover her mouth with her tiny hand and feels no revulsion, no violation, when the air fills with the sound of dry heaves, the phlegm breaking up and rising from the woman's lungs. *Blessed is the fruit of thy womb . . .*

The television set in the corner, suspended from the ceiling, is dark. She wonders what she would see if the screen came to life, a romantic comedy perhaps, or a scene with Catherine and Heathcliff, the latter boyish but irate, promising Cathy the company of his cruel ghost, cursing her with his undying love. *Blessed art thou among women . . .*

A new girl comes into the room and walks up to the sliding glass window. Someone on the other side hands her a clipboard and a pen. She finds a chair and starts writing. A nurse rushes in and the women with folded hands look up. "Ms. Jennifer Roe," says the nurse.

SHE HEARS the laughter of children in the orchard. She glances in the direction of the sound but sees nothing. She imagines them running through the shadows, happy to be hidden by trees and pretending not to hear their mother's call. It's time to leave, she thinks. It's time to walk out of the orchard and ask someone friendly to give me a ride.

She remembers leaving Boston with Cole and driving to Chicago through constant heat and humidity, the car bursting with junk and the radiator boiling over.

She opened the door to the flat, flung a box onto the kitchen counter, and plugged in the phone. It rang. A man's voice talked in a jumble about her application, about a veteran teacher taking a powder. "How's that for professionalism?" said the voice. "A real mess now that he's gone, left us holding the bag, so you must come and check out the school, maybe tomorrow or the next day at the latest."

Grateful for the offer, she signed the contract. She picked up some sensible clothes for the start of classes. She bought a new camera with her first paycheck.

As the months passed, Coleman played casuals and sat in with established groups. They decorated the flat, purchasing furniture, small appliances, blinds, and a Persian rug. They set up an extra bed, mostly for Brian, who, with the birth of CBT, made a habit of coming home with Coleman after work, usually at two-thirty or three in the morning, to unwind and have a drink. "To see," as Brian put it, looking at the gallery of photos, "the best pictures – and the best woman – in town."

She'd often wake in her large bed and drift into the living room to find Brian and Cole sleeping on the sofa. She'd stand on the icy hardwood floor, barefoot, wearing only a thin T-shirt and panties, and shake Brian's shoulder until he'd stir and smile. She'd get him up, say good night with a quick kiss, and point him toward the guest room. Then she'd press herself against Cole, her thighs silver in the moonlight, and nudge him until he finally gave in and struggled to his feet.

She admits that she wanted all of it to last, the safety and intimacy of the flat, the pungent smell of the darkroom, her students asking questions, both silly and profound. But she feels now, walking in the orchard in Michigan, hearing the faint laughter of children, that the fullness of that time was squandered, drained away, until all that remained was a painful breach.

She moves in measured steps like a bride marching down the aisle. She recognizes the walk. It's the one she practiced at her sister's wedding.

She remembers the groom's mother frowning at her son as he recited his vows in a monotone. Gazing at the bride, the minister said, "Your love is the reason for living." The groom's mother cleared her throat and said, "My reason for living is to get ready to stay dead a long time."

SHE TURNS and melts deeper into the orchard and pictures herself, between the rehearsal and the wedding, between the conception and the creation, walking with Coleman in winter, standing with him on a snow-dusted platform near a waiting bus. She can't believe that he's serious, that he's suddenly superstitious about flying.

He won't put it down, she thinks. Not even to say good-bye. He'll drop his suitcase in a puddle, but the other he won't let go.

She glances at the white bus and shivers. "It's bitter cold," she whispers.

"You need a winter coat," he says, pulling her close. "Your lips are turning blue."

"When will you be home?" she says.

A woman's voice comes through the loudspeaker announcing destinations and departure times. They kiss, his free hand slipping behind her neck. More than the kiss, she feels his guitar pressing against her thigh.

"I want you to stay," she says. "I want you to go with me."

"It's too late," he says. "I'll look bad if I don't show up."

"I'll look bad, too."

"Tell your sister I'm sorry. Tell her congratulations. And don't worry. This trip won't change a thing."

"Is that what you think?"

"Yes."

A surge of nausea rises from her stomach. She takes a deep breath. "You're wrong," she says. "We won't be the same."

"You're making too much of it," he says.

She thinks of Pennsylvania, the hills and the barren coal mines. She imagines the bus rising and falling on its way to Philadelphia, the driver going fast so that no one will see the hollowed-out ground, the dark ruts that slowly gave up the earth's fullness.

"I can't make enough of it," she says.

He sighs. "It'll all be the same. I won't pass the audition. I'll come home. You'll go to school. We'll get a call from your sister the minute her honeymoon's over."

"But if you pass the audition, then everything changes."

"It's a long shot," he says.

"Are you going?" she says.

He nods in frustration and checks his ticket.

Shivering in her thin jacket, she stands on the edge of the platform, her shoulder almost touching the bus. "So this is it," she says. She wants to fill the open door. She wants to make it impossible for the door to close.

A blast of wind catches his guitar and knocks him off balance. "It's time," he says. He kisses her on the mouth, picks up his suitcase, and steps up into the bus.

She follows him, drifting like a tired ghost, but then he turns and the shock of his turning startles her. She steps back and another woman rushes aboard.

HEARING her name, she stands and walks toward the wide, heavyset nurse. The door behind her closes, separating her from the women who sit like worried hens and wait, who fill blank spaces with the names and numbers of family members, old friends, people who can be counted on in the event of an emergency. *Hail Mary, full of grace* . . . She can't say whether the nurse spoke or simply pointed the way, but she remembers the metallic taste of the thermometer and the black band gripping her arm. She removes her thin jacket, the nurse having disappeared, and then her shirt, jeans, bra, and panties. She puts on a cotton gown . . . *The Lord is with thee.* Now, she waits again, aware of hushed voices and footsteps in the hall. The tiny room has no window, only a long fluorescent tube hanging from the ceiling. In the sink is a wet pair of latex gloves. The light dims for a second or two as if someone in the next room had plugged in a hairdryer. The dull drone of machinery comes through the wall. *Holy Mary, Mother of God* . . . She wants a sensible person to ask her if this is what she wants, if she's considered all the possible options. If she can answer these questions in a firm voice, then she can proceed without fear.

She sits on the edge of the examination table and hears someone breathing, the sound of paper being shuffled. For a moment, the machinery stops. She rubs the back of her neck and suddenly takes in the floor, the pink linoleum, its long history of scrapes and gouges.

In Michigan again, maybe her third or fourth visit, she finds Coleman smiling, a mix of surprise and satisfaction, when he discovers his old portable radio in his parents' garage. He shoves in fresh batteries and then opens the door to his father's car and bows, offering her a seat.

She laughs. "Early for a picnic, don't you think?"

"This ain't a picnic," he says.

A short drive carries them across the Grosse Ile Parkway and through the entrance to Elizabeth Park. He pulls over where the road parallels the river and shuts off the engine. She notices an old building with cathedral windows and a slate roof.

"Here we are," says Coleman.

"Where?" she says.

He grabs the radio. "C'mon. I'll show you."

She follows him around the side of the building and sees what appears to be a boarded-up casement.

Coleman, without hesitation, slips his fingers behind the plywood and pulls. "Good," he says. "They still haven't fixed it." He puts one leg inside and then ducks through the opening.

She goes in after him. "What is this place?" she says.

"A dance hall," he says. "The Elizabeth Park Dance Hall."

She gazes up at the thick beams supporting the roof.

"The great dance bands played here," says Coleman. "Couples came from all over, especially at the end of the war. Some of the guys came in uniform."

She goes to the window and looks out at the deserted patio. "What about you?" she says. "Did you ever come here to dance?"

"No," he says. "I never did." He sets the radio on an old chair and starts turning the dial, running across several stations, drawing his eyebrows together when the speaker hisses and crackles.

Suddenly, she hears strings, a symphony orchestra pouring out of the radio like a waterfall. She turns and Coleman appears at her side.

"Perfect," he says, taking her hand. "A waltz."

She follows his lead, feeling her body turn and turn again, the two of them making a perfect circle in the room. She closes her eyes and imagines the hall after dark, lights sparkling on the Detroit River, the windows cranked open, and the music rising up into the evening. She opens her eyes. "You told me musicians don't dance."

"I lied," he says.

"You said they never dance."

"I'm a good liar."

"Should I be worried?"

"I don't think I can answer that honestly."

"You're terrible."

"True. But not at dancing."

"What if somebody cut in?"

"There's no one here."

"You're awfully sure of yourself."

"I know the steps."

The waltz ends and she comes to rest, the room still moving around her. She hears a deep, formal voice saying something about the conductor and the recording. Coleman smiles. They stand and face one another, holding hands and breathing hard, waiting for more music.

He looks around the hall. "I thought you'd like the place."

"I do."

The voice on the radio keeps talking.

"We can't dance to that," says Coleman.

"I didn't think you could dance at all," she says. "You kept it a big secret."

"Without secrets, there are no surprises," he says.

"That's what you say about music."

He shrugs.

She takes his perfect hands and plants them on her hips. "So why surprise me now?"

"First opportunity," he says.

"That's crazy," she says. "We've been in plenty of bars where people dance. Parties and weddings, too."

"That's not dancing," he says. "I'm not sure what it is, but it's not dancing."

THE DOOR opens and a young doctor enters the room. He walks to the sink, frowns, picks up the used gloves, and drops them into a metal can. He pumps soap into his left palm and washes his hands under a slow running faucet. He sits on a stool, opens her thin file, and reads.

She looks at his hair, smooth and black, the head of a leading man in a silent film. She can barely hear him breathe. He tells her to lie down. "Any problems since your exam?" he says. She shakes her head. "What about cramps or bleeding?" She shakes her head again. His hands slip beneath her gown. *Blessed is the fruit of thy womb* . . . "Any discomfort?" he says, pressing hard. His fingers are strong and blunt. "You'll be moving to another room," he says. He turns and opens the door. "A nurse will direct you." Then he's gone and the air fills with silence.

I can't move, she thinks. I won't. It took too much to get here. They can't ask me to walk down the hall in this flimsy gown. I won't do it. If I'm quiet, then the nurse may forget. *Blessed art thou among women* . . . Her arms and legs feel heavier than stone. She stares at the ceiling, the stained acoustic tile. I won't complain if she forgets. I won't make a sound.

AT THE Green Mill, before the last set begins, she sits with Brian and Cole and argues with them about whether or not a color can be heard.

"Most people can hear blue," says Brian.

"But hearing a color isn't the same as seeing it," says Coleman.

She sips her drink. "I can hear red just the way I see it," she says.

"Describe it," says Coleman.

"When a saxophone squeals in just the right way, my eyes see a liquid like blood."

"But will two people listening to that sound agree that it's red?"

"Why not?" says Brian.

"If they do, it's only a coincidence," says Coleman. "And what about yellow or green – or pink or purple?"

"Musicians paint in broad strokes," says Brian.

She smiles. "And mostly in primary colors."

They laugh. Coleman stands and heads for the stage. Brian gets up and follows. The waitress clears the empty glasses.

She wants to continue the conversation. She wants to tell them that she hears black and white the best – that for some reason time turns around when the trio plays and everything in sight becomes silver and gray. Of course, Cole would say that that proves his point, that what she really hears is the absence of color. But he would be wrong.

All those gradations of black and white, she tells herself, can't be the absence of anything. It's not possible. She's entirely convinced that all black-and-white scenes, whether photographs or old films, are deeper and more nuanced, one shade bleeding into the next. That's why she chooses to work without color. Kodachrome, she knows, is blunt but ephemeral. She's seen how images, even the most shocking, reveal in black-and-white a sudden elegance and dignity – whatever joy or sadness there is becomes timeless.

The music begins and the waitress comes around for last call. "You're Jennifer, right?" says the waitress. "Cole's told me all about you."

SHE RISES from the table when the door opens. "Is someone playing a radio?" she says. The nurse shrugs and tells her to come along. Walking in measured steps, her gown falling open, she searches for the words that until now had flooded her mind. She takes a deep breath, readies herself to speak, but no sound rises from her lips. She follows the nurse into the hall, where all the surfaces are white, gray, and black. The dull drone of machinery is silver. She notices the nurse's black hair and white uniform. Not like this, she thinks. I won't have it fixed forever. She feels the impulse to pray. She opens her mouth. "In Tobermory," she says, "the houses on the harbor are red, yellow, and blue." The nurse stops. "I didn't get that," she says, checking the file. "Come along, Jennifer. It isn't much farther." She looks down. It pleases her to see that she isn't barefoot, though where the slippers came from she can't say. Her tongue feels swollen. More than anything, she wants a cup of water. In Tobermory, she thinks, the houses on the harbor are red, yellow, and blue.

SHE LEAVES the clinic without acknowledging a single face and rides the Brown Line back to her neighborhood.

On the train, she hears the nurse's voice repeating the caution that someone should stay with her through the night. At first, worried about privacy, she'd resolved to go it alone, but after reading the grim pamphlets and signing the medical release, she made the necessary call, explaining that it's only a safeguard, in case of hemorrhaging or some other complication. Then, this morning, before going with Cole to the station, she'd cleaned the bathroom, changed the sheets on both beds, and managed to step out for groceries. She wanted the apartment fresh and the refrigerator full.

Now, she emerges from the CTA station and walks slowly, her legs trembling, and turns just before the ballpark. She sees Brian sitting on the stoop. She feels a sudden relief when he stands and comes running down the street.

"You okay?" he says.

She nods.

"You're shaking," he says. "I should've been there. I should've picked you up."

"No," she says.

It was her choice. She'd asked him to wait at the apartment, ignoring his insistence about going with her, about taking her to and from the clinic. She didn't want him to see the place, though her reasons were not altogether clear. She went round and round trying to explain, feeling the weight of his stubbornness, until finally she said, "Please don't. It isn't a memory I want you to have."

He stopped pressing the point after that and mentioned it only in passing when she called to confirm the exact day and time.

"Before I turned the corner," she says, "I was afraid you wouldn't be here."

"I couldn't do that," he says.

She leans on him as they go up the steps. "Is that your bag? In all the nights you've stayed, I've never seen you with anything but your bass."

"Well," he says, "I figure I'm staying more than one night."

She pulls the keys out of her purse and opens the door. Stepping inside, she picks up the faint scent of lavender soap. She pauses at the window. The gray light, the overcast sky, and the snow still falling feel calm and soothing.

"I'll make some tea," says Brian. He helps her out of her jacket, wraps her in a wool throw, and settles her on the sofa.

"Earl Grey would be lovely," she says.

He goes into the kitchen, fills the kettle, and puts it on the stove. The burner clicks before the spark fires.

She hears his footfalls and opens her eyes. "I'm so glad to see you," she says.

Brian nods, carrying mugs, cream, and sugar on a tray. "I'm glad you wanted me here," he says. "But I need to ask you something."

"Anything," she says.

"What about your sister? Why isn't she here instead of me?"

"I didn't tell her."

"Why not?"

"She's Catholic."

"Oh," he says. He picks up his bag and takes it into the guest room. A minute later, he's back and sitting on the sofa. "I still think it's shit that he doesn't know."

"You have to promise you won't tell him," she says.

"I already promised."

"And you never will?" she says.

"No. But it's even deeper shit that he left for his damn audition and you're like this – "

"Like what?"

"Alone," he says.

She turns her head. "But I'm not."

"It's too easy," he says. "Cole always gets off easy."

"Maybe this time," she says.

"Most of the time, I'd say. Paying dues doesn't hit with him. He'll probably ace the audition and get the gig. Then he'll come home and fall all over himself explaining why it is he has to go."

"He pays for it," she says.

"I don't believe it."

"He's not easy on himself."

"Yeah, I know. He sets the bar high."

"That isn't what I mean."

The kettle begins whistling, a soft whine that builds swiftly to a steady shriek.

"You know him better than I do," says Brian.

"Maybe not," she says.

He gets up and hurries into the kitchen and shuts off the burner. He pours the water into a teapot and leaves it to steep.

"All I know," he says, "is that he plays like a son of a bitch, better than anyone in his league."

"But he doesn't believe it," she says.

"He will," says Brian.

"No," she says. "That's the thing I mean. He'll never believe it. He'll never believe he's good."

"Are you sure?"

"I'm dead sure," she says.

Brian sits on the edge of the sofa, looks at a magazine on the coffee table, and starts thumbing the pages. "Let's not talk about Cole," he says.

"All right."

"The tea should be ready."

"Stay," she says. "Let it steep."

He leans back, very close to her, and closes his eyes. "It's quiet," he says.

She listens to him breathe.

"Do you want me to put on some music?"

"No," she says. She rests her head on his shoulder.

"Do you love him?" says Brian.

"Yes," she says. "But he'll never believe it."

I REALLY must go, she thinks, as the orchard darkens, the sun falling away somewhere beyond the trees. She'd seen a boy and girl walking together, holding a basket of apples between them. They moved slowly as if they had nowhere to be, as if they'd been here forever.

She thinks of the rooms she won't be going back to, the flickering lights and the dull drone of motors, always the furnace or the fridge, the constant humming that fills her mind with silver. She thinks of the keys she'll carry for a time but then set aside, dropping them into a box with paperclips and loose change.

But now, standing in the orchard, she pictures the apartment: the wood floors, the tables and chairs, and the windows. She thinks of Brian in those rooms, the confusion of him living there – was it four days or five? – making breakfast and dinner, checking on her in the middle of the night, knocking on the bathroom door. "We were better than husband and wife," she whispers, remembering the cold of those mornings, the dread of waking up, but then, like a rare gift, the sudden aroma of coffee and buttered toast.

SHE WALKS out of the orchard and into the parking lot, the sun setting, and finds the car with the door unlocked and the keys under the driver's mat. She isn't surprised that he left it, that he found another way out, but she wanted a clean break, something dramatic, a gesture that felt sharp and unmistakably final. Now the car keeps him with her, his tapes strewn across the backseat, the smell of his hands on the wheel.

She drives to a gas station and gets directions to I-94. She tries to keep her mind occupied, reading road signs and license plates, but the effort proves useless.

She remembers being nervous when Coleman came home because Brian's scent, his warmth, was still in the apartment.

Coleman took a short glass out of the cupboard and filled it with a handful of ice. Then he opened a bottle of vodka and poured a drink.

"Never again," he said.

"Is Philly that bad?" she said.

"No. I mean the bus. Damn near killed me."

"I told you to fly."

They went to dinner, one of her favorite restaurants, and he bought a rose from the old woman who roamed from table to table. He rushed through dessert. He wanted to get home and go to bed. He wanted to have sex. When she refused, he thrashed the bed, tossing and turning like an angry child.

She woke the next morning – and for a month of mornings thereafter – and found the bed empty, found him in the kitchen playing his guitar, no smell of coffee or toast. He spoke rapidly about opportunities and doors opening. He talked about his career, his plans.

She went to work. She corrected papers and turned in her third-quarter grades. She tacked up new photographs in the kitchen, in the bedroom and bathroom, too.

"They're empty," said Coleman.

"What do you mean?" she said.

"Park benches, streets, alleyways – they're all vacant. Even the trees are deserted."

She argued for the simplicity of the pictures, the unbroken lines. "I'm tired of faces," she said. "I see blank expressions all day. Is it my job to spark their enthusiasm? I'm tired of putting on a show."

Coleman flipped through the mail.

"Nothing I do fills them. Nothing satisfies them. They scrape the bottom of every barrel and toss out the remains."

"You need a break," said Coleman. "You need to slow down."

"Or we need to look again. Maybe they're not empty at all. Maybe they're mirrors, pieces of dark glass – "

She sees the junction ahead: I-94 West to Chicago. She brakes and puts on her blinker, though there's nothing behind her but darkness. She turns on the radio and finds a station playing oldies. She sings along, tries to match the doo-wop harmonies. She doesn't worry about singing off-key.

SHE KNOWS, passing the exit for Ann Arbor, that going back to the apartment is more than she can bear. She won't watch him pack. She won't ask for the details of his schedule or the day of his return. She'll refuse to play the woman who's satisfied to wait, as if waiting were her purpose, her duty.

He doesn't know it yet, but today, in the orchard's twilight, she let him go for the last time. I won't follow him, she thinks. I'll go to Evanston and stay with my sister. I'll wait until he's gone, then I'll empty my closet and clean out the darkroom. I'll pack only what belongs to me.

Like her predecessor at school, she'll quit without notice. She'll set off a string of sudden meetings filled with hand-wringing and condemnations. In the faculty lounge, eating a bagel before class, she'll inspire a polite hush. A friend will observe in an offhand way, almost as a consolation, that contracts are made to be broken.

When the time seems right, she'll call on her grandmother and take advantage of Tobermory, the old house, and the promise of absolute calm, a refuge without ghosts or obligations. From there, she'll venture out and visit a place that's new, somewhere she's never been. I'm ready for mountains, she thinks. I'm tired of being a flatlander. She imagines the ground of Colorado rising into the sky. She'll try Boulder. She loves the boldness of the name.

Driving west, she thinks about Chicago and the fact of leaving her hometown for good. Having settled on a course of action gives her a feeling of strength, but seeing Brian and telling him about her plans won't be easy. He'll be distant and very matter-of-fact. He'll wish her luck, of course, and tell her to be careful, but in the sound of each thing he says, she'll pick up notes of anger and disappointment.

Even so, she thinks, it may not be that complicated. We've been long out of touch. He may say he's too busy.

She wanted him, in the time since they'd stopped speaking, to drop in unexpectedly, to walk up the stairs, as he'd done so often, with a bag of carryout food or a bottle of wine. Instead, he kept his distance. She managed to see him once – a Wednesday night at the Mill, a set with Kurt Elling, the songs spiraling upward like flames.

"How are you?" she said.

"Good. Cole out of town?"

"Of course," she said.

Brian looked in the direction of the stage. "They keep him busy."

She smiled.

"I never told you," he said, "but when Cole came back from Philly, he said he'd still have time for the trio."

"I'm sure he meant it."

"Yeah. That's right."

"Why don't you come over sometime," she said. "I'll cook."

"Sure," he said.

She fiddles with the radio and sees from this distance that her invitation was selfish and cavalier. He couldn't help but ignore her. Now, having made up her mind to go, she'll leave a message – awkward after such long silence – and hope that he'll return the call, though she wonders what she'll say to him, trying to remember the comfort of his hands, his voice, trying to convince herself that between them nothing has changed.

It returns to her now without sadness or regret, the night she opened the door, nine months after the abortion, and found Brian standing on the welcome mat, the slush falling off his shoes. She wasn't surprised. Coleman had said, before rushing out in a huff, that she'd be better off with somebody else.

Brian stamped his feet and stepped across the threshold. She closed the door.

"Isn't that Cole's coat?" she said.

"Yeah. He said he wouldn't need it where he was going. Told me to dump my old rag and take it."

She hung the coat on the back of a chair.

"You okay?" he said.

"I'm fine. Why?"

"Cole asked me to come by. He said you needed to see me."

"He said that?"

"Is something wrong?"

"We argued while he was packing. We always do."

Brian nodded. "He was probably concerned – "

"And feeling generous," she said.

Brian sat on the couch. "I told him I didn't need his coat."

"He wants you to have it," she said.

"I guess."

"He likes to give things away."

"He does?"

"Almost everything."

Brian looked up. "You didn't ask to see me, did you?"

"No," she said. "It was his idea."

Then she placed her hand on the back of the sofa, knelt on one leg and slowly moved the other across his lap until she had him between her thighs. She kissed him and felt his muscles tighten.

He squeezed her shoulders. "I've waited a long time," he said.

She kissed him again, her heart pounding.

His hand moved down her arm and slipped beneath her shirt. "You sure you want this?" he said.

"Yes."

"And Cole?"

"He wants it, too."

Brian opened his eyes.

"It's all right," she said. "What he wants doesn't matter."

It ended, she thinks, as abruptly as it began. Brian stopped calling. He stayed away.

She went to the Mill and waited. Then came that Wednesday when he showed up and pecked her on the cheek but wouldn't sit down, anxious about the show with Kurt Elling. Her offer of dinner was, by then, a pointless invitation.

Now, she'll go to Evanston. She'll wait for Cole to leave and then pick up her stuff at the apartment. She'll try to get in touch with Brian. She wonders how anything simple and necessary survives.

There's no going back, she thinks, seeing the sign for Benton Harbor. Tonight, she'll descend along the southern shore of Lake Michigan, passing the ash heaps of Gary and East Chicago, the moon gone and darkness coming down, the color of her skin fading and her smooth arms dissolving, until she feels that her body is without substance, a shadow, a silver mist, moving unseen beneath the city, the ground falling away from her in spirals.

chapter nine

COLEMAN checks the boom vang: the traveler, the double blocks, and the line that runs from the foot of the mast to the ear of the spar. Without this mechanism, the boom, taken by the wind, would naturally ride up and let the main go slack, the sail lifting, twisting, and slipping the air. "If it fails," his father said, "there can be no wing – no hope for control or a perfect curve." He tests the line again just to be sure.

He reaches into his pocket. To his surprise, he discovers that the list he'd been using isn't there. If it doesn't reappear, he'll have to quit for a while and make a new one. He wants to find it right now so he can enjoy the ritual of crossing things off. He scours the boat, turns his clothing inside out, and decides at last to look in his shoes. He feels foolish after that and stops to catch his breath.

He squints at the blue sky. It's still early. He has Humbug all to himself. The air coming off the river feels cool and dry.

He hears the crunch of gravel, glances down from the cockpit, and sees a station wagon pulling into the lot. A cloud of dust drifts through the yard.

His landlord, dressed in a tank top and shorts, gets out of the car and walks toward the boat. "Ahoy there," she says.

"How'd you find me?" he says.

She takes off her sunglasses. "You're always here."

"Yeah, well." He rubs his hand. "I've got a lot to do."

The landlord plants herself just off the stern. "Is she seaworthy? Will you float her this season?"

"Any day now."

"Most folks put in before the middle of June."

"She'll be ready by the end of the month."

The landlord peers at the transom. "What's a *Pequod*?"

"It's the name of a boat," he says.

"I can see that."

He leans over the taffrail. "It's from a book. There's a ship called the *Pequod*."

"What book?"

"It doesn't matter."

"Okay, but it's a strange name."

"Is that what you came to tell me?"

"No," she says. "I came to see how you were doing, seeing that your street's torn up and littered with pipes and big trucks – it's like a war zone."

"I'm fine."

"Toilet okay?"

"Toilet's fine."

"They say it may be weeks before they're finished."

"I've got plenty to do here," he says.

The landlord, looking up, puts her hands on her hips. "Any other trouble?" she says.

He sees that her short hair is shorter still, a cut that shows off the strong line of her shoulders and the symmetry of her arms. He shifts his gaze. "I told you. The toilet's fine. No problem."

"I saw the article," she says, a pained expression on her face.

He nods. He knew it would be like this. After all, they ran the story in the *Sunday News-Herald*. They interviewed the kid who gave a breathless description of the headlock. The mother, who referred to him only as Mr. Moore, threatened to press charges. She said, "A man who can't control himself should be locked up or run out of town."

"If I'm put away or banished, will you cancel the lease?"

"Consider it done," she says, and then her face gets serious. "Someone said you were trying to finish the boy's education."

"No. I wouldn't say that."

"Were you drinking?"

"Not before the ceremony."

"You should ask for the Lord's forgiveness." She points at her breasts.

He sees now that on her tank top is a likeness of Jesus with the word SAVES beneath it.

"And if I were you," she says, "I'd ask for His blessing on this boat."

He thinks about climbing down, but he can't take the risk. He doesn't want another story in the *Sunday News-Herald*. "If there's a problem with the toilet," he says, "I'll give you a call."

"You do that," says the landlord.

"I'll pray that the toilet keeps working," he says.

"You're not a kind man."

"I'm sorry," he says. "I'm out of practice."

After she's gone, he descends and squints at the transom. He'd thought about changing the name before, and now he wonders if he should've gone through with it.

He remembers his father telling him about the drawings he'd made, both ink and pencil, of the boats in Saginaw Bay. His father said, "There was one I especially liked, a cutter, and my mother saw it and suddenly she said, '*Blue Morning*.' It sounded to me like the title of a painting or the name of a song."

He stares at the transom and pictures his father leaning on the taffrail. "You never went so far as a cutter," he whispers. I'll stick with *Pequod* for now, but *Blue Morning* is the right choice – it isn't a fraud or a kind of theft or a sign of spiteful domination.

DRIVING home, the sun going down, he runs into a new barricade, another closed road with piles of dirt on one side and stretches of black pipe on the other. The detour takes him to the river and dumps him on his old street. He sees Maureen's car in the driveway. Rolling by, he glances at the front door and notices the light in the upstairs bedroom. He figures it's a bad time to stop, but then he changes his mind. He pulls over three houses down and parks at the curb.

He slides out of the truck. With the sun gone, the air feels cold. He walks without making a sound and climbs the three concrete steps to the porch. It looks like Heather's in her room.

He rings the bell.

Maureen comes to the door, starts to open it, and then slams it when she sees his face. "I'm thinking about a restraining order," she says.

"For what? I've never touched anyone – "

"Until now."

"You're being ridiculous. C'mon, open the door. I haven't seen Heather since she graduated."

"She won't see you."

"I don't believe that. What did she say? Did she say she won't see me?"

"Yes. And the same goes for me. I think you should leave."

"Tell her to come downstairs. I want to hear it from her."

"I won't," says Maureen. "She's been humiliated enough."

"What humiliation? That kid's a creep. He had it coming."

"Great," says Maureen. "No remorse. You don't get it, do you? Her name's been in the paper. Strange boys call the house. They've heard what the kid said. They ask if the slut's at home."

"Open the door. Let me talk to her."

"She's not here."

"You're lying."

"I'm not. She went out an hour ago."

"Then why's the light on upstairs?"

"I don't know."

He kicks the door. Then he throws his body against it.

Maureen lets out a groan of exasperation. "I'll call the police," she says.

He steps off the porch and walks down the side drive to the rear of the house. He tries the back door. It's locked.

He looks through the window. Maureen is nowhere in sight. He takes the trowel out of the flower box, shields his eyes, and strikes the glass with the bottom of the thick blade. He can hear her coming as he reaches inside and throws the dead bolt.

"Stay there," he says, the glass crunching beneath his tennis shoes. "You're barefoot."

Maureen stops. She begins to cry. "You're a stranger," she says. "After all this time, I can't tell who you are."

He squeezes by and walks down the hall.

"Go ahead," says Maureen. "Don't believe me."

He runs up the stairs, opens the door to Heather's room, and sees that the glowing lamp and the empty bed are the only things there. He checks the bathroom.

Coming down the steps, he hears Maureen sweeping up glass. He rounds the banister and takes in the profile of her body. She's wearing black panties and a T-shirt. She bends. "You're a beautiful woman," he says.

She looks up. Her eyes still filled. "You shouldn't have ruined her graduation."

"I didn't mean to."

She nods.

"Will she see me?"

"Of course. She loves you. You're always the one she loves."

"I'm sorry."

"Sorry doesn't change anything."

"For the door, I mean. I'll pay for it."

Maureen starts to laugh. "That's the one thing about you," she says. "You're always willing to pay."

He holds the dustpan while she sweeps. Then he goes into the garage and finds a piece of thin plywood that's close to the right size. "Where's your hammer?" he says.

She opens the hall closet and pulls out a small toolbox.

He grabs the hammer and a fistful of nails, knocks out two or three of the remaining shards, and boards up the opening.

He finishes the job and sees that she's gone upstairs. He leaves the hammer on the counter, presses the button on the doorknob, and gently closes the door.

·Walking to his truck, he considers the neighbors and feels more than a little self-conscious. He watches for movement, for a drape or a blind closing – or, in an unlit window, the outline of a face that suddenly draws back and disappears.

He hadn't planned to go but now he finds himself in the Black & White Club.

Wes Montgomery's set had been a dream that brought everyone to their feet. Then he played "Down Here on the Ground," a quiet encore, and a hush fell over the house – people even held their breath.

He savored each note and leaped up when it was over and stared at Wes's huge hands until the great man stepped off into darkness.

Still glowing from the performance, he asks the woman sitting with him if she'd like a drink. "I'm fine with water," she says.

"I'll have a vodka martini," he says. "Straight up, extra dry, olives."

"Is that really necessary?" says the woman.

"Absolutely." He smiles. He likes it that her hair is cut short.

"Why did you bring me here?" she says.

He doesn't answer. He missed it at first, but now he sees that her sleeveless T-shirt bears the face of John Coltrane. He points at her chest. "This is a guitarist's club – but I think they'd make an exception for him."

"He's all I listen to," she says. "I play *A Love Supreme* over and over again. I have a shrine in my bedroom. You should come over and see it. A little devotion would do you some good."

"I was once a religious man," he says.

"You don't have to say that."

"I was. I probably still am."

"If you listen to *A Love Supreme*," she says, "you have no choice."

He lowers his eyes and regards his martini. He lifts it and takes a sip. "So you're a fanatic," he says.

"No," she says. "I'm a follower. His playing is like meditation."

"It's prayer," he says.

"Exactly."

Because her hair is short, he can see the curve of her neck and the slope of her shoulder. Something about her skin – its perfect clarity – makes him want more than anything to touch her.

"If you understand me so well," she says, "why don't you ever see me?"

"I have a lot to do."

"I don't mean that. I mean that you've always looked down or away or somewhere in the distance. But you've never looked at me – not really – at least until now."

"I don't like to compete."

Her eyes fall to her breasts. "With him?"

"With anyone."

"That's not very ambitious."

"I used to be ambitious, too."

She reaches across the table and picks up his martini. She takes more than a sip. "So if his face wasn't here, you'd see me?"

"It might be easier."

"I can't take it off," she says. "There's nothing underneath."

"I doubt that anyone would mind."

The woman smiles. She finishes the martini.

He looks up. On the stage, three antique guitars stand in a pool of light. The one in the middle seems to be surrounded by a halo. A security guard walks out and makes certain that each instrument is in the right place.

"I wonder when the next show begins?" he says.

"It starts Sunday."

He laughs and leans back in his chair. "That can't be right," he says.

"Sure," she says. "A Sunday matinee. I saw the sign on the way in."

"That's crazy."

"Why?"

"Do you plan to stay here tonight and all day tomorrow and tomorrow night, too?"

"I don't have a choice."

He glances at the face on her shirt. "But he's not coming?"

"Maybe not," she says. "I'll wait and see."

THE DAYS get warmer.

Coleman goes directly from work to Humbug and spends the night more often than not. The cabin gets stuffy in hot weather, but on breathless evenings the boat feels calm and restful – it makes no disquieting sounds.

Just after the Fourth of July, he looks her over from bow to stern and decides that everything's squared away. It's time, he thinks, for the planning and repairs to pay off. He wants to prove to himself and to anyone who cares that the work he's put into the boat means something, that he's not just tinkering and wasting time. He's also excited by the idea of a long cruise. Heather'll be gone soon enough, he thinks. There's not much reason to stick around.

He visits the house, checks his mail, and pays a few bills. The rooms feel heavy and he sits in the kitchen with the windows open, his small fan clicking as it rotates from side to side.

He leaves a message for Heather, but she doesn't call. He imagines her at work, her mood swinging between anger and disappointment. She can be unforgiving, he thinks, like her mother. They both see things with a hard clarity.

The house is too hot. He drinks vodka on the rocks but it offers no relief. He downs more than he should and thinks about calling a woman, a lover that he completely makes up – tall, dark, commanding. She tells him to come over and he goes without hesitation. She lets him in and he moves outside of time –

no past or future. He lies beside her and listens to her breathing and the sound of cool sheets caressing her skin.

Not long after that he falls forward and hits his head on the wall.

Nodding off on the toilet is fast becoming a hazard. His forehead throbs. He walks through the dark house to the kitchen, puts a handful of ice in a glass, and then fills the glass with vodka.

After an hour or two, in the cool of the morning twilight, having barely slept, he makes his way to Humbug.

He watches *Pequod* rise in her slings. He feels proud, a sense of accomplishment, when her hull touches the water. The putting in is graceful and without incident, but he knows he would've enjoyed it more had he kissed off last night's booze or taken a shot with his coffee to kill the hangover.

He guides the boat to her berth and goes slowly with the mooring lines, repeating the names to himself – bowline, bow spring, and quarter spring – as he rounds a bollard or cleat.

He thinks about the work that remains. He'll need a hand to step the mast, and then he'll trim the stays and reeve the last lines. He knows it'll be a while before he can cast off.

Later, starting his route for the day, he pictures going upriver, across Lake St. Clair and through the narrows, and then out into Lake Huron. He wants to follow his father's course, make the trip to Port Elgin – sail to the place where his father was last seen. Maybe then, sensing the familiar, the old boat will heel and surge, pointing higher than seems possible, footing and careening in a wash of white spray and wind.

He likes the thought of it. He'll take the vacation time he's got coming. He'll listen to the weather, the patterns and the long-range forecasts. He'll try to see Heather.

He drives across the Ambassador Bridge later that morning, loads up the truck in Windsor, and makes the return crossing before lunch. Then he drives north and northeast and delivers beer in Roseville and Warren before turning back and rolling downriver in the late afternoon.

When he gets home, he sees the light on his phone flashing. The time of the message is 12:35 P.M.

"It's Humbug," says the voice. "Looks to me like she's out of trim – and she's not pumping. I'd get over here if I were you."

When he pulls in at Humbug, he glances at his watch – almost six-thirty.

He hurries to the dock.

The boat's too low in the water – half the freeboard seems to have disappeared. He steps down into the cockpit and the boat barely moves. It's stranded, he thinks. The keel's stuck fast in the muck.

He unlocks the hood and slides it forward. He sees water in the cabin. It laps the top rung of the companionway steps.

"Tough break," says the yard manager, peering down from the dock.

"Jesus," he says. "I'm finished with this shit."

"Want me to handle it?" says the manager.

"Yeah. I can't do it."

"It'll cost you."

"I know. Just do whatever it takes."

"I did a search for a cell number – or a number at work – but nothin' came up."

"I don't carry a phone," he says. "Wouldn't have mattered. I was up on the east side."

The yard manager rubs his stubble. "Bilge pump shoulda kicked in."

"I know."

"Could be the battery. Maybe the float switch."

"Battery's brand-new."

"What about the pump?"

"No."

"Well," says the manager, "maybe it got clogged with gunk. Maybe the motor's fried."

"Maybe."

"More likely the float switch."

"Just take care of it."

"All right. I'll pump her till she's near dry."

"Fine."

"And then I'll haul her out."

He looks at the manger's beat-up hands and then at the travel lift standing in the yard.

The manager frowns. "Funny she took on water so fast."

"Yeah, funny," he says.

"You want her in the same cradle?"

"Sure."

"A little makeshift, don't you think?"

He shrugs. "She stood up all winter."

"I can leave her in the lift for inspection."

"No. Lay her up," he says.

"It's your boat."

"I know." He turns and walks away.

"Hold on there," says the manager. "You wanna leave me the keys?"

He pulls the keys out of his pocket and the large yellow float dangles from his hand like a dead fish. "Thanks," he says.

"Don't thank me," says the manager. "Just pay me."

BACK at the house, he tries to occupy his mind with something other than his father's boat. He forgot to open the windows when he first came in after work and now the place feels hot and stuffy. He peels off his clothes, takes a cold shower, and wraps himself in a towel. He stands in front of the open freezer for a long time before grabbing the vodka. He pours himself a double and dials Maureen. A voice in his head says to give her a wide berth, but he wants to get the worst part over with as soon as possible.

Maureen picks up on the second ring.

"Don't hang up." He listens to a long silence.

"She's not here, Jason. You never – "

He cuts her off. "Does she even live there anymore?"

"She'll be home by eleven."

"Wait," he says. "That's not why I called."

"What then?"

"Hold on." He gulps his vodka. "My check may be late again or at least down a few bucks."

"Your timing is unbelievable."

"I know. But accidents happen." He hears her breathing.

"Are you okay?" she says, the words a bit softer.

"It's not me – it's the boat."

"Oh."

"It sank."

"You went out on the lake?"

"No," he says. "I put her in this morning and left her at Humbug. She took on water and went down in her slip. She's more stranded than sunk. Her keel's in the muck."

"What happened?"

"Don't know. Won't know until they pull her out." He hears nothing but static.

"So what do you want from me?" she says.

"Nothing. I just wanted to tell you – I may come up a little short next month."

"Tell her yourself. She's a big girl now. Maybe she can borrow a few dollars from her roommate when she gets to school."

"I always make good."

"Yeah. But in the meantime I'm the one living with the boarded-up door."

He pours another drink. "I'll do my best," he says.

"You do that," says Maureen. Then she hangs up.

He doesn't turn on the light. He hopes the gathering darkness will feel cooler. He sits in the living room and rests the sweating glass of vodka on his leg. Even with the door wide open, the air doesn't move.

He puts his feet up and thinks about not going to work in the morning, calling in and saying he's had an emergency, something that can't wait. But he won't go to Humbug. Maybe he'll try to find Heather, try to apologize for the third or fourth time.

He rests his head on the back of the sofa and hears a car coming down the street. Opening his eyes, he sees light from the car's headlamps flashing around the room – then comes the sound of a door closing and someone walking up the driveway.

The landlord breezes in without knocking. She turns on the lamp. "Oh my God," she says, covering her mouth. She reaches for the switch.

"Don't bother," he says.

She's wearing a tank top, but this time there's no Jesus. Her cutoffs ride low on her hips. Her short hair is wet and combed straight back.

"I saw the dark house and the open door," she says. "Let me turn this off."

"Not now," he says.

He looks at her standing in the light, her breasts rising and falling as she breathes. He sees the lines close to her eyes and mouth, the firmness of her arms – the middle-aged skin, glorious in its imperfection – and her hands, well used, showing signs of work. Her thighs are smooth, not thin, and her flat stomach shows a tiny scar – a mark or two where the skin stretches and shines.

"It's too bright," she says, reaching again for the light.

"Don't move," he says. He stands and walks toward her. "Turn it up."

She hesitates.

"Turn it up," he says, almost flinching, surprised by her touch, her warm fingers grazing his hip.

She puts her other hand on his chest as if to keep him from coming closer. She undoes the towel.

He leans toward her and reaches under the lamp shade. He turns the knob until it clicks. He turns it again. The room overflows with light. He grabs her by the shoulders, his hands aching, and kisses her hard on the mouth.

With the sure strength of a dancer, she climbs and floats free of the ground – the air like water – her arms around his neck, her legs circling his waist.

He pushes her against the wall, wanting to feel whatever grace she carries, kissing her shoulders and the firm slope of her breasts. He lifts her shirt.

She slides it off and tosses it away.

His knotted hand follows the curve of her belly.

"Rip 'em," she says.

He doesn't know if he can. He opens the snap and unbuttons the fly. He pulls. Not a stitch gives way.

"Don't worry," she says.

He steadies his grip and tries again. This time the fabric tears – a sound almost like moaning – and then it flutters and drifts to the floor. In the bright light, he holds her against the wall, the curtains and the front door gaping, the sharp salt of her body on his lips and tongue. The sweat between them feels like oil. She uses one hand on his shoulder for balance and the other to guide him and keep him from slipping away.

Just moments ago, he'd thought the gulf between them was too great –

tenant and landlord, absurd demands, and the constant Jesus talk – that the grim weight of her beliefs, her faith, would drag him down, force him to surrender his original impulse.

But now, suddenly and without struggle, struck by the rhythm of their breathing, he feels himself unfettered, no longer earthbound, her weightless and perfect body joined to his own, the two of them gliding upward like wind.

When it's over, he carries her into the bedroom and lies in the darkness beside her. He rests his hand on her hip and listens to the fan clicking. Sweat covers his arms and chest, and the air moving across his skin feels cool.

He drifts off without thinking about work or the problems at Humbug, without worrying about Heather or anything he's done.

He wakes in the semidarkness to the sound of words, a sad drone, as if someone were reciting poetry in a monotone voice, a way of talking that gives equal stress to all syllables, covering and flattening each utterance – each phrase – like a sheet draped over old furniture. He can't locate the sound's point of origin, forgetting – with his eyes just open – that he's not entirely alone. Then he sees the outline of her thighs kneeling on the bed and the silhouette of clasped hands over his chest. Why does she keep talking? he thinks. Finally, the words slow down. He begins to hear the incantation in pieces, bursts of recognizable sound. He blinks and the room comes into focus.

He stares at her in the gray light praying, sees her kneeling naked on the bed, her breasts trembling and her lips moving like a woman mourning a dead lover.

"What are you doing?" he says.

"Kneel with me," she says.

He tries to roll off the bed but she catches his arm.

"You don't have to pray," she says. "I'll do the praying for you."

On her face is an expression he's seen before, self-assured and presumptuous, qualities that he'd thought were seductive, an appeal only to his manhood and not the question of his soul, but now her all-knowing eyes unnerve him and he sees in her face, as if for the first time, the hard fire of missionary zeal.

"Let me go," he says.

He stumbles into the bathroom and turns on the light. He watches her in the mirror still praying.

I need to get away, he thinks. It's her place, after all. I pay her for temporary use. I need to slip out before she finds a pair of pants and explains why she came over and why it all happened exactly as it did.

The room brightens with the sun rising.

He puts on a T-shirt and jeans and listens to her words. *Let me not, oh Lord, be puffed up with worldly wisdom* . . . Her body is even more beautiful than he remembered.

He stuffs a jacket and clothes into a duffel bag. He opens the medicine cabinet and sweeps all the pills and painkillers on the bottom shelf into the bag. *Give us this day our daily bread . . . And lead us not into temptation . . . Instead, grant me compassion . . . love that never abates . . .*

He can't bring himself to kiss her or say good-bye.

He walks out of the bedroom, moves quietly through the house, and realizes that he left the front door open all night. The sight of her station wagon in the driveway makes his stomach jump. He eyeballs the distance and decides that he has just enough room to get around her.

He goes out through the garage and starts the pickup. He's almost to the foot of the drive when she comes out of the house wearing his bathrobe. I thought I'd get away clean, he thinks.

She raises her hand.

He can't tell whether she's waving or wanting him to stop. He waves, puts the truck in drive, and pulls away without checking the rearview mirror.

HE TURNS the corner and Humbug comes into view. Inside the fence is the giant cruiser that no one ever goes near. Patches of brown and black have blossomed on the hull. He remembers the yard regulars calling it a ghost ship – Humbug's monument to damage and disrepair.

He grips the wheel, his hands aching, and looks again at the old wooden boat. Not today, he thinks.

He stops at the Blue Moon Market and uses the pay phone to call Heather. He leaves her a message, tells her that he won't be around until early next week and that he needs to see her before she takes off for school. He hangs up, puts a few more coins into the slot, and punches the keypad.

He waits. The line rings and clicks. Someone on the other end hesitates, a momentary confusion, and then says, "This is routing and dispatch. May I help you?"

"Hi, Irma. It's Coleman."

"Where are you?" she says.

"I'm not coming in."

"Why not? You sick? You don't sound sick."

"No. I need to start my vacation today."

"You can't do that. You just put in for it."

"I know. But I gotta go."

"There's nobody to cover your route."

"C'mon. You got backups."

"Not today. And even if I did, what about Monday and the rest of next week?"

"Sorry to put you through it."

"It won't go down easy," says Irma.

"You think I'll get canned?"

"I think you can count on it."

He digs in his pocket. He's out of change. "I'll call you as soon as I get back."

"Hope you're going somewhere nice," says Irma.

"Take care," he says.

He goes into the Blue Moon Market and buys vodka, soft drinks, a bag of pretzels, and a sandwich. He looks at the pay phone on the way out and thinks about giving Heather another try. He makes up his mind not to.

He climbs into the pickup and stows the bottle of vodka in his duffel bag beneath the clothes and painkillers. He leaves the other stuff on the seat.

He drives west on Gibraltar Road to I-75 and then heads north, the road rising over smokestacks and slag heaps, the Ford plant at River Rouge – sulfur stinging his nose. The smell brings back his grandfather's voice: "Ford's river," said H.M., "runs redder than blood. Always has. And always will."

Soon after that he sees the Ambassador Bridge and races past the exit and through downtown Detroit. He hits heavy traffic on the ramp for eastbound I-94 and feels a knot in his stomach when the pickup slows. He's in no mood for a tie-up or a bumper-to-bumper crawl. After the merge, he drifts into the far left lane and the cars start moving. He stays there until he sees a cop waiting under the 8 Mile Road overpass. He changes lanes and tries to blend in with the slower cars.

He takes the Metropolitan Beach exit and stops for gas. He cleans the windshield and uses the bathroom. One of the rear tires appears to be low so he takes his gauge out of the glove compartment and checks the pressure. It's worse than he thought. He runs his hand over the treads. Could be a rim leak, he thinks.

A young woman walks over and asks to borrow his gauge. "I think my tires are fine," she says. "But ever since all those rollovers, I worry."

He glances at her suv, sees a small Korean flag, a sticker, on the rear window. He smiles. "Take your time," he says.

She's very petite with luxurious black hair and shoulders the color of dark gold. He wants to tell her that she's beautiful – one of the most beautiful women he's ever seen. He watches as she crouches in front of her tires and completes her transaction at the pump. He watches her walking toward him.

"Thanks," she says. "Great gauge."

He smiles and nods.

Back on the freeway, he turns on the radio, listens to the news, and then scans for a good station. He can't find any real jazz, so he chooses classical: Bach, Orchestral Suite no. 3.

He drives faster than the speed limit, blowing by Mount Clemens and New Baltimore, feeling the sudden pull of Port Huron. It occurs to him that he can make this drive without thinking, without reading the signs or checking the numbers. He likes the comfort in that – the feeling that the road is going precisely where it should.

It seems strange to him now that he learned this route when he was young, driving sometimes with a friend but mostly by himself. Jen was with him once. They were in from Chicago, a long July weekend, but the visit went badly, his father working and sleeping on the boat, a tension in the house despite his mother's good cheer. After a day or two of that, he said, "Let's drive up the thumb. I'll show you Port Austin, the place where I was born."

Now, like before, he goes up 25, opening the windows when he sees the water, knowing that Lexington's not far, but then remembering the drive at sunset with Jen, and how, when she caught the scent of Lake Huron, she took off her shirt and jeans until all she had on was her white bathing suit, the top tied behind her neck and the bottom tied high on her hips, the hue of her black hair and bronze skin made deeper by the narrow swathes of white.

She put the seat back and stretched, letting the fresh evening air wash over her like water. "I'd like to swim," she said.

He glanced at her and saw the profile of her face. "There's Lakeport," he said. "Or we could stop at Birch Beach."

She looked at the lake. "Maybe not," she said. "I think it's the idea of swimming I like and not the actual fact."

"The water'll be cold," he said. "It's a deep lake."

She turned, the red sunlight falling across her hair. "Will you always love me?" she said.

"Yes."

"Even when I'm fat?"

"Yes."

"I don't believe you. You'll leave me when I'm fat."

"You're too beautiful," he said. "I can't imagine." He laid his hand on her thigh, his long, straight fingers pale against her skin.

"I love the twilight," she said.

"There's a hitchhiker ahead. He's got one foot in the road." He slowed the car.

"Do we have to pick him up?" said Jen.

"I wasn't planning on it," he said.

She smiled. "I just don't feel like getting dressed."

He felt the heat of her skin. "It'll cool down fast after dark. You'll get a chill."

"Then I guess you'll have no choice. You'll have to close the windows."

But the night stayed warm and he kept the windows open through Port Sanilac, Harbor Beach, and Port Hope, listening to the sound of Jennifer's words, the rising and falling of her voice, watching from behind the wheel as the pure darkness of her body grew darker still.

He knows he's pretty close at Grindstone City. He wraps up the unfinished bits of his sandwich and brushes the crumbs off his lap.

The first thing to do is find a room. When that's done, he'll drive by the old places and pay his respects, see what's gone and what remains. He won't worry about renting a boat until tomorrow.

Except for getting back and making things right with Heather, he's in no particular hurry.

HE STOPS at the curb and sees that the porch has settled, one side sinking into the ground and the roof sagging.

He still feels guilty for not going to the funeral, for being in Kansas City when Otis died and not having enough cash or energy to catch a plane. He made excuses, of course, and convinced himself that it was already too late, even though the saloon keeper had just heard the news and wasted no time making the announcement. "I don't know about the exact hour or the place," said the man, "but Otis Young has passed, if not yesterday then the day before."

He gets out of the truck. The rectangle of grass that was Otis's front yard is now a patch of weeds. He pictures Otis in the heat of summer dressed in a crisp white shirt and black pants and peering out from behind the screen door, his expression filled with worry and sadness. It's the same face he wore at the Green Mill when he appeared out of nowhere and sipped bourbon and spoke of last wishes before dying. Shivering and sometimes clutching his side, he managed to stay for both sets but didn't breathe a word about his cancer or the burgeoning pain.

After that evening, knowing that Otis was in a bad way, he'd thought about driving to Port Austin and went as far as setting aside dates and servicing his car, but then a complication came up and his plans fell apart at the last minute. He'd felt shameful for not going and for making Otis's visit to the Green Mill their last. In Kansas City, he felt worse.

He argued that funerals are only for the living. He tried to convince himself that he wasn't just selfish and lazy, that sudden demands on his time were inconvenient, too costly, or – after a stiff drink – absolutely impossible. He searched for the easy way out and chided himself for a smallness of soul, a dwindling of gratitude and duty that seemed to make room only for indifference.

He sees the shanty in back and remembers the summer when he moved away and Otis paced the floor and handed him books and music. "Time's run out," he said, "and you still have everything to learn. You've got to play every day so that even when you're not playing, some part of your brain is working out the problems. You've got to learn pedal tones and voice leadings, forms and motifs. There's no end to it. I planned to show you grips that right now you can't imagine."

It was an overcast day and the room was dark. He looked up at Otis, his arms overloaded. "It's hard to balance," he said.

Otis ignored him and rushed to a file cabinet and pulled out a sheaf of papers. "I'm forgetting things. There's more I wanted to tell you."

"I'll come back. You'll remember by then."

"I don't count on second endings," said Otis, still distracted, his words coming out in a whisper.

Trying to hold all the stuff that Otis had given him, finding it difficult to move, he stumbled and a book slipped out of his arms.

"Here, you dropped this," said Otis.

Now, standing in front of the shanty, the windows boarded up and the paint peeling, he feels the weight of thin air. He remembers leaving the books and papers in a jumble near the door and telling Otis that he'd pick them up later, though he never did.

You deserved better, he thinks. Someone who'd go for broke, who'd scramble it and play it backward if necessary. You taught me and gave me advice and showed me what I needed to learn. But I couldn't hold on to everything at once. You deserved someone smarter – someone who'd remember all one can forever. You said, *Never – never forget.* It was thoughtless of me, but when you got up after saying that and straightened yourself against the pain, I didn't think to say good-bye. I said, *Don't worry*. You shivered and buttoned your jacket. I was confused. I didn't know then what you meant.

AFTER dark, he finds a bar, a small place with neon in the window, a slow-moving fan, and peanut shells on the floor. It smells like cigarette smoke and beer. A middle-aged couple sits in the red and yellow glow of the jukebox – a machine that looks to be from the fifties. A woman at the bar stares glassy-eyed at the silent TV.

He pulls up a rickety stool.

"What'll it be?" says the bartender, a wrinkled man with gray stubble.

"Vodka," he says. "On the rocks. Anything but Smirnoff."

The bartender twitches. He picks up a bottle of Stolichnaya and pours. "Where you from?"

"Gibraltar."

The bartender sets the glass of Stoli on a white cocktail napkin. "First time?"

"No. I was born here. But we left when I was in high school."

"Is that right. You got a name?"

"Moore. Coleman Moore. My father ran a marine supply."

"Halyard & Mast," says the bartender, his voice flat, seemingly indifferent. He sips his vodka. "You know it then."

"Sure I know it. And now I don't know whether to shoot you or shake your hand."

He checks the bartender's eyes and keeps a tight grip on his drink.

The old man rubs his stubble. "You're Dorian's boy?"

He nods.

"I knew your grandfather, too. Old Havelock Moore. Owned the big store down in Bay City."

He hooks his heels on the stool's bottom rung. "Were you a sailor?" he says.

The bartender laughs. "God no. And it's a good thing. Otherwise, I might've signed over my soul. Just like everybody else in these parts."

He downs the rest of his drink.

"Want another?"

He pushes his glass across the bar.

"Mind you, I never met Havelock. But you didn't have to meet him to know him. He put men – good men – out of business. Plenty of 'em. He took over this whole territory. If you needed something to stay afloat, then you had to deal with him." The bartender swats a fly with a rolled-up magazine. "I even knew a guy who ran in those singlehander races – said that Havelock Moore could never be beat. Even in a storm, he came out ahead. But you must've been no more than a kid back then."

"Must've been," he says.

"I saw a picture or two of him in the papers, but I never really knew what he looked like."

"He was tall."

The bartender raises his eyebrows. "Here he was the richest man in the neighborhood, and then he shows up one day in Port Austin and blows his brains out – does the deed in that big old boat of his."

"I know," he says. "I was there."

The bartender twitches and leans on the bar. "Now, your father, he was a whole different kettle of fish. I talked to him face-to-face a few times. Kinda quiet. Like something was always on his mind. But he'd give a man credit any day of the week. If you couldn't pay right away, it was okay with him. Keeping the boat up was all that mattered. How's he doin'?"

"He's dead."

The bartender pours a shot of whiskey. "It happens. A little too often to suit me. Here's to your father." The old man throws back the shot and fills the glass again. "What took him?"

"He drowned."

The bartender's face keeps the same flat expression.

"He was lost on Lake Huron. Went into a storm out of Port Elgin. They found his boat grounded on Cape Hurd."

The bartender dries his hands. "I'd say I'm sorry, but what's the point?" He pours more vodka. "So what brings you here?"

He shrugs. "I wanted to see the lake. Thought I might go for a ride."

"A little nostalgia, is that it?"

"Something like that."

"You got a boat?"

He shakes his head. "I thought I'd go over to Captain Morgan's in the morning. See what I can find out."

"The hell with that," says the bartender. "I got a skiff, a '66 Chris-Craft, restored her myself. I call her *Idyllic*, because nothing else is." He takes a pen from behind his ear and writes on a napkin. "Come by in the morning – not too early – and you can take her out."

He hadn't noticed the old man's palsy until now.

"Here you go. My name's Ben." He waves the white napkin like a flag. "You gonna leave me flappin' in the breeze? Or are you gonna take it?"

"Thank you," he says. "I'm – "

"Don't think another thing about it," says Ben. He wipes the bar with a dirty towel. "You're not a pirate, are you?"

The woman who'd been watching TV taps the bar. "Sorry to break up the reunion but my glass is standin' here empty."

He nurses his vodka. He hears the couple behind him talking and laughing. He looks up and sees them in the mirror above the bar. They're sitting at a round table, the smallest one in the room. They act as if they're entirely alone. The man feels in his pockets and shakes his head. Then the woman digs through her purse, pulling out a hairbrush and a small camera. She smiles and slides off her chair and walks over to the Wurlitzer jukebox. She doesn't take long to make a selection. She turns and waits for the music to begin.

He recognizes the tune and the voice of Otis Redding rising out of the speakers. *I've been loving you – too long – to stop now . . .*

He swings around and watches as the woman walks toward the table, her arms outstretched, her hips swaying. The man goes to her and presses himself against her and they dance in the red and yellow light. *There were times – and your love is growin' cold . . .* His perfect hands move slowly down her back . . . *But my love – is growing stronger as our affair – affair – grows old.* He bows his head like a man praying and lifts her from the floor.

He looks away from the couple and glances down the bar. He sees Ben rubbing a beer glass and talking to his other customer. He finishes his drink, leaves a big tip, and nods on his way out.

"See you tomorrow," says Ben.

"I'll be there," he says.

He walks for a while but the cool air does him no good. Everything around him is all at once familiar and strange, known and unknown – the trees and houses flushed with moonlight, ashen and thin, floating in the air like fog.

When he gets back to his room, he opens his bag and pulls out the bottle of vodka. He drinks half of it without ice. He hears the faucet in the bathroom dripping. He raises the window, thankful for a breeze and the sound of white water.

IN THE late morning on the lake, standing at the wheel with the skiff underway, he feels his head clearing.

Back at the motel, opening his eyes to a strange room, he'd felt disoriented.

He'd seen the booze on the nightstand and wanted a mouthful to stop the shaking, but he got up too fast, his hands aching, and his fingers jerked and froze. The bottle crashed on the bathroom floor.

He leaned on the doorjamb and gazed at the puddle of vodka. He slid to his knees and tried to feel for glass. He lowered his lips to the white tile and sucked in what he could.

After that, he drank as much water as his stomach would take and then fumbled through his pills. Eventually, he squeezed a small plastic bottle between the heels of his hands and twisted the cap off with his teeth.

He swept the glass aside with a towel and blew his nose and sat for a while on the toilet. He took a shower, careful to use the handrail when he stepped into the tub. He dozed a little in the warm spray.

When he pulled back the curtain and got out, he felt a tiny bit of glass stinging his foot like a pinprick. He didn't mind the pain. It reassured him. He thought he'd probably be okay.

He ate eggs and drank coffee and then went over to Ben's. The old man took a long time to answer the door. His face was pasty. "Woke up under the weather," he said. "Got a bum ticker." He shuffled out on the porch in his robe and slippers and handed over the keys and took a minute to look at the lake before going back inside.

Now, on the water, he keeps the skiff at low throttle – the sky cloudy but showing no signs of rain. He runs slow and remembers the cold wind out of the northwest that had once made him shiver. On this boat, he doesn't worry about a winch handle or choosing the right moment to come about. He peers out over the bow and knows that he can keep this heading until he's used up half his fuel. He sees the changing colors of the lake, the deep water ahead, and the light at Port Austin Reef.

It's a wooden boat, lovingly restored, he thinks. It's the old man's dream – a last stand against failure.

Running straight out and going slow, he watches for a sign, an indication that he's passed this way before. He feels his body rising and falling, the skiff beating against the current and in some way holding its own.

He knows he should be grateful for the lake's hard beauty – his father embraced it always – but on this day it seems cruel, almost lonely. He tries to stay calm. He wants to hold everything in check, but he feels a pressure in his chest, his heart pounding, and beads of sweat roll down his back.

Without warning, a thin wall within him suddenly gives way. He wants to break something with his hands, to bulldoze long stretches of the past and start building again from the ground up.

He dreams of pouring the lake away. He wants to dam out all water and walk the singlehander's course from Port Huron to Mackinac Island, cataloging the shipwrecks, mapping the caves and trenches, listening as whispers rise up from the seaweed and debris. He wants to search the naked lake bed, cursing the light, cursing the darkness, following the scavengers that circle overhead, their shrill voices calling, until he finds the lost pile of teeth and bones, the bleached remains of his father's body.

He imagines his father grieving, marking the last miles home, steering by clouds and the hunches of birds. He sees him struggling against the weight of canvas, against the sailboat which was once his body. He seems confused by sudden mistakes, errors in judgment, as he watches for the light at Port Austin Reef and tacks across the lake, across its curved and breathing shoulder, checking the channel for big ships, their sad captains thinking of November, ice forming on deserted decks, storms, a long night, and then the shutting down.

He'd like one more day with his father. He'd walk with him on a seawall and force him to speak.

I want to know what was in you, he thinks. What in the end was hard to keep and what was easy to let go? Did you forget the boatswain on his watch, the crow's nest communing with clouds, losing your head and then your footing?

Was it the lake that claimed you? Or was it the last groping for words? You took no time to explain.

Did you reach for lines strung from the light – lines that promised new breath? Did you pull and climb?

What did you think when the weight of your body betrayed you?

Or did you pray?

The skiff rises and falls on steady swells and the fear rising in him is the fear of deep water. "Lord, create in us changed lives," he says to no one, " – even as we drink deep, and thirst, and drink again – whatever the cost."

Now he dreams himself aboard his father's boat, just after the storm, a sea of diamonds flashing at every stir. He paces the cockpit and keeps watch, waiting for spectral arms to reach up from beneath the hull, waiting with broken hands to somehow touch his father, to hold him fast, the boat ghosting and then leaning, for the last time.

He can feel his hands shaking. He grips the wheel and tries to steady himself.

The swells keep coming – four feet, maybe, or five. His stomach churns. He's stayed out too long. Even if he goes farther, he won't find the thing he wants. He remembers being here as a boy and the nausea rising to his throat. He shudders. No boats on the water for as far as anyone can see. Not a soul raising a sail or letting an engine unwind.

He turns the skiff and sees the light at Port Austin Reef. The swells suddenly seem larger, the boat bobbing like a cork on a rippling pond. He looks beyond the light and wonders for a moment if he can regain the shore. Then he pushes the throttle and the pitch of the motor rises and the old wooden boat leaps forward.

c h a p t e r   t e n

HE DRIVES back the way he came, hitting potholes and sudden downpours, the bones behind his knuckles burning. Pills would help, but he can't take them now if he wants to get home in one piece. He watches the road going and feels bad about using Ben's boat and not paying for it. He should've insisted or left some money in the old man's mailbox. He squeezes the wheel. He opens and closes one hand and then the other. Nothing helps.

He punches the cigarette lighter. He opens both windows and turns up the radio. He pulls out the lighter and glances at the heating element glowing red. He presses it against the skin of his forearm. He holds it there, grunting, the smell of singed hair filling his nostrils.

He likes the sensation. It's more immediate, more urgent, than the misery of his hands. He slows the pickup and breathes. He concentrates on the welt – a bull's-eye of pain – and makes it all the way to Gibraltar without stopping.

TURNING the corner, he sees that his driveway is empty, no station wagon there or anywhere in sight. He pulls into the garage and quickly closes the door.

He goes inside and finds the house in immaculate condition.

He gapes, both confused and astonished, as he walks through each room and observes the sharp lines, the absence of clutter, and the vacuum tracks still visible on the faded rugs. He realizes that the landlord, her wondrous body still wrapped in his bathrobe, had seized the moment of his leaving, the opportunity of an empty house, and taken it upon herself to do a late spring cleaning.

It appears that she washed, folded, and stacked his laundry. She organized his closet and placed his shoes in a smart row. She sponged the kitchen counters, wiped the refrigerator shelves, and scrubbed the stainless steel sink. Miraculously, she lifted mildew and flushed away lime until the smallest details of the bathroom – tile, grout, and chrome – sparkled and gleamed.

After inspecting the rooms and making certain that the landlord didn't leave a message – checking the pad next to the phone book, his pillow, and the corners of the bedroom mirror – he begins to calm down. Heather's senior portrait, though straightened a bit, is in the same spot. So are Jen's black-and-white pictures. Then, from the hallway, he notices a string of black beads on the coffee table. She wasn't wearing a necklace, he thinks. He walks over and sees that she's left him a rosary. He picks it up and the crucifix swings back and forth like a pendulum. The figure of Jesus is tiny but exquisitely detailed. He can discern the crown of thorns, the anguished face, and the nails through the hands and feet.

He drops the rosary on the table and the body of Jesus disappears under a pile of beads. He needs a drink. He stumbles to the freezer and yanks the door open and lets out a sigh of relief, glad to discover that his old bottle, half empty, is still next to the ice tray where he left it. He fills a tumbler.

He sets his duffel bag on the counter and tries to unzip it. His fingers refuse to work. He reaches for a carving knife but fails to draw it swiftly and easily out of the block. He makes another attempt and manages to wedge the handle between his thumb and palm. He slits the bag. He chooses a small plastic bottle filled with codeine and puts it on the cutting board. He positions the bottle beneath the wide surface of the blade and then brings his fist down as if he were crushing garlic. The plastic cracks. The lid flies off and skitters across the floor. He swallows three capsules, washing the pills down with mouthfuls of vodka.

He sits on the couch and absorbs the perfect order of the house. He can tell, even at this distance, that his guitar case has been carefully dusted. The air smells good, too – not stale at all, despite all the windows being closed and locked. He stares at the pile of beads next to the neat stack of magazines. He drinks. He thinks about Heather and his father's boat. After a while, he stops thinking. He's no longer aware of his hands. He rests his head on the back of the couch and sleeps.

He hears a thud, his eyes blinking and squinting at the bright light. The floor pitches and the furniture blurs. Not a thing wants to stay in one place. The thud comes again. It's like a log hitting the keel – but he's not on the boat. He's nowhere near the water.

He shuts his eyes and tries to feel his body. His legs seem to be intact. The same goes for his chest, shoulders, and arms. Only his hands are missing.

Another thud, louder this time, jerks him awake like a door closing.

He sits up and everything in the room shifts; the noise strikes him now as a steady thump, a knocking – someone on the porch. Who could it be at this hour? Why is the window flooded with light?

He drags himself off the sofa and shuffles to the door. He throws the dead bolt. He sees red and a patch of blue, then the glare outside blinds him. He shields his eyes and squints at the dark outline floating beyond the screen.

"Well, you look like death," says Brian.

He hears the words and the unmistakable voice. "But you're not here," he says. "You can't be."

"It's me," says Brian, stepping over the threshold. "I'm here. You're the one who looks gone."

He turns and stumbles and Brian catches him.

"You gonna make it?" says Brian.

"Water," he says. "I'd like some water."

Brian helps him to the couch. Then he goes into the kitchen and runs the faucet and fills a glass.

He stares at Brian. He takes the water, his hand trembling, and drinks all of it without stopping to breathe.

"Rough night?" says Brian.

"I don't remember," he says.

"You left pills all over the counter."

"I was driving. My hands were bad."

"How are they now?"

"Okay. No pain at all." He wiggles his fingers. "It's been a while."

Brian jingles the keys in his pocket. "I didn't mean to bust in and give you a scare," he says.

"Where'd you come from?"

"We're in Ann Arbor. At the Bird of Paradise. Being that close, I figured I should visit."

"Oh. The Bird . . . ," he says, his voice trailing off.

"I found Maureen before I found you."

He opens and closes his hands.

"You smell bad," says Brian. "And you look like shit."

"Yeah. Good to see you, too," he says.

Brian laughs and takes in the room. "But you're keeping house pretty well."

"I haven't been here," he says.

"I know," says Brian. "I called all weekend. Left a few messages."

"I went up north," he says. "Port Austin."

"How was it?"

He rubs the back of his neck. "It's not there anymore. Not really."

"Why don't you come to the Bird?" says Brian. "I could send a car for you. The gigs are better these days."

"I hear it's the Brian James Trio."

"How'd you know?"

"I may look it," he says, "but I'm not dead."

"Listen, Cole, I got all day. If you shower and put on some clean clothes, I'll buy you lunch."

"Thanks. I don't think I can eat anything."

"Then you can drink water while I eat."

He rises from the couch. "I've got some unfinished business at Humbug. I should get over there."

"What unfinished business?"

"My father's boat."

"But it sank."

"So you had a long talk with Maureen."

"Long enough," says Brian. "All right, be ungrateful. But you gotta stop by the Bird."

"I will."

"You can't say that and then not show up."

"I won't."

"You won't show?"

"I'll be there," he says.

"We're on the rest of the week."

"I got it." He sees Brian step toward the door. "How long has it been?" he says.

Brian turns. "Eight years, I guess. Or nine."

"Thanks," he says, putting his hand on Brian's shoulder.

Brian hugs him and lifts him off the floor. "I'll watch for you," he says.

"I'll be better in a few days."

Brian nods and walks out onto the porch. "They've busted up your street," he says. Then he gets serious. "If you want to, bring your guitar."

He looks over Brian's shoulder at the red backhoe parked in front of the house. He lowers his eyes. "That's a generous offer," he says.

"Hardly that," says Brian. "If anything, it's selfish."

"See you in a couple days."

Brian lets out a deep breath. "I hope so," he says.

HE ARRIVES at Humbug late in the afternoon and finds his father's boat resting in a small cradle made of steel, a modular system with four vertical legs, two on each side, to support the hull. The legs telescope to the correct height and culminate in a hull pad; the pad rides on a universal joint allowing for a snug fit. A ground frame lies beneath the boat with retainers and blocks under the keel.

He's seen cradles like this before with the legs locking in two or three positions, but this one appears to be homemade, a knockoff of a more expensive design. He notices that each leg fits into a shallow socket on the frame and that it's secured with a bolt, a lock washer, and a nut, allowing, he supposes, for infinite angles and easy adjustment but also for the possibility of slippage. It's a clever but thin rig, he thinks. He decides it's not much better than his previous setup. His wood cradle was rickety, of course – the yard manager must've thought it was shot – but it had kept the boat high and dry for five years.

He puts his foot on one of the legs and tries to give it a shake. It doesn't move. Pretty solid, he says to himself. But he's not convinced. The tubular steel looks flimsy. It seems to him that someone with a heavy boot could kick the cradle to pieces. "It'd be simple," he whispers, "like knocking a leg out from under a table."

He knows he'll need a ladder to get on board, but he chooses to leave that for another time. He doesn't want to go up there now. He has no stomach for throwing himself over the gunwale and stepping into the cockpit. He considers it unwise to open the cabin on an overcast day with a dank smell coming up from below. If he went aboard, he'd feel the boat trembling in its new cradle and glimpse the darkness belowdecks, the gray light piling up like unclean water. At this hour, on the old trembling boat, going down the companionway would be hopeless. Trying to see precisely what happened, trying to see anything at all, would be a hopeless effort. He doesn't want it. He'll leave things just as they are.

HE DRIVES to the Lighthouse Diner, parks in front, and sits in his pickup until Heather, taking an order, glances out the window and recognizes the truck. He watches her as she unties her apron and says a few words to the other waitress. A customer holds the door open and she steps over the threshold and onto the sidewalk. She walks slowly and stops at the curb.

"You still mad?" he says.

"Sometimes," she says. She hooks her thumb on a belt loop.

"Why won't you answer my calls?"

"Mom said you were drinking again."

"I always drink."

"She said you were drunk."

"I've only had water today."

"Should I be impressed?"

"No."

"You look terrible."

He nods. "You look beautiful."

She almost smiles. "Are you working on the boat?"

"No." He catches her eyes but then she turns away. "Are you leaving soon?" he says.

"A week from Monday."

"Can I drive you to the airport?"

She drops her head. "Mom already said she would."

"Okay," he says. "What are you doin' Saturday?"

"Don't know," she says.

"Are you working?"

"No."

"Well, what would you say if I told you we could see Brian James?"

Her face lights up for a second, but then she shrugs. "I think there's a party Saturday night."

"C'mon. Let your old man take you out on the town. He's playing in Ann Arbor."

She comes closer to the door. "At the Bird of Paradise?"

"At the Bird."

She balances on the curb. "I'll have to make a couple of calls."

"I'm sorry," he says. "It's pretty short notice. We could have dinner first and get there for the late show."

"What time would you wanna leave?"

"Let's go in your car," he says. "We shouldn't roll up at the Bird in a dusty truck."

She smiles. "Sure."

"Then it's a date," he says. "Pick me up around six."

She hears people coming out of the diner. "I gotta go," she says.

"Saturday," he says, starting the engine.

Heather runs around the other side of the pickup and leans into the cab and kisses him on the cheek. He lets her slip away and then sees her again inside the diner wrapping herself in a clean white apron.

He listens to the truck's smooth idle and imagines sitting in with Brian at the Bird of Paradise. To get there, I'll have to start now, he thinks, opening both hands and pushing his fingers against the wheel. He congratulates himself for having the courage to invite Heather, but then he's bothered by second thoughts. Having her on board means he can't change his mind. If he runs into a problem, there's no easy way out.

Pulling away, he feels an urge to keep going, to find the place where she once needed him – a night when she couldn't sleep and cried for a story or a song. And where in the world was that place? he wonders. Was I young then? And how young was she? He wants to remember when music was a fast-running stream, an unspoken prayer, when his fingers pressing lightly on the strings could make something beautiful and whole. Now, the music like water eludes him – his daughter, too.

WHEN he gets home, he gathers up the pills in the kitchen, pours the remaining vodka down the drain, and rinses the one glass he used the night before. He runs the water until it's cold. He bends and puts his mouth under the faucet and drinks more than he thought his stomach could hold. He tosses his dirty clothes in the laundry and throws out his duffel bag. He plumps up and arranges the sofa's green pillows. He wants to keep the house exactly as the landlord left it.

Below the sink in the bathroom, he finds a bar of lavender soap. He doesn't know how it came to be there. He peels off the plastic wrap, his fingers stiff but able, and carefully lays the bar in the soap dish on the rim of the tub.

He showers in cool water, enjoying the spray on his neck and back, the narrow streams falling down his body like silk. He lathers his arms and chest and fills himself with the scent of lavender. He lets out a deep breath and feels wobbly. He leans against the tile wall and tries to focus on the bottle of shampoo and, next to that, the razor. The dizziness passes and he bows his head beneath the drenching nozzle – the water rushing and bubbling in his ears.

He sleeps that night without disturbing the bed and brews coffee in the morning before making oatmeal for breakfast. After washing his bowl and spoon, he sits at the table and makes a shopping list. He'll go to the market and bring home fish, vegetables, and rice – maybe some pork. He'll set a small basket on the counter and fill it with tomatoes and peaches.

Over the next couple of days, he establishes a routine. He showers in the early morning and again in the evening. He cooks uncomplicated meals and eats in the kitchen. He drinks hot tea or bottled water. When he finishes what he's doing in a particular room, or in a particular corner of that room, he immediately picks up after himself. He keeps the newspapers and magazines in separate piles. If he moves the footstool or a chair, then he uses the markings on the rug to put it back in its proper place.

Having changed the strings and adjusted the neck, he takes his guitar out of the case and plays for two hours in the morning and two hours in the afternoon, his mind blank but his fingers remembering. By the fourth day, his left hand is surprisingly nimble, and the ache in both hands is almost dull, manageable, a pain he can live with, at least for the moment, without pills.

BY SATURDAY at six he feels a year or two younger. He stands at the picture window and waits for Heather to appear. He smells rain on the air, the sky darkening to the northwest. It makes him glad that the house is in good order. He can leave and lock the door and not be preoccupied. Humbug remains, of course, tasking him like a paper cut, but he won't think about the boat until tomorrow or the next day.

Heather pulls into the driveway. He slips into his sport coat, picks up his guitar, and walks out onto the porch. He rotates the key and hears the dead bolt click.

"I don't believe it," she says, stepping out of the car.

"What?"

She points at his guitar. "You're going to play?"

"Maybe."

"Don't be a tease," she says. "You've already made up your mind – otherwise, you wouldn't bring it."

He walks down the steps and marvels at her confidence, the perfect ease of her movements. "It's good to see you," he says.

She hugs him. "Thanks."

He holds her tight. "I'm glad you came," he says.

"I would've said yes right off if you'd told me you were going to sit in."

He smiles. "How do I look?"

"You clean up nice."

He puts his guitar in the backseat. "Boy, you even got it washed," he says, seeing his reflection in the roof of the car.

"It's clean," she says. "But don't open the trunk."

"I won't."

She takes in the sky. "Those are some mean clouds. Did you remember your windows?"

"They're all set."

He watches the way she turns the key in the ignition and drops the car into reverse, checking the mirrors and then glancing over her shoulder. She drives – talking all the way to Ann Arbor about her ambitions for school and how much she'll worry about him while she's away.

"Without you here," he says, "there's not much reason to stay."

"What about the boat?"

He shrugs.

"You can't sell it," she says.

"No. I suppose not."

"What then?"

"Leave it in the yard, I guess. It seems to like it there."

"Where would you go?" she says.

"Not sure. Maybe Chicago." He notices the blinker on the dashboard flashing.

She changes lanes. "And you'd start playing again?"

He laughs. "No. I don't think so."

"You should see a new doctor – a young doctor – about your hands. I bet there's some sort of modern therapy you could get."

He looks at his crooked fingers. "I could probably find a lot of young doctors in Chicago."

She stops at the traffic light. "You'll never go."

"You never know," he says. "But in the meantime I could find a better job."

"Like what?"

"Does it matter?"

"You say it matters for me."

"It does. It's your time."

She gives the keys to the handsome valet who opens the door and stares at her legs when she slides out of the car.

He takes his guitar into the restaurant and requests the table for four at the edge of the room directly across from the bar. He asks the hostess, despite her obvious displeasure, to remove the extra chair on the side where he'll be sitting. He sets his guitar there and leans it against the wall.

Heather catches the waiter's eye. The young man stops and asks her if she'd like a drink. She orders a Coke.

He glances at the waiter. "I'm fine with water," he says, then waits for the guy to leave. "I know I've said it before, but I'm sorry about graduation."

"Is his mother suing you?"

"Not that I know of."

"You caught me off guard," she says. "It wasn't like anything I'd ever seen you do."

He nods.

"Do you have a secret life?" she says. "Do you put on a mask and go out at night and look for damsels in distress?"

"What if I did?" he says.

"I'd say you were silly."

"Now you sound like your mother."

"Ouch."

"Well, what if I did make up my mind to go out and do things – help the needy – or get a cat down out of a tree?"

"I'd be worried," she says. "Especially for the cat."

He laughs. "Okay, we're even."

The waiter delivers the drinks and then lingers.

"Give us a few minutes," he says. "We haven't opened the menu."

Heather watches the waiter turn to the next table. "I don't need protecting, you know."

"Are you sure?"

"I can take care of myself."

"I know. But I think you started too young. If I'd been there – "

She bends the straw in her drink. "Let's not talk about that."

"I don't completely understand it myself," he says. "When I saw that kid try to grab you, when I heard what he said, a part of me gave way – it was like a door or a floorboard cracking. I couldn't stop myself." He sips his water. "At first, it didn't strike me as foolish."

"If I tell you something," she says, "you have to promise not to tell Mom."

"No chance," he says.

"When it happened, I was embarrassed – mortified, really. But afterward, a part of me felt another way – almost proud."

"You don't have to say that."

"I'm not making it up," she says. "Mom goes on about how it was a crazy and pathetic thing to do. And it was crazy. And then, at the same time, it felt like you didn't care about anything else but me."

"That's kind," he says.

"No," she says. "It's true."

"I wish we could go back," he says, "and start over."

"Why?"

"So I could be there more and make you feel safe."

"You did enough of that," she says. "Why go back? We'd all be the same anyway. Do you want me to be different?"

"No," he says. "I can't imagine you any other way."

She smiles. "Then there's no point in going back."

THEY take their seats at the Bird of Paradise just as Brian walks into the spotlight and welcomes the audience.

Heather fools with the position of her chair and then leans toward the stage, her eyes bright with seeing Brian after so many years.

The piano begins the set with a cascade of notes that calls up the ghost of Art Tatum. After twelve bars, the hi-hat kicks in, crisp and steady, and then

Brian runs up from below. At a right angle to the piano is an electronic keyboard. The guy playing reaches over as the music builds and lets fly a few heartbreaking riffs, the lines fluid and deep and sounding like they've come from an old Hammond organ.

Brian's solo is modest, creating a generous field for both the piano and drums. The trio is tight, cleaner and purer than anyone would think possible, and what comes through right away is the wisdom of Brian's mature style, how he listens for each nuance and keeps himself open to mood, color, and movement. When Brian drops in a new idea, the drummer smiles and tries to answer with something fresh.

The good listeners in the crowd, those who've followed the trio's progress, understand that Brian can stay back or step forward with perfect ease. For Brian, it's not a question anymore of showing what he can do. It's an effort now to be true to the song, to stay with it and find its direction. He's learned to acquiesce, to let go, and no warm-up appears to be necessary. He surrenders to the sound and rhythm and in doing so finds a place for himself that feels right.

The next tune pays homage to Charlie Parker, an incredibly fast, dense, and elliptical charge with the hands of all three players moving in a constant blur. He lets it wash over him and remembers some of the ancient bluesmen in Chicago talking in a scattershot and cryptic street language that seemed to mimic the bebop phrasing of Parker's saxophone. He hears it now in the conversation between Brian's bass licks and the sharp, staccato cries of the piano. He glances at Heather – she rocks back and forth and her head dips and then rises – and he wants to ask her exactly what she hears. He senses now that the audience is on board and the trio, taking the opportunity, works to keep everyone together, pulling the crowd through waves of emotion and energy, carrying them far from shore and then returning them to a place they recognize as both familiar and new.

With the set two-thirds gone, Brian calls him to the stage.

Heather, already moved by the music, kisses him on the cheek and whispers, "I'll be listening," her voice wavering, tearful, filled with a smoky kind of joy.

He plugs in and tunes and hears Brian's voice but not the introduction itself and then Brian wipes his face with a towel and turns to the musicians and says, "Let's go easy and find a groove. Blues in E."

He looks at Brian and takes a deep breath as Brian counts off the beat.

At first, his fingers won't cooperate, all of them heavy and stiff, almost clumsy, but as the piano and bass move through their turns he starts to feel loose, getting off fills and phrases that surprise him for their voicings and speed. When Brian points to him for the next solo, he takes off and plays three or four choruses, working higher and higher on the neck, enjoying a strong and youthful momentum. In the middle, he catches a glimpse of Heather at the table, her head tilted to one side, a look of quiet satisfaction on her face. The drummer grabs the last lead and does the run-up to the end and the final chord vanishes in a glittering crash of cymbals.

He wants to celebrate his good fortune. He realizes that he can't make some of his old moves, but when an inspiration comes, he finds other ways to compensate. He smiles at Brian. "What's next?"

"I'll think of something," says Brian. Then he turns to the audience and speaks into the microphone. "We'd like to feature Coleman Moore on this next tune – a classic from Brazil that Cole and I played when we were young – 'Manha de Carnaval,' otherwise known as 'Black Orpheus.'"

Coleman begins without accompaniment, making the first notes a plaintive and legato whisper. Then the drums step in with a stammering rhythm, a mellow samba, and the guitar repeats the opening measures, this time with a feel that's cool and lyrical. He opens his eyes and sees that the magic of the bossa nova has transformed the room into a sultry, smoke-filled bistro with the people, the tables, and the walls all beginning to sway. A woman approaches the stage with a camera. He notices her black hair and the sculpted line of her shoulders. He blinks and clears his head.

He listens as the piano carries the theme through the first verse and chorus. In response, he creates a descant and touches on a few harmonies, hinting at variations to come. Later, during Brian's solo, a spiral of descending registers, he plays short bursts of the melody, eruptions of fire, while his guitar seems to shift and change, the body and neck somehow growing pliant, supple – even weightless.

He takes over after that, ascending in scales like a man climbing out of darkness. Following each phrase, he lets out an exhalation of breath, almost a groan, and listens in the next beat, in the brief space of silence, hoping for reassurance, for the echo of someone moving and breathing nearby.

He forgets his hands and the slow plodding of his feet, and then, as the room fills with audible light, the music soaring, he lifts his fingers, a slight hesitation, and sees that the stage has suddenly become a boundary, a far shore, where he waits in silence and bends his ear to the wind and finally looks back, knowing in that instant that he's turned too soon, a lack of faith, of judgment, always and again, the melody straining and falling away, disappearing on the air like dust.

Sensing the turn, Brian finds him and buoys him up, the long dark notes like water. Then, reasserting his presence, relying on the precision of his hands, Brian pulls on short melodic lines strung from the light, his fingers striding between strings and discovering new patterns, his progress steady, the bass growing brighter, more poised, as he bridges the distance between the guitar and drums.

Coleman bows his head and drifts, giving himself to the sound, surrounding himself with it, a union more complete than harmony. In that moment, even as the music fades, he feels whole, utterly at peace, utterly cleansed.

AFTERWARD, with most of the crowd having gone, he orders a shot of vodka on ice and sits with Heather and sips his drink. The woman with the camera and dark hair stops at the table and asks if she can take another picture. He puts his arm around Heather and the flash fires.

"Are you coming out?" says the woman.

"Pardon me?" he says.

"Of retirement. Brian James said in his introduction – "

"I never retired," he says.

The woman smiles. "Then you're planning a comeback?"

"Nothing quite so ambitious."

"But you do intend to play."

"Maybe. But not to make a living."

"Then how will anyone hear you?"

He shrugs.

She smiles again and waits for an answer. When it doesn't materialize, she taps her finger on the table like an impatient schoolteacher.

"Is there anything else?" he says.

"Comebacks take a lot out of a man."

"I imagine they do."

"How old is she?" says the woman, still smiling.

He puts down his drink.

"You're outrageous bringing her here," says the woman. "You could be arrested."

Heather's face goes sour. "I'm his daughter," she says.

The woman laughs. "Nice try, sweetie." Then she scowls and stamps off.

Heather scoots over and rests her head on his shoulder. "I'm sorry," she says.

"For what? It's not your fault."

"I know. But I wanted to stay and talk about the songs – enjoy it with you for a while."

"It's okay."

"No, it's not."

"Really. It's fine. It's a good reminder."

"But she ruined it."

"No." He shakes his head. "She can't. Let's talk about something else."

"It was strange," says Heather.

"What?"

"Seeing you and Brian together. I mean – the last time I must've been only seven or eight."

He stares at his glass.

"But there were moments tonight when you seemed like two parts of the same person – like you were moving in him and he was moving in you."

"Is that what it looked like?"

"No. That's what it sounded like." Heather sweeps her hair to one side. "Was it always like that?"

"Maybe it was."

Heather's words make him think of Jennifer and the first nights that he worked with Brian at the Green Mill. He remembers the small, awkward stage, the thick smoke, and his firm belief that no one would stay for the second or third set.

He sees Jen drinking bourbon over ice, her camera waiting on the table. And he thinks of her now in Tobermory and of the last time they spoke, a phone conversation just after midnight, a cold New Year's Eve.

"You should be celebrating," she said.

He heard the concern in her voice. "I am."

"I always hated New Year's Eve," she said.

"Me, too."

"You did not. You liked the bigger paycheck."

"That's true."

She didn't say anything then, so he raised his pint and took a quick pull. "I'm surprised you weren't asleep," he said.

"I was."

"Sorry."

"Is there a reason other than New Year's?" she said.

"I keep seeing a picture of yours. A bench in Chicago. I can't get it out of my head."

"I didn't think you liked that picture."

"Did I say that?"

"I don't remember. You never said it was good."

"It's better than that," he said.

"Cole," she said, "you should come up here. Stay as long as you want."

"You'd do that?"

"Just drop everything and come up."

"I'd have to explain to Heather," he said.

"I know."

"And the boat still needs work."

"What difference does that make? It's not going anywhere."

"Maybe I will," he said.

"Good," she said. "Anytime."

In the morning, he couldn't remember hanging up or saying good-bye. He meant to call her, of course, but then winter dragged itself into April, and he only went as far as the yard at Humbug.

The waitress stops for last call and he asks for bottled water. Heather orders coffee. Brian comes over and takes a seat at the table.

"You were incredible," says Heather.

"Thanks," says Brian. "But your old man brought down the house." Brian smiles. "How was it for you?"

"Like before," he says. "Only better."

Brian nods. "Too bad we closed tonight. I'd invite you back."

"You around tomorrow?"

"No. Early flight out."

The waitress returns. Heather clears a small space on the table. "But you'll be playing here again," she says.

"I suppose," says Brian. "Don't know when though."

"I'd like it if you could stay," says Heather.

"Watch out, Brian. She's playing the guilt card."

"No I'm not."

"It's all right. It won't work on Brian any better than me." He watches as she stirs her coffee. "That really smells good."

"Want a sip?" says Heather.

"Sure." He savors the aroma. The coffee looks very black inside the white cup.

"I'll see you," says Brian, offering his hand across the table.

He takes it and feels glad, his gnarled hand almost disappearing in Brian's grip. "Thanks," he says. "For everything."

Brian lets go. He kisses Heather on the cheek. She hugs him. Then Brian stands and turns and slips out the door without looking back.

Walking to the car, they hear thunder groaning in the distance. The storm has come and gone, leaving large puddles like mirrors on the asphalt. He catches a glimpse of himself together with his guitar and Heather. The parking lot is empty. The fresh-scrubbed air smells like honeysuckle.

"Are you tired?" he says.

Heather puts her arm around him. "I'm a little sleepy."

"Give me the keys," he says. "I'll drive."

HE FEELS close to a hangover in the morning, though he'd taken only one drink, a tiny shot of vodka, at the Bird. He opens the fridge and manages the carton of orange juice without much pain. He brews tea and toasts a plain bagel. He washes the fork, knife, and salad plate he'd left in the sink.

He showers, puts on a clean T-shirt and jeans, and makes the bed.

He brings in boxes from the garage and begins to pack all the tapes and photographs of the CBT Trio. He pulls out and takes down all of Jen's loose pictures and places them carefully between the pages of a scrapbook. He pauses over the three images in the black frames – an ethereal, onstage shot of Brian and two self-portraits of Jen. He pads each of these with thick paper and slides them into the carton.

He dumps the contents of his dresser drawer on the bed and picks up his grandfather's letter and carries it out to the patio. He strikes a match and holds it to the corner of the envelope. Then he drops the letter into a metal can and watches it flare up and curl into ashes.

After that, he looks through folders of old arrangements, chord charts, and original songs. He comes across his cardboard "Circle-O-Keys" slide rule and is amazed to discover that it was published in 1957 on North Wacker Drive in Chicago. He packs it with a blues harp and his antique pitch pipe.

Starting a new box, he takes down his photograph of Wes Montgomery and wraps it several times in a thin blanket. He thinks of Otis and Lucille's sister and for a moment gives free play to his recollections, trying to gather up and keep what details he can: Otis in a white shirt and black pants waiting at the screen door, the dozen or so grips that he knew for every chord, his sense of time, the ease of being with him, his belief in a student's will, his faith.

He seals the carton and carries it into the living room and sets it on the stack next to his amplifier and guitar.

He empties his closet, the medicine cabinet, and several of the kitchen drawers and crams the stuff into suitcases, backpacks, and shopping bags. He slips Heather's picture into a briefcase along with a short stack of letters and a crayon valentine that she'd made somewhere in the past.

He runs out at midday to the Blue Moon Market for a sandwich, bottled water, and a pint of vodka. He wolfs down the smoked turkey on wheat in the parking lot and chugs the cool water. He stops at the gas station and fills the tank and squeegees the windows. When he returns to the house, he puts the vodka in the freezer.

In the afternoon, he sweeps the garage, ties up newspapers and magazines, and tosses out a dull tin snips and a corroded screwdriver. He decides to bequeath his workbench to the next tenant. He organizes his toolbox and loads a heavy length of towing chain into the rear of the pickup. He'd been lugging the chain from one side of the garage to the other for years now, after using it to pull out a stump for Maureen and then thinking he'd someday haul it to Humbug and just leave it in the yard.

He eats a bowl of cornflakes for dinner.

He showers. He trims and files his nails before picking up his guitar and playing into the evening and well beyond sunset, the amplifier low and the door closed so as not to disturb the neighbors.

He unplugs at midnight and lays his guitar in its case. He goes into the kitchen and washes his hands and sets a glass on the counter and pours two fingers of vodka. He drinks. He grabs his keys, walks out to his truck, and opens the garage door.

WHEN he rolls in at Humbug – driving slow with the headlights off, gravel crunching beneath his tires – he listens for the sound of voices. He notices three cars in the lot. Sleepovers, he thinks. They should be dead to the world at this hour.

Now, at the height of summer, except for a few wrecks and his father's boat, the yard looks deserted, a vacant lot flooded with moonlight. Everything he sees is black, gray, or white. He peers at the shadows and waits for the slightest movement, a brief glimmer or a shifting outline. No ghosts tonight, he thinks.

He turns around and backs the pickup toward the middle of the boat, stopping a short distance from the starboard side. He shuts off the engine and grabs the pliers and box wrench that he'd placed on the passenger seat after packing his tools.

He kneels at the forward leg of the cradle and for a moment looks up. Curving away from him is an endless expanse of white. He clamps the pliers on the head of the bolt and slips the wrench over the nut. His hands are warm and without pain. He leans forward, letting the weight of his shoulders do the work, and the nut gives way. After two more rotations, he spins it off, removes the lock washer, and slowly slides out the bolt. The leg, a slim shaft bearing the load of his father's boat, stays in its socket. He lets out a breath – almost laughing – and sweat drips off his forehead. At the aft leg, repeating the process, he listens hard for any unexpected creak or groan.

He opens the tailgate and drags out the heavy chain and lets it drop to the ground. He finds the red link in the middle of the chain and hooks it to the towing bar. He yanks one end toward the bow, loops the chain around the forward leg, and runs it back. He pulls the other end toward the stern and loops the aft leg.

Suddenly, a thin squeal strikes his ear. He freezes. He stares at the white hull, the moonlight icing it down, but nothing comes to him except the river and his breathing. He hooks both ends of the chain to the truck's chassis.

He checks the marina. The boats in their wells are motionless; no one seems to be stirring. He starts the engine and creeps forward until there's plenty of clearance and no more slack in the chain. Then he puts the truck in low gear. He leans out the window and turns, craning his neck for the best view.

He presses the gas pedal. He feels a mild strain and the cradle's legs pop out like toothpicks.

The boat shudders. It tips and moans. It wavers for a split second as if it were struggling to right itself, and then it falls on its side like a beached whale, the keel snapping and the hull splitting, the boom and the unstepped mast spilling into the yard.

LATER, having returned to the house, his hands and face washed, he lies down and drifts, the gray light enfolding him, all the noise and debris collapsing into silence. He wonders if this is what it means to be entirely at peace.

He tries to speak with the ferryman but feels a weight on his tongue like silver. He chokes on the coin. He spits it out.

In the next instant, the ferry shudders, it pitches and rolls. He loses his grip and slips over into darkness. He falls with the efficiency of stone, dropping until he can no longer stomach the sensation, until his arms and legs begin thrashing and kicking, his fingers reaching for a line, a narrow ledge, first slowing and then stopping his descent.

After a time, he finds himself floating, suspended between two worlds. An ache for breath, for speech, swells in his throat. Weight and resistance fall away. He opens his eyes to the gray light. "You can scuttle the boat," someone says.

Finally, before dawn, drifting on a white whale, he hears something familiar – a thud. It sounds like a wet sandbag hitting the galley floor. He turns and moves toward the companionway. Nothing there. He starts making a list; *shattered hull* is the first item, then *broken rudder* and *bent shaft*. He wants to forget, to sleep without worry or fear. The noise comes again like a fist punching a wall or a door closing. What can he do but choose? The only way is to choose – take sides with truth or memory, sanity or madness, the real or the imagined. But how will he separate one from the other?

A footfall thumps in his ear. He stares at the companionway. No shadows or shifting outlines. Nothing now but a clear passage.

A clamor in the air wakes him.

He sits up and throws his legs over the side of the bed. He yawns. He scratches the stubble on his face. It occurs to him now that that pounding isn't just in his head. He puts on his jeans and a clean shirt and walks barefoot into the living room. He hears Maureen's voice between the knocking. "Jason," she says. "Jason, are you there?"

He opens the door.

"Your bell's not working," she says. "Where were you?"

"In bed."

"You never sleep this late," she says. "I would've called – but I was on my way out and I drove past Humbug – "

"Come in," he says. "It's too bright on the porch."

Maureen steps into the house. "Jason, I hate to be the one to tell you – "

"Don't call me Jason," he says, cutting her off.

She furrows her brow. "It's your name."

"It's not my first choice."

"For God's sake, Jas – "

He raises his hand.

"All right," she says. "I'll try."

"Thank you," he says. "Now. What's the problem?"

"Your boat fell over."

"It did?"

"It bit the dust. It's in the yard this minute lying on its side."

He rubs the knuckles of his left hand. "Thanks for letting me know."

"Is that all you're going to say?"

He starts for the kitchen. "Would you like some coffee?" he says.

Impatience seeps into her face. "No. I don't want coffee. You have to get down there."

"For what?"

"I don't know. Talk to somebody. Find out what happened. You'll have to call the insurance company."

"It's not insured."

"What do you mean?" she says. "Of course it's insured."

"No. I let the coverage lapse. It was that or child support."

Then Maureen sees the boxes, bags, and suitcases sitting next to his amplifier and guitar. She leans against the sofa to steady herself. "Where are you going?"

"I'm leaving."

Maureen doesn't say anything after that. Her eyes seem suddenly surprised by the bare walls.

He goes into the kitchen. She follows.

"You sure you don't want some coffee?" He spoons fresh grounds into a French press. "What are you staring at?" he says.

"I'm not sure." She runs her hand across the counter, her fingers trembling. "The place is so clean," she says.

"Yeah. I'm breaking the lease. I figure it'll be easier if I don't leave a mess."

She lets out a sigh of amazement. "I'll be damned," she says. "You did it. It was you – "

He cuts in, "I'll say good-bye to Heather and then go."

In the flat morning light, Maureen looks tired. She fusses with her hair. "What about your furniture?"

"I'm giving it to the landlord. She can keep it or sell it. It won't make up for the rent, but it's all I can do."

"Where are you going?"

He hesitates. "I'm thinking Canada."

She seems startled by something outside the window. "I was ready for one of you to go," she says softly, "but not both." She tries to smile.

"I'm sorry," he says.

She nods. "I should leave," she says, glancing at her watch. "I'm late."

He stops her at the front door and kisses her on the cheek.

"Will you call?" she says.

"I'll have to," he says.

"That's not what I mean."

"Yes," he says. "I'll call."

At noon, he rushes through the house and looks for the last time into closets, cupboards, and drawers. He writes a note to the landlord and apologizes for his abrupt departure and asks her to accept his furniture, sorry though it may be, as compensation. He lays the note on the kitchen counter and piles the rosary on one corner and the keys to the landlord's kingdom on the other.

After securing and covering his goods, the guitar and amplifier stowed in the cab, he leans on the tailgate of the pickup and catches his breath, satisfied that he's taking only those things that he wants. A Monday feeling hangs in the air. The neighbors are all at work, he thinks, forced out of bed by alarm clocks and obligations.

He opens the door, settles into the driver's seat, and starts the engine. He rolls into the street and speeds away with his eyes fixed on the unfolding road.

Minutes later, he pulls up in front of Maureen's house and sees Heather sitting on the porch steps. He gets out slowly and walks up the driveway, the midday sun beating down on his head like a spotlight.

"Can we go inside," he says. "I can't handle the glare."

Heather leads him into the small room just off the front hall where Maureen still keeps the piano.

"Mom called and told me about the boat. Did you really knock it over?"

"Your mother must've been the first to see it."

"Maybe. But when I showed up – "

"You went to Humbug?"

"I had to," she says. "When I got there, lots of men were standing around the wreck as if it were a crime scene. One of 'em recognized me and asked if I knew where you were. Someone was trying to call."

He sits on the piano bench, his back to the keys. "I cancelled the phone."

Heather laughs. "Mom says you did it."

"What else did she say?"

"Nothing. Just that you'd be here to say good-bye. But I knew that."

"I'm surprised she didn't say more."

"Like what?"

"Like your old man's gone off the deep end."

"No. She didn't say that."

"So you're leaving a week from today?" he says. "On Monday?"

"Why don't you stay?" she says. "You can help me pack."

"You've packed already."

"That's true. But if you stay, we could do some other stuff."

"I'd like to, but I can't. I'm trying to miss the landlord."

"Oh," says Heather. "A delicate situation?"

"It's always delicate when you break a lease."

"I wouldn't know."

"But you're all set for the airport, right?"

She nods.

"I'll visit as soon as I can," he says. "As soon as I get settled."

"Sounds good. But you have to promise, Dad, no headlocks."

"I promise."

"I'll miss you," she says.

"You will?"

She sits next to him on the bench. "I always loved the music. I missed it for a long time, but then, when I heard you again with Brian, it seemed like it was never gone." She touches his crooked fingers. "How are your hands?"

"Never better," he says.

"You need to take care of them."

"I will. I'll even wear gloves in the winter."

Heather smiles. "I liked watching the old movies, too. Especially the ones in black and white."

"You said they were slow."

"I did not."

"And you fell asleep."

"Not all the time." She rubs his hand. "And I loved your stories about the Black & White Club."

He groans.

"No. I really did. The place was completely perfect and strange. Do you still go there?"

"Not so much," he says.

"Because I do. I daydream about it sometimes."

"Sorry," he says.

"Stop it. You always made up the best stories."

He wants to memorize her face. Carry it with him the way it is now for as long as he can. "What's your number at school?"

"I don't know. But I'll find out as soon as I get there."

"Okay. I'll call your mom." He touches her hair. "If you need anything – "

"I know." She follows him to the door. "I feel scared," she says.

"You're just nervous. You're not afraid of anything," he says. "I'm proud of you. I've always been proud of you."

She hugs him.

"I'd planned to write some stuff down," he says. "Or at least tell you what to watch out for."

"I'll be okay," she says.

"I know. But I wanted to make it special – give you some words to carry along."

"I'll be all right," she says. "I've got plenty. More than I'll ever remember."

He lets her go. "Take care," he says, stepping over the threshold.

"You, too."

After a moment's hesitation, in the brittle sunlight, he walks down the steps and across the lawn to his truck and climbs in behind the wheel.

HE STOPS at the corner and thinks. To go anywhere near the mess at Humbug doesn't seem wise. He'll give it a wide berth and use something other than his usual route to get out of town. He glances in the mirror. Heather is nowhere to be seen.

Now he'll head west for a while before turning and traveling northeast. He can't make up his mind whether to take the tunnel or the bridge to Canada. He'll wait until he's on the freeway and then choose.

In Tobermory, the houses on the harbor are red, yellow, and blue.

The idea strikes him as far-fetched. "Don't count on a second ending," said Otis, his long finger pointing at the music. But he wonders now if Otis was right. It isn't always true. He's seen one or two exceptions to the rule.

Once the river is behind him, he'll drive north through Ontario and along the eastern shore of Lake Huron. He'll arrive in Tobermory and stay as long as he can, and he'll welcome the coming days when the trees turn brown and the sky becomes an endless field of gray. And there'll be nothing sad or colorless about it.

After passing the slag heaps at River Rouge, the sulfur and the heat, he settles on taking the bridge. He'll make the crossing. He'll reach the far shore and resist the impulse to look back.

In Tobermory, the houses on the harbor are red, yellow, and blue.

archipelago books
is a not-for-profit literary press devoted to promoting
cross-cultural exchange through classic and
contemporary international literature
www.archipelagobooks.org